OFF KILTER

"If you fancy a quick, inexpensive trip to the Scottish Highlands, then *Off Kilter* is your ticket. Join writer Eden Elliott as she journeys to Glenkillen to research and write her first book, then go along for the investigation into the death of the town's sheep-shearer. Hannah Reed's new series will please Scotophiles everywhere, and they'll soon be eager for another trip to Glenkillen."

—Miranda James, *New York Times* bestselling author of the Cat in the Stacks Mysteries

"*Off Kilter* is a brilliant mystery, rich in charming characters set against lush depictions of the Scottish village of Glenkillen. With her kind heart, quick wit, and savvy smarts, Eden Elliott is my new favorite amateur sleuth. She is fun and feisty and a delight to spend time with. Hannah Reed writes an engaging tale full of belly laughs and white-knuckle moments. I thoroughly enjoyed this romp through the Highlands and I can't wait for the next one."

—Jenn McKinlay, *New York Times* bestselling author of the Cupcake Bakery Mysteries and the Library Lover's Mysteries

"Hannah Reed's series debut captures the appeal of the Highlands, and features a plucky, determined heroine surrounded by a cast of quirky but believable characters."

—Sheila Connolly, *New York Times* bestselling author of the County Cork Mysteries

continued . . .

Praise for
Hannah Reed's Queen Bee Mysteries

"A great setting, rich characters, and such a genuine protagonist in Story Fischer that you'll be sorry the book is over when you turn the last page."

—Julie Hyzy, *New York Times* bestselling author of
Home of the Braised

"Action, adventure, a touch of romance, and a cast of delightful characters fill Hannah Reed's debut novel. *Buzz Off* is one honey of a tale."

—Lorna Barrett, *New York Times* bestselling author of
the Booktown Mysteries

"Hannah Reed sweeps us into her world with skillful and loving detail."

—Cleo Coyle, *New York Times* bestselling author of
the Coffeehouse Mysteries

"Reed's story is first-rate, her characters appealing—Story's imperfections make her particularly authentic—and the beekeeping and small-town angles are refreshingly different."

—*Richmond Times-Dispatch*

"Will appeal to readers who like Joanne Fluke and other cozy writers for recipes, the small-town setting, and a sense of community." —*Library Journal*

"A rollicking good time. The colorful family members and townspeople provide plenty of relationship drama and entertainment . . . This series promises to keep readers buzzing."

—*RT Book Reviews* (4 stars)

"A charming beginning to what promises to be a fun series! . . . A yummy treat for fans of cozy mysteries." —*Fresh Fiction*

OFF KILTER

HANNAH REED

BERKLEY PRIME CRIME, NEW YORK

THE BERKLEY PUBLISHING GROUP
Published by the Penguin Group
Penguin Group (USA) LLC
375 Hudson Street, New York, New York 10014

USA • Canada • UK • Ireland • Australia • New Zealand • India • South Africa • China

penguin.com

A Penguin Random House Company

OFF KILTER

A Berkley Prime Crime Book / published by arrangement with the author

Berkley Prime Crime Books are published by The Berkley Publishing Group.
BERKLEY® PRIME CRIME and the PRIME CRIME logo are trademarks of Penguin Group (USA) LLC.

For information, address: The Berkley Publishing Group,
a division of Penguin Group (USA) LLC,
375 Hudson Street, New York, New York 10014.

ISBN: 978-0-425-26582-6

PUBLISHING HISTORY
Berkley Prime Crime mass-market edition / October 2014

PRINTED IN THE UNITED STATES OF AMERICA

10 9 8 7 6 5 4 3 2 1

Cover illustration by Jeff Fitz-Maurice.
Cover design by Sarah Oberrender.
Interior text design by Laura K. Corless.

To my Scottish ancestors.

*Armed with pistols and swords, they came knocking
inside my head, demanding that I pay a visit
to our homeland. I dared not decline their "offer."
This is what grew from my modern-day adventures
in the Scottish Highlands. The weapons have changed,
but the munros and lochs remain the same,
as do people's motives for murder.*

CHAPTER 1

Sometimes my best friend, Ami, can go way overboard. Like earlier this month, when she presented me with her gift of a round-trip ticket to Scotland. With a return date six months out! What had she been thinking?

"I hate to appear ungrateful," I muttered under my breath as we stood beside a security checkpoint in one of Chicago O'Hare's international terminals, "but going away from July to December is just too long. I shouldn't have agreed to this craziness." I was seriously reconsidering how easily I'd caved to Ami's whims. It was the story of our friendship, really, her bossing me around—though the truth was, her whims were usually pretty good ideas in retrospect. That's also probably why she was such a successful businesswoman. And she'd been so adamant—pushy is more like it—when she set out to take full advantage of my fragile state of mind with her surprise gift. I'd tried to turn it down, but it had been too late. She'd taken care of all the arrangements in advance. I was stuck.

"You can come home to Chicago anytime you want to," she repeated now, just as she had every time I'd expressed regrets out loud. "You don't *have* to stay all six months, but you wouldn't make it through customs without a return ticket. Thank God for smart travel agents. According to her, the max you can stay on a tourist visa is six months. I didn't know what to do, so I went for it."

What kind of logic was that? "You could have asked me first."

"I was flustered."

"You're never flustered. Are you trying to get rid of me?"

"Of course not. I'm looking out for you. Stay six months or come home next week, it's your choice. But for now, relax and enjoy, Eden. You deserve it after what you've been through."

What I'd been through was the year from hell—I was thirty-eight years old, freshly divorced after six years of marriage, almost one year to the day after my husband had filed, and two days after I'd buried my mother, who'd finally given up a long, ugly battle with MS last month. For a long while she'd stabilized, but over the last five years I'd watched her fade away and finally pass on peacefully. After I'd witnessed the extent of her suffering, the end had been a welcome relief for both of us. I'd gotten married right before my mother took a turn for the worse, and while I'd felt responsible for her, my husband had resented the attention I'd given her instead of him. We never really had a chance. And now those two events, the loss of my mother and the finality of the divorce decree, each right on top of the other, had rocked my world. And I don't mean that in a good way, either.

What exactly was I to do next? And more importantly, what was the point of it all?

I'd been awarded my mother's small life insurance payout as a consolation prize, and my ex-husband bought out my share in the condo we'd owned together, although there hadn't been much equity in it. After he'd filed last year, I'd moved into my mother's small apartment to care for her, leaving all the furnishings we'd purchased together behind, taking only my personal belongings. I hadn't wanted constant reminders of what had ceased to be.

The unexpected bit of cash allowed me time to pause and examine my life up to now. Not much of interest to report, I'm afraid. Nothing concrete to fall back on. I'd done some freelance editorial work in the past, as well as one ghostwriting gig, and had really enjoyed both, but as my mother's condition had worsened and my marriage imploded, I'd put aside my ambitions. Until now.

"Look," BFF was saying over the airport din. "You can do this."

I nodded, toying with my boarding pass and passport. "Of course I can do it. But *why* should I? I'm having second thoughts. Third and fourth thoughts, actually." Numbers five and six flitted through my mind as well. But there was also something else. Was that excitement underlying the pounding of my heart? Or simply a nervous response to an uncertain future? Was I ready for this?

Ami went on cheerleading. "You had to fly free eventually. And I mean that figuratively as well as literally. It's time you stopped working special projects for me and started working for yourself. You're more than talented enough. . . . You are. Don't look at me like that!"

I studied my longtime, dearest, most loyal friend, who had been with me through thick and thin since our good old college days. How much fairer she'd weathered the storms. Ami Pederson wore her marriage to her beloved husband, Brad, like a diamond necklace, while even before my divorce I'd worn mine like an albatross around my neck. She hadn't married the wrong guy or had to care for a terminally ill family member. Nothing so common for Ami

Pederson. Yes, *that* Ami Pederson—the bestselling, prolific, world-famous historical romance author. Millions of copies sold of every single novel, dozens of exotic foreign translations. I'd lost count of how many by now.

Ami could grace the cover of one of her own novels. She's tall and slender, with long-flowing locks, and always perfectly groomed as though perpetually ready for a television interview. Lights, camera, action: that's Ami from the moment she rises in the morning to the time she wraps up her writing late at night.

Me? I was already feeling rumpled and wrinkled, and I hadn't even boarded the first leg of my journey yet. I'd memorized the drill: seven-plus hours in the air, arrive in London in the wee hours of the morning, a lengthy layover at Heathrow, then a flight to Inverness in the Scottish Highlands, then pick up a rental car for a short drive to my final destination, a small town called Glenkillen. Ami had been to the village once and highly recommended it.

I shifted my carry-on from one shoulder to the other, resigned to whatever fate awaited me in the Highlands.

Ami must have sensed my surrender, because she gave me a warm, wide smile, and said gently, "Remember why you're going to Scotland in the first place. Because you just happen to be under contract to a New York publisher to write your fabulous book!"

The thought did give me a blush of pride, which I quickly damped down. "Which I couldn't have accomplished without your help and connections." Not to mention that Ami had been extremely involved in the outline for the story and had suggested the Scottish Highlands setting.

"Nonsense!" Ami said. "You're a great writer. And you've been hanging around me long enough to learn all the ins and outs of writing romances. All I did was help you brainstorm and then get your work in front of the right editor."

Ami's comment about my familiarity with romances was true enough. I'd read every one of her books, along with many by her contemporaries. I was a romance junkie from way back. And to be fair to myself, I *had* written my opening chapters without Ami's input. Right this minute, though, I was feeling a little fearful. The publisher was taking a chance on me mainly because of my friendship with Ami. I didn't want to let her or the publisher or myself down. That was a lot of pressure.

"Another wonderful reason for your trip comes to mind," Ami continued. "Because your ancestors on your father's side came from the Highlands. Lucky you! It will be such fun to check out your ancestral homeland, trust me. I'd join you if I didn't have a deadline looming."

The mention of my father wasn't a welcome one. The man had abandoned me and my mother long ago, back when she'd originally been diagnosed with MS. Yet we'd both continued to use his last name—Elliott—maybe because it was the only thing we still really had from him. At first Mom had waited patiently, certain that my father would return. My mother had been more charitable than me, more forgiving; until the end, she always wondered if something had happened to him, rather than his having left us behind. Later, by the time she'd given up, she was too sick to care about pursuing a divorce. Either way, there'd been no second chance at love for her.

Ami was still talking up my destination. "All those hunky Scottish men! A romance novel set in the Scotland Highlands . . . Well, it's a fantastic location for a romantic interlude. Both on the page"—Ami gave me a conspiratorial glance—"*and* off."

Not this again. My best friend was bound and determined

to see me involved with someone as soon as possible. I had other plans. More realistic ones that better reflected my personality and the more recent past.

I'd been an introvert my whole life, whether by choice or by demand, it didn't really matter. I'd learned to cherish and protect my personal space and time. As far back as I could remember, reading had been my escape. It was only a matter of stages: I started trying my hand at writing journal entries, then progressed to short stories and the discovery that the creative process gave me a much needed outlet.

In my teens and early twenties, I'd been a voracious fiction reader, mostly romances, but at this stage in my life it was time to learn to sort fact from fiction. The whole concept of Prince Charming was unrealistic, a fantasy. Happy endings were best suited for fairy tales—and all the best romances. But those things didn't happen in real life. Opposites attract, that's for sure, but lately I'd been reconsidering whether they made for good matches. I'd married one—extroverted to my introverted, someone with enormous energy who loved people and parties while I preferred a good book and spent my efforts doing what I thought was right, which was tending to my mother until the end.

Would a man with traits more like mine have understood and stayed by my side?

Well, it was way too late to know. And I had better uses for my time than regretting the past.

Yes, the more I thought about it, the more I decided that the future belonged to me—by myself, alone. I wasn't about to share it with someone who expected me to do piles of laundry and serve him meals in front of the television set, all the while trying to maintain my own career around his demands.

Besides, I rarely suffered from loneliness and I wasn't afraid to be alone.

What did I need a man for?

Absolutely nothing, that's what.

"I better go," I said to Ami after checking the time and glancing at the long line of travelers snaking through security. I shuffled over to the end of the line.

"Remember, turn off roaming," Ami warned, tagging along. "In fact, don't use your cell phone at all; it's way too expensive. We'll keep in touch through e-mail. Take a few days to acclimate, then get to work. You're booked into the local inn for two weeks, but you can always extend that if you decide to stay longer."

The line moved a few inches, then a few more. Ami stayed with me.

"You can't go any farther," I told her when it came my turn to show my boarding pass at the first security checkpoint. Ami hung back but didn't leave. As I grabbed a bin and began to unload my things into it, she shouted out her parting words, much to my dismay: "And make sure you find out what's really underneath those sexy kilts!"

Several travelers turned and followed Ami's gaze back to me.

Maybe I *did* need some time away.

The flight from Chicago to London went fairly smoothly. I'd chosen a window seat way in the back, and the others in my row weren't interested in making conversation. But while I still couldn't sleep for several reasons—mainly because I'd never perfected the art of dozing off in a sitting position, and my wayward heart wouldn't stop beating to its own Scottish tune at the realization that I was on my very first trip out of the country—coming in for the landing at dawn the next day revived me.

Unfortunately, weariness set in during the layover, and I promised myself a nice nap on the flight to Inverness.

It didn't happen.

Almost as soon as we'd boarded, Chatty Cathy's twin sat down next to me in a seat that didn't completely contain her.

"Vicki MacBride," she said, introducing herself while I caught a strong whiff of her perfume, a combination of rose and jasmine. "I'm from London, until very recently. Now headed back to live in the place of my birth." Her accent didn't sound very English, even though she'd just told me she was from London. It was a blend of some sort, and I wondered if she'd lived elsewhere as well.

Vicki wasn't a huge woman—plump but not fat, strong-boned but not manly. I guessed her age to be somewhere around mid-forties. She wore her blonde hair tied up in a knot on top of her head and gave me a wide-toothed smile as she dug in a tote and pulled out a beautiful skein of yellow and blue yarn along with knitting needles, and began adding rows to a few existing ones without stopping her flow of talk. "And who do I have the pleasure of meeting?"

I readjusted in my narrow seat, scooting as close to the window as possible in search of a little personal space. "Eden Elliott," I said by way of introduction, then paused when she asked the reason for my trip to the Highlands. That was a good question. Was I searching for something? A new beginning? Purpose to my life? I went with a more concrete, less introspective response. "I'm going to write a novel."

"Really?" Vicki's eyes widened. "What kind of novel?"

"Contemporary romance," I said. Gillian Fraser, my heroine, would be a strong modern woman struggling with present-day issues and conquering them. I hoped to get into character.

"Lots of sex on the page, I'd imagine?" Vicki said, nudging me with her elbow.

I laughed weakly. "I'm not that far into it yet." Several thin, first-draft chapters after a polished first chapter didn't amount to much. I hadn't yet tried Ami's advice, to write one of the love scenes first. "Your story will grow organically from there. And don't be afraid to add lots of juicy details," she'd said with a wink.

"My favorite reads are romances about American cowboys," Vicki told me, her knitting needles clicking away. "The hotter, the better. Make sure some of the scenes are right steamy and it'll be a bestseller."

"Mmm," I said noncommittally, then leaned back into the headrest and closed my eyes as the plane gained altitude.

Unfortunately, Vicki MacBride wasn't the sort to take obvious hints that a person wanted to be left alone.

"I hope Pepper and Coco are doing all right in the hold," she said, sounding anxious. "They're my two wee West Highland terriers, and they aren't used to travel."

I sympathized with her anxiety over her dogs. Sometimes I think I like animals more than people. Correction: more than sometimes. Change that to "almost always." They are so much more loyal and aboveboard—loving, caring, never wavering from a constant state of affection and devotion. They don't run off when you need them the most. And they don't win your heart, then snap it in two like an insignificant twig.

Once an animal befriends you, it's for life. Unlike some ex-husbands I could think of.

It was his fault I'd been without the companionship of a pet. Him and his allergies. And my mother's apartment hadn't allowed pets. When the lease was up in a few months, I planned to move someplace pet friendly and get one of my own.

"We were supposed to be on an earlier flight, but our

plane had mechanical problems and we were all herded over to this one," Vicki lamented. "I'll be lucky to make it back in time, what with collecting my boys and finding my car in the lot. Good thing Glenkillen isn't too far from the airport."

"Glenkillen? That's where I'm going," I said, opening my eyes in surprise.

"Well, fancy that! We'll have to stay in touch. Are you in need of a ride over? I have room, if you don't mind budging up with my little pets and our luggage."

"That's very nice of you," I said. "But I've reserved a rental at the Inverness airport."

"Ah, of course you have. Will you be staying at the Whistling Inn or with friends?"

"At the inn." I yawned. So exhausted! I only half listened as she talked for the better part of the flight.

"My half brother and half sister used to be my best little pals," I heard at one point, listening to the faint sound of the needles working away, my eyes once again closed. "I'd visit every summer from London and we'd run wild on the Highland hillsides, scaring the sheep, dressing the newborn lambs in baby clothes, all of us without a care in the world. Ah, those are fond memories. Then my mum moved us to the States—California—when I was thirteen. You know how teenagers are, so busy with their own lives they forget about everybody else."

"But you're living in London now?" I asked, opening my eyes.

"I needed a change of scenery, and London was as good a place as any, one where I knew my way around. That's all changed now. I'm on my way back to Scotland for my father's funeral and to move into the old family house there."

"I'm so sorry about your father," I murmured.

She went on, "It's fine, really. My da wasn't much of a father to me. It was his second wife, Moira, who encouraged me. She was the one who rang at the beginning of each summer and invited me. After that marriage ended, my father never rang to ask me to visit. But by then we had an ocean between us."

"I know exactly how that feels," I told her. "My dad took off when I was a kid and never came back. I don't even know if he's dead or alive."

"You poor dear. But you have a good mother?"

"Had. She was the best. And you?"

"A wonderful woman, passed on now as well."

"Then we were both blessed."

Vicki smiled. "But now my da's up and died, and suddenly my circumstances have changed overnight. Earlier in the week I flew to Glenkillen to meet with the solicitor, who's also acting as executor of the estate, and imagine my surprise to find I've inherited the whole lot! Until then, I was a part-time pet stylist on the dole, unable to find permanent work and running out of funds. Now I'm moving out of the city and may never have to work another day in my life unless I so choose. Life's full of surprises."

That was quite the inheritance—as an only child to an ill single mother, all I'd inherited beyond her house and life insurance were the bills. Even if other family members had existed to make claims, there hadn't been much in the way of material possessions to argue over when my mother passed away. But if I ever found myself in that situation, I swore I'd just give everybody whatever the heck they wanted and back away. It just wouldn't be worth the hassle.

Vicki's head was down as she concentrated on her knitting. "Wonder what I should do with all of my time now that I'm secure," she said. "It won't be spent catching up with my half siblings, that's for sure. They didn't take kindly to my return and to the terms of our da's will. Maybe I'll write a story, too, Eden Elliott. What do you think of that?"

I must have dozed off after that, because the next thing I knew we were beginning our descent. The fog had lifted, giving me a breathtaking view out the airplane window of the countryside surrounding Inverness and a spectacular view of the River Ness, home to the famous Loch Ness Monster. Everything was so lush and green!

"I'll look you up after I tend to my family business," Vicki said as we deplaned. "I could use a friend."

Couldn't we all, I remember thinking as my flight companion hurried off to claim her terriers and I went off to claim a rental car.

CHAPTER 2

Somewhere between Inverness and Glenkillen, my rental car broke down.

After trying everything I could think of to get the thing going again, I gave the tire a swift kick in utter, absolute frustration. My foot connected, the impact hurting me much more than it did the car. Which only angered me more.

My foot was in mid-swing again when I heard the sweet sound of another vehicle approaching. *Finally!* But it was too late to halt what was already in process, proving the theory that a body in motion stays in motion. Or in this case, a leg in motion.

A white Land Rover pulled up behind my rental car on the curvy, impossibly narrow excuse for a road. More like a mountain-goat path, if you ask me. I adjusted my attitude into a semblance of cool, calm, and collected for the benefit of the driver. I needed road assistance, and acting like a lunatic wasn't likely to get it for me.

I plastered a welcoming smile on my face and really hoped it didn't make me look totally insane.

The driver's window slid down, and a guy around my age stuck his head out. "Winning the fight, are ye?" he said, in a lilting Scottish accent that I would have found attractive under normal circumstances. But I was too cranky to be charmed. Between my jet lag, the need to constantly remind myself to stay on the opposite side of the road from the right as I was used to—not to mention driving from what felt like the passenger seat—and the discovery that I'd rented a car with a manual transmission (a skill definitely *not* on my bucket list), well . . . things weren't going exactly as planned.

"The steering wheel started pulling hard to the right," I explained, calling back. "Now the stick thing won't move." I winced at my lame attempt to describe a mechanical problem. Who knew that most rental cars in Scotland were manuals and that you had to specifically request an automatic in advance? Not me, clearly. And, wouldn't you know it, by the time I realized my mistake, there hadn't been a single automatic left. The rental agent had been sympathetic and even gave me a lesson in shifting and clutch work, but to say I was completely frazzled would be an understatement.

Thank God everyone here at least spoke English, or some version of it anyway. I was only processing about half of what had been said to me since landing on this unfamiliar terrain. Coming from Chicago, I was used to hearing foreign accents on a daily basis, and I'm usually pretty good at deciphering most of them. But this Scottish one had to be the hardest.

The guy slid out of his vehicle and came toward me.

Now that someone had finally stopped, my stranger-danger warning bells went off, and I wondered what the odds were that this guy got his kicks out of committing atrocities on stranded female motorists. Leave it to the airlines to take away a woman's line of defense. I'd forgotten all about the little canister of pepper spray in the bottom of my purse when I'd gone through security in Chicago. The body search hadn't been pleasant.

But a quick glance at his Land Rover showed that he was towing a fishing boat, and besides, he had a cute border collie riding with him. In a split second of decision-making, I applied a partially formed opinion of his character, using good old intuition to decide he was A-OK. What animal lover (an assumption I made based on his canine friend) could possibly be a bad guy? Besides, I figured I had to trust him. Who else did I have to turn to out here in the middle of nowhere? Still, I planned to remain alert to any trouble.

I rubbed the back of my neck, considering the symptoms of whiplash after so many sudden starts and stops. I'd heard it takes a few hours for aches and pains to settle in. "I'm fine, really," I told him.

"Ye don't look so fine," he said, then, apparently realizing that I might misinterpret his remark as a critique of my personal appearance, amended, "I mean, *ye* look fine, but . . . uh . . . yer situation doesn't." He gave me a slightly crooked smile. "Did ye use yer mobile to call for help?"

It wasn't as though I hadn't considered that option, but my cell phone hadn't worked since I'd landed (not a fact I wanted to broadcast to unfamiliar men; it would be like using a black magic marker to write *Helpless Prey* on my forehead). Never mind that I hadn't the faintest idea who to call. Ami, back in Chicago? Not much help there. What was the magic number for emergencies here anyway? It certainly wasn't 911.

"And how exactly do I do that?" I said instead, immediately realizing I'd made a stupid mistake in showing my ignorance.

"In the future, ye call nine-nine-nine," he informed me. "Yer from the States, then?"

I strained to catch a tone of disdain in his voice, but, to my relief, didn't hear anything negative. He was simply making a statement. I was aware that we Americans weren't exactly beloved worldwide. Trying to beat up an innocent car was a perfect example of how not to act in a foreign country.

I admitted I was, and he studied the car situation while I covertly studied him. He really was a nice guy, I could tell. And it didn't hurt that he was also tall and attractive, with sandy blond hair and a little natural red facial hair, like he hadn't had time to shave this morning. He was wearing jeans and a plaid shirt with the sleeves rolled up, showing well-muscled arms, and he smelled nice, too, like fresh air and open fields—unless that really *was* the great outdoors giving me sensory overload. And he had those Scottish blue eyes I'd been admiring since landing.

Everything about this guy seemed relaxed, from the casual way he wore his clothes to the hair on his head (just a little too long, which happened to be just right in my book). I wanted to think I had the same sense of self-confidence that wafted from him, but I had to admit, in the short time since I'd arrived in Scotland, some of my poise—all right, most of it—had bailed on me.

He opened the driver's door, slid in, started it up, and tried to shift through the gears. Yup, they were locked in place for him, too.

"Can you fix it?" I asked anxiously, wrapping my cardigan a little tighter around my body, realizing that the temperature here was much cooler than a July afternoon back home. I'd have to replace it with one made from Scottish wool.

"Did ye hear any loud noises?" he asked, a hint of amusement twitching his lips.

"Yes. A big bang."

He got out and tinkered under the hood. The internal workings of cars have always baffled me, so instead of observing I walked over to the rover's partially open passenger window and introduced myself to the border collie. "Eden Elliott," I said as the dog stood up and wagged her tail madly. I reached in and gave her a pat on the head along with an ear scratch. "You're a sweetie."

I heard the hood close, and I walked back to my car for the damage report.

"Eden, is it?" the guy said, inclining his head to the dog. "I overheard ye introduce yerself to Kelly there. I'm Leith Cameron at your service. Yer not all that familiar with a manual, are ye?"

"Not really. This is . . . was . . . my first attempt."

Leith's eyes swept over my faulty transportation. "The transmission is fouled up a bit. That extra pedal on the floor is a clutch, in case ye were wondering."

"I know that. I had a lesson before driving off."

"Must o' been a wee one."

"I told the rental person it was a big mistake not to make more effort to locate an automatic for me."

We both looked at my big mistake. I'd been right—as usual—when it came to my lack of mechanical abilities. When they'd passed out those brain connections, I must have been in a far corner reading a book.

"Where are ye heading?" he asked next.

"Glenkillen."

"Let's grab yer things, then," Leith said. "Glenkillen is right around the bend, and it's where I'm goin'. I'll see tae the car, but I'll need the hire agreement."

I fished around in the front seat and handed over the paperwork.

Leith pulled the keys out of the rental car's ignition, popped the trunk (or rather the "boot," as the rental agent had referred to it), and transferred my bags into the backseat of his Land Rover, moving so quickly that I didn't have a chance to pitch in and help.

"Ye don't mind sharing a seat with Kelly, do ye?" he asked.

"Not at all," I said, climbing in.

"Ye'll be staying at the Whistling Inn?"

"How did you know?" I asked warily.

"Only place around these parts to stay."

Ah. True. Research had told me tourists usually made Inverness their home base and traveled from there on day trips to take in the sights. But I'd wanted more total immersion. In spite of Glenkillen's popularity as a coastal town, it didn't encourage overnight revelers. In fact, I'd read that it closed up relatively early each night. It was exactly what I'd been looking for, and Ami had agreed.

"You won't be able to run to the comfort of other Americans in a place like that," she'd said with a wicked little grin.

She'd certainly been right about that. And if only she could see the Scot who'd come to my rescue. She'd absolutely flip with glee.

"Well, Eden Elliott," Leith said, "let's get ye to yer destination."

And we were off, heading through the rolling hills of the Scottish Highlands. I finally had an opportunity to sit back and enjoy the scenery. Right outside my window, which I rolled all the way down to enjoy all the sensory delights, were glorious purple-hued heather-covered hills on both sides of the road. Mountainous peaks rose in the background. The air smelled very much of honeysuckle, sweetly and powerfully fragrant.

Sheep dotted the hills and valleys like clumps of cotton, some all white, others black-faced but with white bodies, as well as the occasional proverbial black sheep, all grazing contently. Hand-built stone walls edged both sides of the road, sometimes branching away and meandering off over the tufted grass, crumbling here and there with age.

"Did ye come for the funeral?" Leith asked rather loudly, since we both had our windows down.

"What funeral?"

"James MacBride's. Should be quite the turnout for it," he said.

He must be talking about Vicki's father, I realized, deciding to feign total ignorance, curious what Leith would say about James MacBride and the rest of the family.

"An important man?" I asked.

"Ye could say that."

That was all the prompting he needed. The gist of it, if I understood right (which was questionable, considering Leith's brogue and my unfamiliarity with several Scottish idioms he threw in), was that the elderly James MacBride had been an important community member who'd recently suffered a rapid series of strokes. The last and final one had stopped his heart for good. He'd owned a large hill sheep farming operation where, not only were sheep raised for their wool, but all stages of the process to create yarn for retail sale and for commercial wool product distribution was conducted. MacBride's place was one of many tourist attractions in these parts, with regular sheep-shearing demonstrations and a gift shop specializing in all kinds of finished wool products and yarns.

Despite having done a fair amount of research before this trip, I hadn't come across anything about the MacBride farm, probably because it was on the outskirts of Glenkillen.

I was more eager to visit the village pubs and shops. At the top of my list was a pub called the Kilt & Thistle, Glenkillen Books, the Whisky Stop, and A Taste of Scotland, which advertised sweet oaties, Dundee cakes (whatever those were), and six flavors of shortbread. And the Whistling Inn, where Ami had reserved a room for my extended stay that included a full Scottish breakfast.

"The funeral is today at five o'clock, and the family is feuding something fierce," Leith gossiped as Kelly and I got to be pals. "Story is, James MacBride left everything to his oldest daughter, who he hadn't seen since she was a bairn. Worse, his two grown children from his second marriage were left out of his will altogether, and one of them even runs the family business with her husband. An' none of 'em will cry baurley-fummil."

That last part flew right past me, although I was pretty sure the barley part didn't involve any grain.

"Whose side are you on?" I asked, genuinely curious.

"I don't take sides. 'Live and let live' is my motto."

We crested the top of a hill, and Glenkillen and the North Sea came into view. In its harbor and as far out into the ocean as I could see, sailboats rode the waves, their colorful spinnakers flying. A few fishing boats were heading out into the vast rolling water, and other boats of varying sizes were tied to moorings, rising and falling with the waves. Through my open window, I breathed in salty ocean air.

"What do ye think of it?" Leith asked with obvious pride.

"It's more beautiful than I imagined." My tiredness gave way to excitement. Soon we were driving along Castle Street with its quaint shops, exactly like the images I'd seen online. People crowded the streets, shopping, eating, drinking, milling about. I loved seeing this village and all its energy, even in my travel-weary state.

I heard a bagpipe jig coming from inside a pub.

" 'Biddy from Sligo'," Leith muttered, glancing my way.

"Excuse me?" Was he calling me a biddy? And if so, did that mean the same thing in Scotland as it did at home?

He laughed when he noticed my expression. "Name of the jig, that's all."

I laughed, too, at the misunderstanding, one of many more to come, I was sure.

Leith pulled over next to a discreet hotel sign, hopped out, gathered my bags, and deposited them inside the entry-way, again refusing my assistance when I tried to offer it. I thanked him, then turned to his companion.

"Good-bye, Kelly," I said to the friendly canine through the open window. "Hope we run into each other again."

Leith grinned. "Don't worry there." He opened the driver's door, then turned back. "Ye should come to the pub tonight," he said. "Everybody's invited after the funeral, for a proper send-off."

"Doesn't sound like my kind of event," I told him, thinking of the MacBrides and their personal problems. "Especially if the family is fighting like cats and dogs."

Leith grinned. "Ye don't strike me as a woman who tip-toes around. Ye certainly weren't tiptoeing back when I found ye, now, were ye?"

"No, I guess I wasn't." More like trying to kick the car into a zillion pieces.

"If ye come, I'll buy ye a pint," he said, his smile its own form of enticement, "And give ye an update on yer car."

"Another time, perhaps," I heard my voice saying. What was wrong with me? Why was I making excuses instead of taking this handsome knight in shining armor up on his offer? Ami would be deeply disappointed in my behavior.

Leith seemed a bit disappointed. Or was that my imagination? "If ye change yer mind," he said, "I'll be there." Those blue eyes met mine. "Ye better stay off the roads until ye learn how to operate that car properly," he advised me. "Our roads can be treacherous if ye aren't used to them."

I didn't say so, but I had absolutely zero interest in learning how to drive that particular one. I wanted an automatic car, one without all those gears and extra pedals and the need to multitask the entire time. Tomorrow, I vowed, I'd call the rental company and beg for a different car.

It was the safest thing for me, and for all of Scotland.

I watched his Land Rover pull away, Kelly's nose pressed against the window, her border collie stare drilling into me. Had I lost my mind? One of these days, I'd have to work on the introverted side of my personality, beat it out of the forefront, where it seemed to always control my actions. Those pesky old habits were hard to overcome, though.

I paused at the entrance to the inn to take in the lively and colorful view up and down the street.

Here I was, standing on a cobblestone street in the heart of the Scottish Highlands, savoring the exciting possibility of romance and intrigue . . . even though I'd turned down my first opportunity a few minutes ago. Serenity, reflection, acceptance, creativity. It all could be mine.

I finally made it to Glenkillen. Thank you for giving me the push I needed, Ami.

If I'd only known what awaited me, I would have been on the next flight home.

CHAPTER 3

The Whistling Inn was a family-run bed-and-breakfast, rather simply designed with cream-colored stone on the exterior and pastel colors within. The owners lived on the premises and cooked for their guests each morning. A warm and inviting breakfast room was off to the side of the registration desk. The inn met my needs nicely, with Internet access available and the single bedroom en suite. No way would I feel comfortable trotting down the hall to a shared bath. My own bathroom had been a requirement from the very beginning.

"Yer paid up two weeks in advance," a young woman with a heavy Scottish accent said from the opposite side of the desk. "So yer all set. I'm Jeannie Morris, if ye be needin' anything."

Jeannie couldn't be more than in her early to midtwenties and though she had red hair, none of her brassy highlights had the natural beauty of Leith Cameron's or some of the other heads of hair I'd seen. Hers were clumps of fiery copper, mixed with about six other man-made shades. Definitely from a box, or rather from several boxes. And she wore a nose ring. Not a discreet jeweled stub, but rather a large hoop that reminded me of a bull's ring.

If Jeannie wasn't exactly the best first impression, the room was everything I imagined it should be: cozy, with wonderful natural light from my second-floor window, a desk that would function perfectly for my writing, and a thick lush duvet on the bed.

After sending Ami a quick e-mail to let her know I'd arrived safely, and briefly mentioning the breakdown and the guy who'd picked me up, I put my things away and stretched out on the bed for a few minutes of downtime. As I lay there, I heard bagpipes on the street below. This time I recognized the piece: "Amazing Grace," which always makes me cry. Being played on the bagpipes turned it into the most mournful, soul-wrenching rendition I'd ever heard. Sure enough, tears ran down my cheeks. I sang along softly: "I once was lost, but now am found, was blind but now I see."

I got up and peered out my window to see some sort of procession passing through the village. A solitary piper was in the lead. Next came a horse and a cart adorned with strips of plaid ribbon, carrying a coffin. An actual horse and cart! This had to be the MacBride funeral. Mourners at the front of the advancement were dressed in kilts and colorful clan tartans, except one woman—off a bit from the others—who wore an ankle-length black dress. Sure enough, I recognized her as Vicki MacBride. The others must be her half siblings. They were followed by a bevy of folks I assumed to be locals, many also in kilts. If it weren't such a sad occasion, I would have thought the sight very festive.

Despite my jet lag and bone weariness, why wasn't I out

there? I reminded myself that absorbing Scottish culture and observing local traditions firsthand was exactly why I'd traveled to the Scottish Highlands. And Vicki looked so sad and lonely as she passed by. She'd said she needed a friend, hadn't she?

I made an impulsive decision. I splashed water on my face and rubbed my hands along my wrinkled shirt in another attempt to smooth my clothing. With a burst of energy induced by sheer willpower, I left the inn for my little adventure. I hurried out into the street, following the mourners to the village cemetery.

From my position at the back of the crowd, most of the ceremony was lost on me. I still hadn't completely adjusted to the Highland dialect. The jumble of words that drifted over my head from the front might just as easily have been in Swahili. Even when I thought I caught some phrases, I was often confused—like with the concluding remark: "Deep peace o' the running waves tae ye." *What did that mean?*

Toward the end, a woman directly in front of me glanced up into a nearby hawthorn tree, and pointed out something to the man beside her. "A corbie," I overheard her say. "Nothin' good aboot that."

The man, an elderly gentleman with unruly salt-and-pepper gray hair and an enormous walrus mustache that covered his entire mouth, turned slightly to follow her gaze. "Aye," he said. "Nothin' at all good."

Scanning the tree for this corbie creature, I spotted a large crow. Or maybe it was a raven. Either way, the bird cocked its head and turned a wary eye on me before taking flight and disappearing from view.

A corbie. Huh.

Frankly, I was starting to wonder if the travel guides I'd studied were going to be much use to me here.

After the graveside service, the mourners began assembling at the Kilt & Thistle, which turned out to be conveniently located right next door to my accommodations. And the whole village really was invited, judging by the number of people flowing through the outer doors.

The Kilt & Thistle had great atmosphere and welcomed me in from the moment the door opened. I glimpsed a warren of small, oddly shaped rooms tucked away here and there, with the main pub area sizeable enough for a gathering of this magnitude.

"Well, who do we have here!" I heard from behind me. "Come get a hug, Eden Elliott!"

I turned to see Vicki bearing down on me with a big, friendly smile and her arms spread in preparation for an embrace. Call me easy, but I let her. Although I wasn't sure I had a choice. After a strong squeeze enhanced by the equally powerful musky aroma of roses and jasmine I remembered from the plane, she backed away, beaming at me.

"How was your drive from Inverness?" she asked. "It takes some getting used to, doesn't it?"

I shuddered, remembering. "I doubt I'll ever get used to it." Then: "I'm so sorry about your father. Are you okay?"

"I barely knew him," she reminded me. "Mostly, I'm in mourning for what could have been. But now . . . it's the living I need to reconcile with, and that's going to be the hardest part."

"I have faith in you," I told her. From what I'd seen, Vicki seemed like a warm and genuine woman. She'd manage just fine.

A lone man began to sing, his voice powerful and rich.

Others joined in until the entire room resonated with raised voices.

"Scotland's national anthem," Vicki said quietly. "Flowers of Scotland." I saw tears form in the eyes of those nearby just as mine had when listening to "Amazing Grace."

"Well, new friend," Vicki said when the song was finished, tucking her arm through mine, "thank you very much for coming. You've renewed my strength, which tends to ebb in times of turmoil and conflict. Now let's get some nibbles, shall we?"

Whisky and ale flowed freely, and a band complete with bagpipe, fiddle, and accordion started playing Gaelic tunes.

The MacBride family had to be well-off to offer up such a smorgasbord of meat pies, sausages, fish and chips, and cheese-and-fruit platters to such a large gathering. With my new friend's encouragement, I helped myself to a small plate of assorted food items. I tried to sample a little of everything, not realizing until that moment how hungry I was.

When one of the servers called Vicki away to make some small decision regarding the menu items, leaving me alone, I moved to the bar. I really enjoy a good beer, but decided to wait and indulge another time—considering how little sleep or food I'd had over the last day or so, I worried it would go straight to my head and I'd make a public fool of myself. What I wanted more than anything was to be accepted by the locals, to blend in. To assimilate. Not to become a laughingstock.

I'd read that Irn-Bru was the national nonalcoholic drink of Scotland, at least according to the travel guide. I figured now was a good time to try it.

"Aye," the bartender said in the local lilting accent when I asked if they carried it. He was blond and goateed, and when he brought my drink, he gave me a friendly, conspiratorial wink as though he knew I didn't really belong here.

Eden Elliott, funeral crasher. That's me. Vicki had been welcoming, but maybe the other family members would consider me an intruder.

I took a cautious sip of the beverage. It was overpoweringly sweet, metallic, and bitter all at once. Just as my face scrunched at its fizziness, I heard a familiar voice by my side.

"What're ye havin', Irn-Bru?" Leith Cameron said. "Either ye like it or ye don't. There's no in-between."

"I suppose it takes some getting used to," I replied, although it was definitely not to my taste.

"I'm glad ye changed yer mind about coming."

"Me, too."

"Now, let me get ye something drinkable." He slipped onto the stool beside me. "Ye strike me as an ale woman."

"Good guess." I laughed, impulsively throwing caution to the wind. One drink couldn't hurt, right? "Sure, why not?"

We bellied up to the bar like old friends. Leith put me at ease right away. He came across as trustworthy and transparent, and my mind wandered into his personal life. If he was so great, he must be taken, or spoken for. The good ones always are.

Whatever his real-life availability, however, I decided that Leith would make the perfect Scottish model for the romantic interest in my novel. I delved into my research by keeping him chatting.

"I ran into Vicki MacBride a minute ago," I told him. "Turns out we were on the same flight up here. Which ones are her family members?"

He took a swallow of the whisky he'd ordered before shifting his eyes across the room. I followed his gaze. "Over there," he said. "See the large, bearded man in the kilt? That'd be Vicki's brother-in-law, John Derry. He manages the farm and tends the sheep. Beside him is her half brother, Alec. He's the only one of the lot that isn't involved in the business. Beside Alec is his sister, Kirstine, who manages the wool shop and handles the accounts. She's married tae John."

All three wore kilts—the men's were more ornamental and traditional, but all three had the same blue-and-yellow plaid pattern. Kirstine, who I pegged to be in her mid-thirties, wore hers several inches above the knee, paired with stylish knee-high black boots.

"Vicki's the oldest," he went on, "by at least four or five years. Alec is the youngest. We were in the same year at school. Vicki would sometimes watch over us when she'd visit in summer. Seems not that long ago, but it was."

"So you knew her well in those days?"

"We all played together. Then Vicki and her mum moved away, and that was the last we saw of her. Until recently. Sometimes it takes death tae bring a family back together. I hope this one works things out."

"Me, too," I agreed.

Leith clinked his whisky glass against my pint of ale, and said, "Time tae cock the wee finger."

"Whaaaat?" I wasn't sure I'd heard that right.

"Cock the wee finger. That means drink up."

Oh. I caught him playfully rolling his eyes at me.

"So tell me a bit more about yerself, Eden Elliott," he said next. "What brings ye tae Glenkillen? I blathered on so much about the MacBrides on the way down, we never discussed yer plans."

I paused. What to say? What would this man think of me and my purpose if he knew I was writing a romance? "I've always wanted to write a novel," I told him, dodging the specifics. "I'm here to do that. Something adventurous and Scottish."

"Ah, everybody thinks about writing a book, but few

follow through. Although, ye don't look like a quitter. Good for ye."

I took another sip of my ale before responding. "Aye," I said, trying out a Scottish lilt of my own. "That I'm not, sir." We grinned at each other.

Was I really flirting with a Scottish man? And was he flirting with me?

It felt good. A bit silly, but good.

We would have continued our banter, except right then we heard loud, angry voices rising above the din.

And suddenly, the music died.

CHAPTER 4

Just like in a scene out of a movie, every single thing in the immediate vicinity of the action seemed to grind to a halt. Everybody stopped what they were doing to watch. I know I did—it was the first fight I'd ever personally witnessed that didn't involve popcorn and a big screen TV or a surround sound movie theater.

It was almost as though we all experienced collective paralysis. Maybe it was the element of surprise. We were supposed to be celebrating a life and mourning a loss, not brawling. If the musicians hadn't stopped playing, those closest to the outbreak might have been the only ones to notice, and that would have been the end of any further public displays of rowdiness. But the room quieted to a hush.

"You're a bloody liar!" we all heard a woman's voice exclaim.

"Get your hands off me, you heathen!" Was that Vicki MacBride's voice?

An immediate circle of spectators formed. Leith made several attempts to push through the crowd, but he couldn't penetrate the mass of bodies. I stood on my barstool to see what the brouhaha was about, and saw Alec MacBride, the kilted son of the deceased, working his way through from the opposite side of the room. Unlike for Leith, the crowd gave way to Alec.

"You don't belong here," I heard Kirstine spit at Vicki, giving her a shove. "You reek of bad news. If I didn't know better, I'd suspect you killed my father just for his money. That's the only reason you're here. To collect what isn't rightfully yours."

For a moment, I thought I was acclimating to the Scottish lilt, because every word Kirstine said came through loud and clear. But then I realized her Scottish accent was much less pronounced than the others I'd heard since arriving. Not so her husband, John Derry, who shouted something unintelligible to my untrained ears. But from the anger and excitement that twisted his face, he clearly wasn't trying to defuse the situation. Rather he was instigating more aggression.

"Stop it right now." Alec finally got between the two women and grabbed each by an arm. His accent sounded just like his sister's. "Making a scene at a family funeral? I can hardly believe the indecency." This he directed at Vicki rather than at Kirstine. The hostility between the three was palpable. He swung around to the musicians. "Play!" he ordered, and they instantly struck up a lively tune.

Vicki shook free of Alec's grip and headed for the door. Leith rejoined me, but I said, "I'm going to make sure she's all right." I didn't wait for a response. Instead, I jumped down from the stool and rushed after her.

"Wait, Vicki!" I called as she hurried away.

She stopped and turned, giving me time to catch up. "No

one saw, did they?" she asked, wiping her face with her fingers.

"Saw what, the fight?" *Uh, everyone saw that*, I thought but didn't say.

"No, me crying. I cannae let anyone know I'm this upset." Vicki's accent thickened as she struggled with her emotions and brushed away evidence of her tears. "The whole village is against me, and if they see any weakness, it will only make matters worse. It was a mistake coming here. I should've stayed in London, where I belong."

By now, we were walking abreast in what I guessed to be the direction of the sea. My shorter legs had to hustle to keep up with her angry strides. We turned right onto a street called Saltmark, and right before the end of the street, Vicki made an abrupt turn onto a beach. The briny, fishy smell of the seashore filled the air. Powerful waves crashed against the shoreline nearby. She kicked off her shoes and walked barefoot through the cool white sand until her knees folded and she sat down, stopping just short of the incoming tide.

"I'm sorry for what happened," I said, sinking onto the sand beside her. "This can't be easy."

She turned a tear-streaked face to me. "Why? I keep asking myself. Why did he do this, make it all mine? His other children hate me for it, and I don't blame them a bit."

"Maybe your father simply forgot to update his will," I suggested.

"That's what Kirstine believes. She's fighting the will, claiming that since he didn't specifically disinherit her and Alec, his intentions must've been to distribute the estate more equitably. In the meantime, the farm continues to operate as before. And me alone in my father's house with what seems like the whole world against me. They've turned the villagers their way, too, I'm sure of it. I see the looks they give me."

For a few minutes I stared at the waves, then I looked back at her. "Is his estate really that large?" I asked. Not that it was any of my business.

Vicki nodded. "It's involved, that's for sure. I couldn't possibly run it by myself even if I wanted to. For now, Kirstine and her husband are handling the operation, mainly because they don't want me to run the estate into the ground before they get it back."

She composed herself a little and changed the subject. "How do you like your accommodations at the inn?"

"It's really nice," I answered. "I'm looking forward to sampling a full Scottish breakfast tomorrow morning."

"You'll have to try haggis soon," Vicki said, clearly trying to make light conversation even though her stress was apparent. "It's not part of the traditional Scottish breakfast, so you'll have to seek it out."

I can eat almost anything. Or at least try most things; I draw the line at insects and reptiles. And possibly at haggis. I knew it was the traditional dish of Scotland, but I wasn't too sure about sheep liver and lung cooked in stomach lining. "I'm not ready for that quite yet," I admitted.

"Either you like it or you don't."

I laughed. "That's exactly what Leith Cameron said about Irn-Bru. That there's no in-between."

"Did you try Irn-Bru, then?"

"I did."

"And?"

"It isn't my favorite."

"Well, you're going to love haggis."

Vicki and I sat quietly until the waves crawled up and kissed our toes. I noticed that the sun was just starting to

set, even though it was past nine thirty. I vaguely remembered reading that summer days in Scotland were longer
than those at home, and today had certainly felt incredibly
long to me, filled with travel frustrations. But I'd also met
two new, friendly people, making my first day in Scotland
a good one.

"I almost forgot why I came down this way," Vicki said,
getting up and brushing sand from her clothing. "I wanted
to pop in on Gavin Mitchell."

"Gavin Mitchell?" I rose with her and we walked away
from the water's edge.

"He's the local sheep shearer, and a longtime family
friend. I remember him well from my summer visits. He
used to let me help him with the animals."

Sheep shearing? Not a lot of call for that back in Chicago.
But of course, this was sheep country.

"I didn't see him at the funeral, though," Vicki continued,
"which surprises me, since he's the one who called to tell
me about Da's passing in the first place." At the edge of the
beach, we brushed sand off our feet and slipped back into
our shoes. "He lives on this street here. If we'd kept going
instead of turning toward the beach, we'd have ended up at
his cottage."

In spite of the lingering sunlight, I could see that all the
other cottages along the row were lit up because of a canopy
of thick, heavily leafed trees that cast deep shadows. But
not a single light shone from any of the windows of the
cottage at the very end of Saltmark.

"That's Gavin's place," Vicki said.

"He must be away," I said, stopping and studying the
cottage.

"We should make sure, since we're already here."

"It really doesn't look like he's home," I said, again

noting the darkness of the place. "Maybe he's gone to the pub." But Vicki started up the narrow walkway leading to the front door, so I followed.

"You might be right," she said. "We'll know soon enough."

We were at the door. Vicki called out, "Gavin Mitchell, are you in there?"

We listened for a response. Nothing.

We looked at each other. She called again, louder this time. "Gavin Mitchell!"

Still no answer. Vicki tried the door. It was locked. She stared at me. "Come on. Let's try in back."

We crept around to the side and peered through a window. Total darkness. The two of us stayed close to each other. We rounded to the far side of the cottage to a back entryway. The door gaped wide open.

My heart skipped a beat, and I heard Vicki suck in her breath. "Something's wrong," she said. "He might need immediate help. What if he's had a heart attack or something like that?"

I thought about suggesting we call 999, like Leith had told me, but she had a point. Gavin might need us, and every second could count.

Vicki didn't move, so I gathered my wits and courage and took the lead. My exploring fingers found a light switch on the wall right inside the entryway. I paused, hesitating, fearing what I might see, then I flipped it. A dim overhead light came on.

We were in a kitchen. And what a mess! Dirty dishes, a smelly trash can that needed emptying, evidence that the occupant hadn't bothered using the cupboards. Clearly, Gavin Mitchell was a longtime bachelor who had developed bad habits and didn't have the benefit of an outside cleaning service.

But no sign of anything amiss.

The kitchen light cast its weak rays into the front room of the tiny cottage, where I made out a television, one of those old cabinet styles, directly ahead beneath a window. I moved farther in and switched on a lamp that was sitting on a table within arm's reach. I noted an indentation in the dust on top of the television and papers scattered at my feet.

Right behind me, Vicki gasped. "Oh no!"

The lamplight illuminated a man lying on his back on the floor between the couch and an armchair that had seen better days, a large file box beside him. I made a safe assumption that this was the missing sheep shearer. And as much as I had wished his absence from James MacBride's funeral to have had an innocent explanation, it was not to be.

First, because of the vast amount of blood pooled around his body.

And second, the weird-looking metal handle protruding from his chest.

Vicki gave up gasping and started screaming.

CHAPTER 5

The walls of the sheep shearer's tiny cluttered cottage closed in around me. My throat constricted as though a taut piano wire was tightening around my neck. I couldn't swallow or breathe or think. Moments ago, when we'd first entered his home, my head had been screwed on straight. But now my mind seemed to be flapping senselessly about with no direction at all.

Surrealism at its most unreal. *This can't possibly be happening.*

If not for Vicki's earth-shattering, ear-piercing shrieks, I might have thought I was in the grip of a harrowing nightmare and would wake up soon. But there was so much blood! Even my vivid imagination couldn't have produced this much.

Thanks to Vicki's powerful set of lungs, neighbors came pouring into the tiny cottage.

"What the . . . ? Oh my God!" I heard.

After they saw what had caused all the screaming, Vicki and I were led outside and watched over, whether out of a sense of compassion or to make sure we stayed where we were, I didn't know or care. Vicki clung to my arm while we waited for what seemed like an eternity.

The police finally arrived.

"Don' any of ye be leavin' yet," a plainclothes cop flashing official identification warned us. Not that my legs were going to carry me far anyway. I could barely stand. The combination of jet lag and finding a murdered man had taken a huge physical toll on me. Not to mention the emotional impact.

The dead man's neighbors huddled together on the edge of the porch, at arm's length from Vicki and me, whispering and casting furtive glances our way. In spite of my overall numbness, I could read their body language only too well. A growing suspicion was welling up amongst them. If they'd turned cold shoulders to Vicki before, they were absolutely frigid to her now.

Not only were Vicki and I outsiders, and therefore suspect to begin with, but by virtue of being the ones to find Gavin Mitchell's body, we were also the bearers of really awful news. The continued glances shooting my way spoke volumes; this bunch wasn't about to greet me with the same warm welcome that Vicki had met me with earlier tonight.

Talk about making a bad first impression on a small community.

I began to work on my "story," even as I wondered why I felt I needed a story. I had no intention of making stuff up, but I wanted my account to be rational and linear. And most of all, believable. I knew we were innocent of any wrongdoing—at least, *I* was—but somehow I'd been made to feel guilty anyway. Dagger glares and collective whispers just out of earshot will do that to a person. I felt like a target. And the neighbors had ample arrows.

Had Scots been the first ones to shoot the messenger? I remembered that the phrase originated with the English, or at least from one of Shakespeare's plays. *Antony and Cleopatra.* England was close enough geographically to fuel a real concern.

Vicki and I were split up and questioned, as were the neighbors. Eventually, they were all released to return home, until it was only Vicki and me. We were the best saved for last. The original cop approached me and waved Vicki over from her position alongside another police officer.

"Inspector Kevin Jamieson," the police officer said by way of introduction, then quickly commanded, "Yer names, if ye don't mind."

As though we had a choice. The inspector mentioned that he already knew of Vicki from what he called local "blether," which I interpreted to mean gossip, but as a complete unknown, I had to give him all my personal background information. I was prepared for those questions—*How long have you been here? What's the purpose of your visit? How long do you intend to stay?* Standard airport customs questions—but still found myself fumbling.

"I'm not sure," I said, responding to his question about the length of my stay.

He gave me a piercing look.

"A few weeks," I muttered. "I only arrived today."

Had I really only been in Scotland for one day? It was the longest one of my life! And as to how long I planned to stay—at this rate, I'd get a plane home tomorrow if I could.

"I'm doing a little local research for a book I'm writing," I concluded, "and was hoping to see the sights." These weren't exactly the sights I'd had in mind. A dark glimpse into a murdered man's life.

"So yer basically on holiday?" Detective Inspector

Jamieson said, writing everything down in a little notebook. He was left-handed, with that exaggerated hovering-above-the-paper curled wrist most lefties adopt to avoid smearing drying ink. I always noticed a lefty, since I'm one myself.

I guessed him to be somewhere in his late fifties, based on the frown lines etched across his forehead, although those could be the effect of responsibilities he carried. He had dark hair, not a bit of red, but he did have those classic Scotsman's piercing blue eyes, which were even more intimidating when flashed by an officer of the law.

He also wore a wedding ring that had been on his finger for a long time, and I could tell he wasn't in the habit of taking it off, because his knuckle had expanded over time. Chances were, it would have to be cut off, or left where it was. This was a man truly devoted to his wife. Something I had little experience with.

"I need the circumstances, step-by-step," Inspector Jamieson demanded, his eyes riveted to Vicki rather than me.

Vicki, having finally calmed down, related to him her growing concern for the sheep shearer after he hadn't attended the funeral, the graveside gathering, or the reception at the pub. "I'd spoken to him on the phone before I came to Glenkillen, and"—at this point, Vicki came close to breaking down again. Her eyes welled with tears and her voice shook—"I decided to check on him, and Eden happened to accompany me."

"So ye hadna ever met with him face-to-face while he was alive?" the inspector asked.

"What? . . . N-no . . . not recently. I hadn't seen him for years. Why would you think that?"

"It's a line of inquiry only," he said, glancing up sharply from his notes.

Vicki shook her head emphatically, and said, "No, we

only spoke on the phone when he rang to inform me of my father's death. I *did* know him, though, from my childhood days at the farm. He was a nice man. And I was looking forward to seeing him again. But not like this."

Vicki burst into tears, and it took some time to help her get herself under control.

Fortunately for both of us, after that we could back each other up on the rest of the details.

"He'd been stabbed in the chest," I finished, "but with what? What was that thing?"

Even in my state of shock, I recalled the unusual image of the murder weapon only too well. Its metal handle had ended in what appeared to be the shape of a heart, and the thought that it had been used to stab a beating heart made me shudder.

The constable glanced up from his notepad. "Gavin Mitchell was clipped with his own sheep shears, that's what," he informed us.

Vicki gasped. I covered my face with my hands, rubbing them up and down in hopes of erasing the image inside the cottage. It didn't help.

The inspector remained professionally detached. "Where can I reach the pair of ye?" he asked.

"I'm at the Whistling Inn," I told him.

"The MacBride farm," Vicki said. "At the main house."

"Stay in town until I say otherwise, the both of you. I'll be having more questions, I'm sure."

I'd barely arrived and here I was, stumbling across a murder victim, getting involved with the local police, and ordered in no uncertain terms to remain in Glenkillen.

How had this happened?

Chapter 6

Despite how horribly my first evening had ended, somehow I slept later the next morning than I thought possible, wrapped up in a fluffy duvet. I crashed hard from the combination of jet lag, time differences, stress, and emotional roller coasters. When I finally awoke, light slatted through the venetian blinds, streaking across the bed. I stayed where I was awhile longer, listening to the sounds of activity on the cobbled street below—voices, traffic: business as usual.

And then all the details of last night's terrible discovery came back to me in a rush, stranger than any fiction I could have created. Imagination, I've learned, is always a runner-up to the real thing.

At least we hadn't barged in while the killer was still there. What if that had happened? We could have ended up just as dead as the sheep shearer.

To stop my thoughts going from dark to darker, I quickly rose from the bed, hoping for a better day.

Breakfast was included in the cost of my room, and although I wasn't hungry, I dressed and went downstairs, thinking I'd skip the traditional Scottish breakfast and instead eat light—yogurt or a bowl of cereal. Jeannie, the same young woman who'd checked me in yesterday, led me to a table beside a window overlooking the street, slightly away from several other guests.

Before I could tell her I wasn't hungry, she placed an enormous plate on the table in front of me. Toast covered with baked beans, some kind of hash, cooked tomatoes, a thin slice of ham (which I'd find out later was the Scottish version of bacon), and runny poached eggs.

"So this is a traditional Scottish breakfast?" I asked, and she nodded. I pointed at something on my plate that looked round and dark and fried, but that I couldn't identify. "What's that?"

"Blood puddin'," Jeannie casually informed me.

Blood? That brought back gruesome memories from last night. All the blood pooled around Gavin Mitchell's body. The round fried thing could have been a cow pie and I would have been more okay with it. Well, maybe not, but really? What the heck was blood pudding?

"What's in it?" the researcher in me just had to ask.

"'Tis only sausage with a bit o' pig's blood and some suet and other stuff that won't hurt ye," she said, setting down a cup of tea in front of me. "Go ahead. Give it a try."

She trotted off, leaving me staring at the suspicious, unappealing thing. I took a small taste of everything on my plate except the pudding.

"Ye want porridge instead?" Jeannie asked a little later when she brought more hot water for my tea and noticed that my heaping plate was still heaping.

"No, thank you. I'm not very hungry, that's all."

"I'm not surprised, after wha' happened last night."

"You know about that?" In my growing paranoid state, I searched for any trace of hostility from her, but found none.

"Poor Gavin!" she went on. "Who would do a thing like that tae him? He didn't haff an enemy in the whole world." Before I could engage her further, she said, "Well, take yer time. I'll come back and check on ye in a minute or two."

And she went off to wait on other guests. I screwed up my courage, remembering why I was sitting in front of this particular plate in the first place. My story needed the kind of authenticity that only comes through actual experience. That meant digging in and eating a traditional Scottish breakfast. If I needed something to take my mind off yesterday's events, maybe this experience would do the trick.

Reluctantly I picked up my fork, broke off a tiny piece of the blood pudding, and popped it into my mouth. There. That hadn't killed me. Although, it was dry and overcooked in my opinion. I took another bite, thinking that I'd take good old American sausage any day over this.

Soon after, Jeannie was back and noticed my effort. "Yer a sport," she praised me.

"Tell me," I asked her, "are you part of the family who owns the inn?"

"Aye, me and me da keep it running. If ye can call him a help rather than a hindrance."

"And how old are you?"

"Almost twenty-five," she said.

"That seems so young to be running all this."

"I grew up with it." She shrugged. "An' I hardly have a choice."

"What's there to do with your free time in a small village like this?"

"There's nothin' tae do at all," she replied, a cloud

passing over her features. "I'd love tae travel, see the world, leave this place far behind me, but my da needs me help. He cannae handle it all himself. He's disabled."

"So you're stuck, just like George Bailey in *It's a Wonderful Life.*"

"Right, eh? But I'm not staying stuck forever like wha' happened to that poor bloke in the film."

I wanted to ask Jeannie more about her father's disability, but she turned away and disappeared through the kitchen door. Perhaps another day I'd learn more of her story.

Leaving the dining area, I was surprised to find Leith Cameron, my hero from yesterday, waiting for me in the lobby.

"Enjoy your breakfast?" he asked.

"I wasn't very hungry."

Leith gave me a studied gaze. "I hear Gavin Mitchell's dead," he said. "And that ye and Vicki MacBride were the ones tae find him."

"Yes. It was . . . awful."

"A bloody bad business, that."

"I'm so sorry. Did you know him well?"

"Well enough. He was born and raised here, and he trimmed sheep for everybody in the area. He'll be missed by all. His murderer best be brought tae justice fast. It's a sad affair, but what about ye? How are ye doin'?"

"I'll be okay."

He gave me a small, rather sad smile. "Come on, then. Ye and I have unfinished business tae take care of."

We walked outside, and there it was: The car from hell.

"She's all set to go," Leith told me.

Terrific, just great.

"A driving lesson would do ye good," he added. "I just happen tae have some spare time."

"Now?"

He nodded, then hopped into the driver's seat, which reassured me for a moment . . . until I remembered that he was on the *wrong* side of the car. Over here, that was actually the passenger seat he was sitting in.

"These streets are too narrow," I told him through the open window, not moving from the side of the car. "I'm not used to them. Plus, after last night, I couldn't possibly drive," I tried next. "I'm shook up. Wouldn't you be, if you'd found a dead person?"

"This will take yer mind off all other troubles."

Well, of course it would. The sheer terror of the winding narrow roads and the speed at which these people drove would wipe out pretty much anything else I had on my mind. On the other hand, I also ran the risk of wiping out the two of us permanently, not to mention any unwary pedestrians unlucky enough to cross my path.

"As a reward, I'll show you how to get to the MacBride farm," he added, still sitting there all relaxed. That would change very soon, I knew, once I got behind the wheel.

"You could just drive me there," I suggested.

"Get in the car, woman. It's only about eight kilometers down the road. Besides, I have tae save Glenkillen's residents from certain destruction. Ye've got to learn, eh?"

"Where is Kelly?" I asked, still stalling but also hoping for an ally in the sweet dog.

"Are ye mad? I wouldn't risk her life!" And then he laughed.

Those eyes, that face. And the temptation he'd thrown out to me, to visit Vicki's farm, to see how my new friend was doing after last night. What choice did I have?

I marched around the front of the car and slid into the driver's seat.

Leith first gave me a verbal refresher on the mechanics of the vehicle, then went through the motions of using both feet and both hands at the same time, and had me shift through all the gears before turning on the engine.

After that, he had me wait until there wasn't a single other moving car in the vicinity. Then we hopped and skipped out onto the middle of Castle Street.

If I killed this kind and handsome man, I'd never forgive myself.

CHAPTER 7

Leith hadn't mentioned that those mere eight kilometers it took to reach the MacBride farm involved driving along a very curvy, very narrow road, or that the trip would take well over twenty minutes. Maybe a more experienced driver could have made it there in less time, but this was me behind the wheel.

Neither of us chitchatted much on the drive. Steering and staying on the narrow road took every ounce of my concentration, and I assumed Leith was speechless with terror. The very worst moments of our harrowing drive came at roundabouts, which we had to enter heading left (so wrong) and which had way too many lanes to choose from and far too many exit options. And I used to think the traffic circles at home were challenging!

One of my favorite parts of the journey was when we got to stop for a bit because rugged-looking cows had taken over the roadway. They had thick red coats and impressive horns with shaggy manes of hair falling forward over their eyes.

"Highland cattle," Leith told me before getting out and shooing them to the side.

By the time we pulled into the entrance to the farm, Leith had lost his lazy grin. His calm, cool demeanor had gone missing as well. So had mine, if I'd ever had one in the first place. I'm sure every sheep and cow alongside the road had smelled my fear right through the steel armor of the car.

Leith reached over and pulled the keys from the ignition, literally leapt from the car, and declared: "I'll drive on the way back."

"But I'm just starting to get the hang of it," I lied, deciding it would be bad form to follow my instinct, which was to drop down on all fours and kiss the ground in relief.

I'd barely had any time to appreciate the scenery while driving, but when I stepped out of the car and gazed around, I found myself in what I can only describe as Shangri-la. Rolling green farmland, pastures covered in purple heather, lush mountains in the distance.

Leith had directed me to park next to a stone building that housed a shop called *Sheepish Expressions*, according to a sign out front. A few other cars were parked there, too, and as I gaped at my surroundings, a tour bus pulled in. A gaggle of tourists, mostly women, exited the bus and made their way inside the building.

"I thought we'd start here at the shop," Leith said, "but since the tourists have descended, let's leave the car here and walk up the lane a bit tae the house. The view is best appreciated on foot anyway."

"Where is the house?" I asked, not seeing another structure of any kind up ahead, just a country lane that ascended ever so slightly.

"Around the hill up ahead. Let's go."

The MacBride "farm" wasn't what I'd imagined a working sheep farm would be like. It was a massive estate with magnificent views in every direction. As we strolled up the gravel lane with sheep grazing lazily about, Leith explained that this area of the Highlands was highly traveled through the summer months, and Sheepish Expressions was a woolens shop, and a favorite destination with the tour bus operators. "After searching for whales along the firth," he explained, "or following the whisky trail, they stop here for a bit of shopping on the return tae Edinburgh, Glasgow, or Inverness."

"Look!" I said, pausing as at least a dozen sheep began to flock and walk toward us.

"They're curious about our newcomer," Leith said with a laugh.

The sheep stopped twenty yards or so away and stared at us.

I noticed a swath of pink paint on their hindquarters and asked about it. "Pastures in the Highlands are most often shared," Leith explained. "The markings help us sort them out if they get mixed together. For example, my land came with communal grazing rights. If I raised sheep—which I don't—mine could roam freely amongst the MacBrides', and I'd just mark them differently."

"Your land? Is it anything like this?"

Leith laughed. "Hardly, but it's enough for me. It's right next door tae here. Ye'll have to visit sometime."

"Doesn't the paint wear off the sheep?"

He shrugged. "If it does, their ears are also marked."

We watched a border collie halfway up a hill round up scattered sheep and move them toward another pasture under the direction of a man a good distance out.

"That was amazing," I said, following as Leith walked along. "Is that John Derry whistling his commands to the dog?"

"That's him. He tends the sheep, trains the working dogs, and keeps the farm in running order."

"He and his wife put on quite a show at the funeral last night, didn't they?"

"They'd all been drinking more than their share, and the situation was stressful tae begin with, and not much time tae get used tae the changes. James MacBride passed away on Monday, the family found out about the terms of the will on Tuesday, and the burial, as ye know, was only two days after. They've hardly had time tae adjust."

"What will happen next?" I asked.

"The others are going tae fight to get the farm back. And they'll likely win. They still tend the sheep and handle the shop as before. None of the family members want to see the place fail in the meantime."

At least there was that. I could imagine pettier people willing to destroy the business out of bitterness.

Right then, the lane curved to the right and the farmhouse came into view. It didn't look anything like a traditional American farmhouse. Instead of the kind of white clapboard Victorian-style building with a wraparound porch I thought of as a farmhouse, this was a plain rectangular two-story stone building with a gray sloping slate roof, gabled dormer windows on the second level, and no porch to speak of. Smoke spiraled from two chimneys, one on either side of the house.

"This is so beautiful," I couldn't help uttering. It really did take my breath away.

In spite of his reportedly large holdings, it seemed James MacBride had chosen to live a simple life. Several outbuildings were visible back behind the house, the closest one a barn made of honey-colored brick. Other, smaller ones farther out didn't look to be currently in use, at least not judging from the overgrowth surrounding them.

Vicki appeared in the farmhouse's doorway and waved in welcome. She was followed by two white West Highland terriers, whom I assumed to be Coco and Pepper. "What a relief to see some friendly faces for a change," she called out. "Thanks for driving Eden out, Leith."

Leith smiled, though it again had a certain sadness to it that reminded me that this village had just lost a dear friend. "Actually, it was Eden who did the driving," he told Vicki.

"And we made it without any accidents or breakdowns," I added.

"Are you accident-prone?" Vicki asked me.

"Apparently," I said with a laugh.

"Ye just need some more practice," Leith said more kindly than a few moments ago. He turned to me. "If ye don't mind," he said, "I'll borrow the car for a wee bit, check on a few things over at my place, then come back and collect ye."

"Of course," I said, appreciating the chance to spend a little time alone with Vicki to discuss yesterday's events.

With that, we made arrangements to meet up again in an hour outside of Sheepish Expressions. Then he left us, striding quickly down the lane in the direction of the car.

"That Leith is easier on the eyes than I remembered," Vicki commented as we watched him go.

I couldn't have agreed more. "What's his history?" I asked.

Vicki shrugged. "No real idea. Other than he lives on the farm up the road, same as his parents before him. It's been a long time since I was in Glenkillen. Everybody's grown up, all in different directions. Why do you ask? Do you fancy him at all?"

I waved off her suggestion with a snort. "He seems like a nice guy, but I'm not really looking. I'm in Scotland to relax, do a little writing, and recover from a very bad year."

"You deserve to find true love," Vicki said, "and you will."

I could have replied that as far as I was concerned, true love didn't exist off the pages of one of those romance novels I was intent on writing, but instead I said, "Now that I'm free to do what I please and go where I choose, I don't want any responsibilities or commitments other than to myself."

Was that true? Or was I trying to convince myself of it?

"A man is a heap o' work," Vicki commented, in full agreement.

"My caregiver days are over." And that part was absolutely true. No way would I ever willingly take on that role again, and from what I've seen of most male/female relationships, women were the ones who usually took on the supportive role.

It would take a strong, confident, and independent man to catch my eye the next time. If there ever was a next time.

"Sounds like there's a story lurking in there."

"Another time perhaps," I said, then changed the subject. "This place is beyond beautiful, Vicki. But looks like it requires a ton of maintenance, what with all the sheep to tend to and the shop to run."

"The family might not like me personally, but they're committed to the business and are carrying on as though I don't exist. My brother and sister still want nothing to do with me," she said sadly.

"Because of the will," I said, stating the obvious.

"Believe me, it was as much a shock to me as it was to them."

"Hopefully time will heal their hearts."

"You're a good soul, my friend. How did you weather the night? I hardly slept a wink myself."

I didn't want to admit that I'd slept like a log, so I shrugged and refocused my attention on Vicki's dogs, who were chasing each other around the yard.

"That one is Coco." She pointed at one of them with obvious pride, although I couldn't tell them apart. "And that's
Pepper, she has the tiniest bit of black marking on her belly.
They've been trying to make friends with a cat named Jasper
that lives in the barn, but he's not cooperating."

I looked off past the barn toward the neglected buildings
off in the distance. "What's over that way?" I asked.

"Cottages," she said. "Farm workers used to live in them
years ago. The one is past repair—it'll have to come down—
but the other just needs a little work. It's in rather good shape
considering the age of it. To be honest, I haven't done much
more exploring the grounds yet, mainly because I'm wary
of running into the others."

"That must be difficult," I said.

Vicki tucked her arm through mine, and said, "Having
a friend is going to help me get through it. But I sure do wish
we hadn't been the ones to find Gavin's body. What a stroke
of bad luck that was."

"Not nearly as bad luck for us as for the sheep shearer."

"If only I'd thought to visit him earlier. We might have
scared off his attacker and saved his life," Vicki said
mournfully.

"It's not as if you'd have had any time before the funeral,"
I reasoned. "He must have been dead already by then. You
couldn't have saved him."

Even as I worked to reassure Vicki, though, I wondered
if the sheep shearer might have been fighting for his life
while the funeral procession made its way to the gravesite,
while I'd stood in the back, listening to the service and gaz-
ing into the tree at the bad-luck corbie.

A bad sign that was indeed, I thought, as a shiver raced
down my spine.

CHAPTER 8

The next moment, our attention was drawn to the lane leading from the road to the house, the same lane Leith and I had walked. I heard the sound of a car engine approaching. The sheep who had been grazing now looked in the direction of the shop. Was Leith back already? No; it was a Honda CR-V with a solid yellow stripe running horizontally across the side, framed by a smaller stripe with blue and black checkers. I recognized it from last night—those were Scottish police vehicle markings.

The car came to a stop near us, Inspector Jamieson was in the driver's seat, another man beside him, barely visible through the front windshield of the Honda. Jamieson opened his door and stepped out, then leaned back in. "Stay right where ye are," I heard the inspector order his protesting passenger with a forceful tone, then he slammed the door shut. I would have thought the other man was a prisoner if not for his black shirt, which I'd seen was trimmed with a row of insignias along each shoulder, indicating a law enforcement position of some sort. A rookie maybe?

"I've more questions for ye," the inspector said to Vicki after an almost imperceptible nod of greeting to each of us. "But since Miss Elliott is on my list as well, I'll speak with her first."

I wondered nervously why he needed to speak with me again. When neither of us moved, he added, "Alone would be best."

"Oh," Vicki said, worry in her voice. "Of course. I'll be in the kitchen. Would you like tea?"

"Another time perhaps."

And with that she hustled inside the house, leaving me alone with the inspector.

"Right at the moment," he said to me, "yer about the only person in Glenkillen who has been cleared in the murder of Gavin Mitchell. You're free tae come and go as ye please."

My relief must have been visible, because the inspector actually chuckled. "Ye left a trail to follow as wide as this glen. First a broken-down vehicle and Leith Cameron to vouch for yer whereabouts. Then the innkeeper's daughter keeping an eye on ye and goin' so far as tae list the time ye arrived and what ye had for breakfast this morning. Pity ye didn't care for the blood pudding." He smiled, then looked serious again. "Unfortunate that ye got yerself involved in coming across a body, but that's the extent of it."

"I appreciate you letting me know," I told him, relieved to no longer be a suspect, but at the same time a little uncomfortable that he'd been looking into my every movement since my arrival in Scotland. Not that I had anything to hide. But still.

In the light of day and under calmer circumstances than we'd encountered last night, I decided that Inspector Jamieson was a handsome man with expressive and kind eyes. He came across as the genuine article, someone I wanted to confide in. That is, I would feel that way if I had anything to confide.

"Let's go over what happened at Gavin Mitchell's cottage again, but this time with more detail, if ye can recall any."

I saw Vicki watching us from a window inside. The man waiting in the car was also staring our way.

My mind went back to the moment when I'd turned on the light, and I remembered accumulated dust on the TV and a rectangular area that was free from it. "It looked like something had been removed from the top of the television set."

The inspector registered surprise. His reaction gave me a small amount of pleasure.

"You have a keen eye," he said. "And in a bad situation at that."

"There was a box on the floor beside the body," I replied. "It could have been what was moved. Maybe his killer was looking for something and perhaps found it in there."

The man inside the police vehicle opened his door.

"Stay right there!" Inspector Jamieson called over. But his words had no effect.

"I'm Special Constable Sean Stevens," the man announced as he rushed over, literally pushing his way between us. I guessed him to be in his early thirties, a bit younger than me, and shorter, too—no taller than five five and fine-boned.

"Special constable?" I asked. "Are you the inspector's partner?"

"No, no, no. He's a volunteer," Jamieson said, looking extremely miffed and barely able to keep the scorn out of his tone. "Nothin' *special* aboot him at all. He's naught but an overeager trainee. Seems the powers-that-be are under a lot o' pressure tae cut costs, and in their infinite wisdom decided to accept volunteer police officers tae assist the force."

Volunteer cops! My gosh, that seemed risky. Although Scottish police didn't carry firearms, which I supposed made it somewhat safer. I couldn't imagine this happening in the States though.

Sean Stevens did look extremely enthusiastic, with his chest swelled out and his head held high. "Years as a security guard have prepared me for this moment. My future plan is tae apply for a regular position with the police after I prove myself in the field."

The inspector began to turn an unhealthy shade of pink.

"I'm here for the Highlands," Sean continued with pride.

Jamieson's skin tone colored a few shades deeper. "Sixteen hours a week I have to put up with this."

"Tacklin' crime," Sean said to me as though his superior wasn't complaining about him right to his face. "Making the streets safer. I've been trained tae carry whatever power of arrest the inspector here carries."

"If ye don't shut up this very minute, I'll show you the power of arrest," Jamieson declared.

Officer Stevens clammed up at that threat and walked a distance off but stayed within earshot. For the next ten or fifteen minutes, as the volunteer examined his fingernails and pretended not to be listening in, Inspector Jamieson grilled me on one singular subject—my newfound friend, Vicki MacBride. I bristled at this new direction of questioning, but I stayed calm and patiently answered his questions. I explained how we'd met on the plane over to Inverness, related the argument between Vicki and Kirstine that I and everyone else in the pub had witnessed, and described how I'd caught up with Vicki outside and accompanied her to the seashore and then to the sheep shearer's cottage.

I sensed that he already knew much of this already.

"So she didn't coax ye tae go along with her?" he asked when I finished.

"No, I followed her outside." I remained calm on the outside, but I felt my jaw tighten with tension. "She'd looked like she could use a friendly face."

"After the beach, did she persuade ye tae go with her to Gavin's?"

"No, I offered."

"And why did ye go inside first? Did she ask you tae?"

"That was my decision also," I said, losing my grip on cool, calm, and collected, and growing angry. "I don't appreciate your implication that Vicki used me as a cover."

The constable gave me a small smile, and said, "Yer a clever woman."

I thought about Vicki and any opportunity she might have had to murder the sheep shearer. The flight and funeral had kept her busy yesterday. Before that, she had been in London making arrangements to move and pick up her dogs, which was likely easy enough to confirm. But she'd previously been in Glenkillen either Monday or Tuesday, and based on the inspector's focus, I took a guess. "Gavin Mitchell didn't die yesterday, did he?" I asked. "He'd been dead a few days, hadn't he?"

The inspector didn't reply. Instead, he handed me a business card with instructions to call him if I remembered anything more. I tucked it into a pocket, and he turned to go talk to Vicki. I watched him walk toward the house, Special Constable Stevens hot on his trail.

CHAPTER 9

I still had a few minutes to spare before I expected Leith back to pick me up at Sheepish Expressions, so I walked down and entered the shop. I was a little apprehensive over what kind of reception I would receive if any of the other MacBrides were around, but I told myself I was being silly. The family probably wouldn't recognize me as Vicki's friend. I wasn't even certain they had seen me last night. They'd had other concerns. And if any of them had heard about my role in finding the sheep shearer's body—which, given the way news seemed to travel around here, I was sure they had—they would know me by name, not by sight.

Or at least that's what I hoped.

I walked in and quickly ducked around a corner when I saw Vicki's adversary, Kirstine, checking out customers at the register, but she didn't glance up from what she was doing. Her presence behind the counter didn't surprise me, although I'd hoped she'd be in a back office buried under stacks of paperwork instead of out here, where I might risk exposure.

I didn't worry long, because Sheepish Expressions was a visual delight in every sense of the word. Half the store was devoted to colorful yarns—stacks and stacks of skein after skein, wicker baskets full and cubbyholes brimming—with a cheerful little room tucked off to the side where a small group of knitters had gathered. Books filled with patterns were scattered about on a long worktable, available as resources and idea guides.

I couldn't help touching and feeling all the wonderful varieties of wool I found in the shop. What a feast for the senses! Every skein of yarn was from Scotland, of course. Lambs' wool and silk blends from the countryside. Shetland yarns from the northern islands. Cashmere and angora from the Isle of Skye. But the real star of this show, which dominated over all the others in terms of quantity and variety of color, was from this farm: Glenkillen yarn.

The panorama of colored yarns before me were every hue of the rainbow and even beyond. And the textures! I wasn't a knitter, having suffered through too many frustrating instructions early on from right-handers who thought I should simply adapt and learn to knit right-handed. As if it were as easy as that. It would have been helpful if another left-handed knitter had been around during those failed attempts to reprogram my brain, but none of my own kind had appeared and I'd ended up moving on. But this visual experience was enough to make me want to try my hand at it one more time.

The other half of the store was devoted to finished woolen products: kilts, argyle jackets, tweed driving caps, sweaters, capes, scarves, all arranged as artfully as the yarn section. Clans and tartans rushed to mind from some of my pre-trip research. I knew that every clan in Scotland has its own tartan design, including my very own Elliott clan. Ours was a lovely bold blue, crisscrossed with deep yellow stripes. After a futile search for my family pattern, I wandered the aisles, careful to stay out of Kirstine's line of sight. Another tour bus arrived, filling up the shop with more new customers eager to spend money on souvenirs and gifts.

Not wanting to make Leith wait, I reluctantly left the shop sooner than I would have liked but with a sly grin of amusement at having toured it without being detected by enemy forces. I felt like I'd done a little undercover work for Vicki; not that I'd learned much other than that Sheepish Expressions appeared to be doing extremely good business. After my short visit to the MacBride farm, I was unsurprised that the family was up in arms over the contents of the will. Who *wouldn't* want to own this magical place?

Outside, I swept my eyes over the landscape and thought about Vicki's inheritance and James MacBride's overlooked other children. Why in the world would any father disown the very children who had kept his business in such excellent working order, who'd worked so hard to make it profitable? Was it really just an oversight? Someone in his sort of financial position surely had advisors. An oversight seemed unlikely.

Something wasn't quite right.

But all thoughts of family disputes and last wills evaporated as the rental car from hell came into view and Leith pulled up next to me in it. I'd like to say it was due to the sheer thrill of his presence, but in truth it was gut-wrenching anxiety that bubbled to the surface when Leith unfolded from the driver's seat and held the door open for me, sweeping his arm in a grand gesture that clearly implied the seat was all mine.

"We agreed you'd drive back," I reminded him, fighting against a blast of stress sweat.

"I've recovered from the first leg o' this exciting journey and am quite prepared for another go-round. *And* I truly believe with all my heart"—here he dramatically clutched his chest and grinned—"it will be more tranquil on the return."

Don't panic. Convince yourself that this is for the best, I told myself firmly.

It really was. If I wanted to experience the Highlands the right way, I needed wheels to get around. This car was all I had, so I plastered a happy smile on my not-very-happy-at-all face, something I was rather accomplished at. I slid in and waited for Leith to go around the front of the car and get into the passenger seat, and we were off. A little jerky at the onset, but I did believe I detected some minor improvements since the drive out.

I focused on the next roundabout coming up ahead, threw in the clutch, downshifted, and prepared to enter the circle of vehicles traveling at the speed of light and shooting off in every direction. "Take the third left," Leith said, guiding me through the spider's web.

Is it my imagination or is his voice a little shaky?

And, yes! We were through the roundabout!

After we arrived back to Glenkillen intact, Leith suggested lunch at the Kilt & Thistle. I suspect it was because he needed a stiff drink.

The same goateed bartender who had taken my order for Irn-Bru the night before greeted us from behind the bar. He wiped his hands on a bar rag, and gave my hand a hearty shake. "I'm Dale, the owner of this establishment. I would've properly introduced meself last night if I'd known ye were stayin' in town." He turned to a woman with cropped dark hair and a pale complexion at the other end of the bar and raised his voice, "And that's Marg, me wife, and those"—two young boys with flaming ginger hair ran past, roughhousing—"are our twins, Reece and Ross." He raised his voice in their direction. "And take that roughhouse play outside, ye troublesome bairns."

"I'm Eden Elliott," I said, laughing at the boys' antics. "Very nice to meet you."

"Elliott. 'Tis a good, strong Scottish surname."

"On my father's side, yes," I said.

Leith gave me a concentrated stare. "I see it now. Yes, ye *are* a Scottish lass."

"Wha' will ye be havin'?" Dale asked.

"What do you suggest?"

"We've a nice ale from Stirling."

"Ok, I'll try that, then."

"I'll have the same," Leith said, "and a whisky. Glenfiddich."

A whisky *and* an ale? I guess he really did need a stiff one.

Once we were seated at a table with a pint in front of each of us—Leith had tossed his whisky back in one swift motion while still at the bar—we placed the rest of our lunch order, both of us deciding on fish and chips, which I figured would be a nice safe bet with no surprise ingredients. Then our talk turned to murder, as I'd suspected it would.

"Gavin Mitchell's death is the main topic in all o' Glenkillen and far intae the countryside," Leith said. "He traveled all over for his shearing and was well thought of by all. He didn't have a single unsatisfied customer, let alone any enemies that any of us knew about, so ye can imagine what a shock it's been."

"I keep hearing what a wonderful man he was," I said. "But no one could possibly be that perfect."

"Gavin was. He never had a bad word for anybody and

he minded his own business. He provided a necessary service for the community and performed it better than any other person could, plus he frequently bought rounds here in this very pub, which ye can imagine went a long way in establishing loyalty."

I thought about what Leith and others had said about the sheep shearer. "If what you say is true, then maybe his death *was* a random act," I suggested, taking a sip of my brew and finding it deliciously rich and malty. "Like a robbery that went wrong. Gavin could have surprised someone in the act, maybe arrived home unexpectedly, they struggled, then the intruder picked up the shears and it ended badly. A robbery-turned-murder."

"It's certainly a possibility," Leith agreed. "But it takes a certain type o' wicked person tae kill another human in that manner."

I agreed. A stabbing was so . . . personal. "We have more shootings in the United States," I admitted. "We're a land of guns. And frankly, if I had to choose between dying from a gunshot wound or a deadly blade, I'd take the shooting any day."

"Guns aren't all that common here. Ye read mostly about stabbings in the newspapers," Leith explained. "But this is the first time one's happened in our village. Inspector Jamieson is good at his work, though, and with a bit of luck tae go along with his skill and experience, I trust he'll get tae the bottom of it."

"I spoke with him at the farm before you came back to pick me up. He came out to talk to Vicki, but he had a few more questions for me as well." I decided to withhold the fact that he seemed to be targeting Vicki in his investigation. "He doesn't seem to have overlooked anything. I have faith that he will find the killer."

"He throws himself intae his work, that's the truth."

"That must be hard on his wife," I said, thinking of the wedding ring on the inspector's finger.

"She died a few years back," Leith told me. "She fought the good fight, but in the end the cancer got her. Too young."

"No children?"

"He has a son, but from what I hear they aren't close."

We sat quietly after that, and I thought about how we all suffered our own losses—be they divorce, terminal disease such as my mother and the inspector's wife endured, or sudden death, as had been the sheep shearer's fate.

"Did Gavin Mitchell have any family?" I ask after a few moments of internal musing.

"He was a lifelong bachelor, the last of the Glenkillen Mitchells. And if he enjoyed the company of a woman on his travels, it was beyond my ken."

"I've been reminded of just how precious time is. And of course, I have regrets."

"Aye, we all have those."

I raised an eyebrow. "Really? You don't seem to have a care in the world."

"Now, why would ye be saying that?"

"It's true, isn't it?"

Leith raised his glass to his lips. Just before taking a drink, he said, "We all get tae keep our own secrets, now, don't we, Eden Elliott?"

CHAPTER 10

I spent the evening holed up in my room hovering over my laptop, thankful for the Whistling Inn's Internet connection. Checking my e-mail, I found that Ami had sent several, all variations on a theme: "Is the guy who saved you on his white horse, single? Cute? You really need to get back on the horse that threw you. Ha-ha. Have you checked out kilts yet? And if not, why not?"

"Okay," she'd written in the last one, "so maybe your introduction to Scotland wasn't the smoothest (although I'm telling you, that guy has serious possibilities), but at least you made it to the Highlands in one piece. The rest of your trip will probably be smooth sailing from here on out."

If only.

Back in Chicago, Ami wouldn't have been awake yet. She wasn't an early riser, and with the time difference she wouldn't see my return e-mail for several hours more. I could only imagine her expression as I wrote up the events that had occurred since my comparatively tame earlier adventure with the rental car breakdown. Finding the sheep shearer's dead body, and my subsequent introduction to a Scottish murder investigation, sure trumped a little car trouble!

After giving it a bit of thought, though—and to give myself a little breathing space from my overly concerned friend—I went back and downplayed the criminal aspects of my trip and added a little scolding about her pushiness. "You," I wrote back, "are so transparent! Please read my virtual lips: I. Am. Not. Looking. For. A. Romantic relationship! Now I'm off to write." And I signed off by reassuring Ami that "I might go off-line here and there but only to devote time to the novel. Don't worry about me. Everything is peachy!"

Right. Just peachy.

With that, I closed my e-mail and turned my attention to my work in progress, *Falling for You*.

My heroine, Gillian Fraser, returns to her hometown in Rosehearty, Scotland, after having her heart broken and is working for her brother's dive shop, taking divers out into the North Sea to explore shipwrecks and view sea life. (I'd done some fascinating research on diving but knew I'd have to get out there to experience it firsthand as well sometime.) She encounters rugged, sexy Jack Ross, wealthy owner of a local distillery who doesn't believe in love at first sight until he meets Gillian, and then . . .

Well, this was where I was a bit stuck. Could Gillian and Jack discover a love strong enough to last?

I certainly hadn't.

But this was fiction. Anything could happen, and I had every intention of making their relationship work.

So, with renewed commitment, I lost myself in the story, adding some of the Highlands' amazing scenery into the first chapters. My best friend might have been correct when she told me I had to experience its beauty to make it come alive on the page. I wrote, or rather revised, until around midnight, when I'd finished reworking several chapters. Writing always transports me to a place far removed from the real world, but now my blurring vision told me it was time for bed.

I changed into my standard nightwear, a well-worn over-sized T-shirt, and climbed into bed. I'd kept busy all day, surrounded by people and activities, so I hadn't had time to think much about the murder victim, or the protruding sheep shears, or all the blood on the floor. Until now. Those disturbing images would be with me for a long time, maybe forever.

Unlike last night, tonight sleep eluded me. I tried counting sheep, which seemed apropos, considering my current location. I'd never counted sheep before, but it must have worked, because the next thing I knew, the clock on the nightstand had fast-forwarded several hours and someone was shouting in the hallway.

"Where's it coming from?" I heard a man yell. He sounded close, right outside my door. "We have to find the source!"

Right then, I smelled smoke, the feeling of it raw in my lungs, leeching precious oxygen from the room. I slung the covers aside and leapt from bed. At the same time I heard banging on my door.

"In here!" More banging. "This way. Break it down if you have to."

I quickly unlocked and flung the door open before whoever was out there started smashing it in. A wave of bodies rushed in, almost trampling me in their haste. Something in the air was seriously irritating my eyes.

Glancing into the hallway, I could see that the other guests were awake and making their way toward the exit.

Voices continued to shout.

"Wait outside!"

"Go on, hurry!"

"Fire!"

Someone opened my bathroom door. Thick smoke billowed out. I began to cough.

"Everybody get outside!"

It finally registered with my confused, oxygen-deprived mind: The inn was on fire! I had to get outside before I inhaled any more smoke. My throat contracted, and I found myself coughing uncontrollably. How long had I been sleeping while smoke was wafting into my room? It didn't matter. I was alive, and if I wanted to stay that way, I had to get out.

My mind was a jumble. Should I take my things with me? Money? Passport? I couldn't think straight with all the commotion. Someone decided for me. A man gave me a shove. "Get going if you want to see the light of day."

My gaze fell upon my laptop. I grabbed it and ran out into the hallway, tripping along, realizing I was one of the last guests to vacate when Jeannie practically shoved me from the building. She followed swiftly behind me, glancing back, a worried expression on her face.

"Is your father out?" I called to her.

"Aye. He's safe and sound," she answered, moving off.

A fire-and-rescue truck had arrived, a miniature version of the kind of fire trucks I was used to seeing in America, immense vehicles with every kind of lifesaving piece of equipment and long, powerful hoses. This one seemed dinky in comparison. Could it really get the job done?

Outside, fresh, cool air cleared my mind. I shivered while taking a quick inventory of all I'd left behind . . . which amounted to almost everything. Except for my manuscript, tucked away safely inside a file on my laptop. We all have our own priorities in an emergency, and this had been mine. Adding my cardigan or a blanket to the list would have been a nice touch.

As I stared up at the building, at the window of my room, where smoke rolled out through the now open window, one of the other guests turned to me, angry and fearful. "This is yer fault!"

"Mine! What?" I'd had nothing to do with this.

"Smokin' in bed, that's wha'!" another guest decided.

"I don't smoke," I said in my defense. "I've never smoked. Maybe it was faulty wiring."

No one seemed convinced.

By now, the emergency fire brigade was taking charge, rolling out hoses, handing out equipment, all operating as one well-oiled machine. Thankfully, I hadn't seen any flames inside, but smoke was still making its way out of the building. Had the fire been contained? *Please, be contained.* I kept glancing down the street, hoping another fire truck would arrive. Because this little one could use some help.

"Aren't more trucks coming?" I asked whoever wanted to listen.

"This is the only one within close tae fifty kilometers." Metric conversion isn't my strong suit even on a good day, and it must have been apparent because the person speaking helped me out. "That's about thirty miles."

The only one within thirty miles? From my extremely limited but highly memorable experience with the Highlands' narrow, windy roads, I knew it could take a good hour or longer to travel thirty miles. It had taken me much longer than that coming the forty or so miles from Inverness. By the time backup arrived, the entire town might burn down.

No flames yet, though.

"It's yerself again," I heard from behind me, and I turned

to find Inspector Jamieson addressing me in a rather resigned, exhausted manner. "I haven't had a good night's rest since ye arrived. It's like having a newborn pup keeping me up till all hours o' the night."

His gaze traveled down to the hem of my shirt, reminding me that all I was wearing beneath it was my underwear. He quickly turned his eyes elsewhere. "Yer shivering, lass. We'll have tae get ye covered up somehow," he said. "And find ye lodging elsewhere."

I hadn't thought about actually abandoning my room and all my belongings for longer than it took to contain the source of the smoke. I clutched the laptop. "My car keys are up in the room, my money, everything. How can I go anywhere?"

The inspector's look shifted over my shoulder. "I'm guessing a ride is here fer ye," he told me.

A ride? Sure enough, as I turned in bewilderment, I saw Vicki MacBride making her way toward me with a blanket under her arm. Inspector Jamieson moved off as Vicki swept me into her arms and squeezed.

"I can't breathe," I managed to choke out when she didn't let go.

"Oh, sorry," she said, releasing me and wrapping the blanket around my freezing body. "It's that I'm relieved is all."

"How did you find out about the fire?" Small-town gossip couldn't have made its way to the farm—and certainly not to Vicki—so quickly. She nodded to where I now saw the volunteer police officer from earlier talking to several inn guests. "Sean Stevens called and warned me that you might need a friend," she said. "I almost had a heart attack when the phone rang at that hour of the morn, but I'm glad he let me know." She looked down at my bare legs, still exposed to the crisp night air.

"Everything I own except this computer is up in my room," I told her. "Passport, cash, shoes, everything."

"Come home with me, then, and we'll fix you up."

"I can't leave yet. What if they let me back into my room?"

Vicki took a moment to study the situation—the fire truck and the smoke still escaping from the open window. "It won't happen for hours, if then. Plus, you smell like a chimney and you're half-naked under that blanket. Let's get you a shower and you can wear one of my nighties. It'll be a bit big for you, but I suspect you won't mind."

Vicki led me to her car, where her two West Highland terriers, Pepper and Coco, were waiting for us.

Glancing up into the cloudless sky, I thanked my lucky stars for this new friend. I didn't know what I would have done without her.

CHAPTER 11

The next morning, Pepper and Coco greeted me by jumping up on the bed, an amazing feat, considering their small sizes. The Westies lavished me with attention in the form of wet kisses and moist, cold nose rubs. One of them rolled over for a belly rub. "You must be Pepper," I said, spotting a telltale black marking.

Outside the window, the sky was steel gray and rain streaked the glass. Vicki had given me a nightgown at least three times too large and then had ceremoniously thrown my odorous, sooty T-shirt in the outdoor trash.

What day of the week was it anyway? It took a moment to remember that it was Saturday.

"I've got porridge cooking on the stove," Vicki said when I made an appearance in the kitchen. She looked much fresher than I felt. "And I put the kettle on when I heard you stirring. You sure slept a long time, but I expect you needed it."

She placed two individual pots of tea next to place

settings, then sunk down in one of the chairs. "The tea has been steeping long enough. Go on, sit."

I sat down and looked around the kitchen. It was large, a combination kitchen and dining room, with a built-in washer and dryer.

I imitated my hostess by pouring a cup of tea and adding a dash of milk from a small pitcher. After taking a sip, I judged it to be the way I'd drink tea from now on. Delicious.

"How do you make your tea?" I asked her. "It's wonderful."

Vicki beamed. "Nothing to it really. Just steep one bag of tea for each cup, then add one for the pot. And don't forget to cradle the pot in a nice tea cozy."

She made it sound so simple.

After a few minutes, she rose and transferred a bowl of dark fruit from the counter to the table.

Vicki confirmed my suspicion. "Prunes. They're good for you."

Had I ever eaten prunes before? Not that I recalled. But after tasting them, I decided I liked prunes.

Next, she scooped up porridge from a pot on the stove, filled two bowls, and came back to the table.

"I have news," she told me, placing one of the bowls in front of me. "Some good. Some not so good."

"Great," I said with a dab of sarcasm.

"Which would you prefer to hear first? The good? Or the not so good?"

"The good news," I decided, digging into the bowl of oatmeal.

"Well, first is that that nice Officer Stevens fetched your car and dropped it off this morning with the help of another bloke. The keys are in the vase next to the door."

I wasn't sure that was good news.

"*And* the Whistling Inn didn't burn beyond repair," Vicki said. "But your wing suffered smoke damage, and apparently the fire was set off in your room. No question about it. How do you suppose that happened?"

"I have no idea," I said stiffly. "I hope you're not implying that I set it intentionally."

"Nothing of the sort. You see, though, here in Scotland, and in most parts of the UK, we have a real fear of fire and take every precaution against it."

I suspected as much, considering every establishment I'd entered had fire extinguishers front and center.

Vicki went on, "For example, we don't typically have electric outlets inside bathrooms like you do in the States. Lord, that's just asking for trouble, in a Scot's opinion. But there may have been an outlet in yours for men's shavers only and a sign warning as much. You didn't try to stick the hair dryer plug into it, did you?"

I shook my head. "No, of course not."

"The voltage here has twice the strength of that in the States. If you tinker around and get a zap here, it isn't a little shock to the system like you're used to. A bolt of it will drop you dead in your tracks. That's a future warning from a friend who doesn't want to see you perish."

I hadn't touched the outlets, but it was apparent Vicki didn't believe me. And if she didn't, nobody else was going to believe me, either.

"Well, however it took place," Vicki said, "good thing somebody on the street noticed smoke pouring out your open window or we might not be having this conversation. You'd be dead from smoke inhalation, and then I'd have lost a friend as soon as I'd found her."

I lost my appetite with the spoon midway to my mouth. Open window? I hadn't left the window open. I'd seen one open when I watched from the outside, but I'd assumed a firefighter had opened it.

I set the spoon down. "Are you sure the window was open? Who told you that?"

"The inspector, so I have no cause to doubt it."

Had someone started that fire in my room, perhaps entering—or exiting—through the bathroom window? It wouldn't have been difficult; my room was only on the second floor, not that hard to scale the outer wall. Once inside, they could have set the fire and exited the same way they'd come in while I was sound asleep in the next room.

I shuddered at the thought. How creepy would that be? Who would do such a thing? And why? And would anybody believe me when I insisted I had nothing to do with what happened?

But if Vicki's good news was that the fire had begun in my room, I didn't want to hear the not-so-good news.

"The other news," she went on before I could properly prepare myself, "is that the inspector is coming round, and it can't be for a social visit." She glanced over my shoulder in the direction of the entryway. "And speak of the devil, there he is."

Sure enough, her words were followed by a knock on the door. Pepper and Coco started barking after the fact, and Vicki rose to let a very damp Inspector Jamieson into the house.

I wondered if I'd have been so quick to let in the police if this had been Chicago. Letting a cop into your home without a warrant wasn't the American way, especially if said cop is out to get you. But here was Vicki not only welcoming the inspector, but offering him tea while taking his umbrella and seating him across the table, where he could study me with those questioning, intelligent, penetrating eyes of his.

I shifted awkwardly, self-conscious in Vicki's nightgown. At least I'd showered and washed the smoke out of my hair last night.

"According tae the fire chief, it wasn't an electrical fire," the inspector announced, addressing me. "Besides, yer electric appliances were still packed away inside yer luggage with the proper transformer beside them."

Despite his clearly intending this to console me, knowing he'd gone through my things felt like a major violation. What exactly were my rights in Scotland? Did I have any, as a guest in their country? I forced myself to relax, deciding to face his interrogation with confidence. After all, *I* knew I hadn't set the fire.

"Perhaps," he continued after preparing his tea, "it wasn't accidental at all."

"Yes. Perhaps," I retorted, feeling myself bristle, even though I had no idea what he was implying, "it really was arson on someone's part, that someone *not* being me."

"We'd never think you had anything to do with it," Vicki said. "Not on purpose."

I continued firmly, wanting to force the inspector's hand. "Now that you've ruled out an accident, isn't the only other explanation that it was set intentionally?"

The inspector remained silent, staring at his teacup.

I kept going. "I didn't stuff flammable material in the garbage and light it on fire before turning in for the night, if that's what you think. What kind of nut would that make me?"

Okay, so he didn't know me. I could be a nut.

"I've had just about enough of your insinuations," I burst

out angrily, even as part of me realized that the inspector had actually said very little. It was what was left unsaid that was most important. "I'm sure you are perfectly aware that my background is spotless."

"I'm aware o' that."

I raised an eyebrow.

"Background checks are routine," the inspector said, rather stiffly, "in situations such as these."

"Fires, you mean? Or murders?" I was so angry, although I had to admit to myself that my anger might be misdirected at this man who was charged with investigating, when it was the circumstances themselves that had me frustrated and fuming.

"Now, calm yourself down," Vicki said. "Do either of you want a nice almond biscuit?"

I wasn't finished with him yet. "Do you mind everybody else's business so thoroughly? How about Vicki? Did you do a thorough background check on her?"

A moment of silence ensued.

"Well, did you?" Vicki said, hands on hips now that his investigation might broaden to compromise her personal life as well.

Of course he would have. But apparently she hadn't thought that far.

"I do my job as I see fit," he replied to her, not answering directly, then he turned to me. "I apologize if I've offended ye, but ye might be more sympathetic if ye looked at the situation from my point o' view."

"It's been an exhausting few days," I muttered in my defense. A real understatement.

"I'd like tae hear yer opinion o' what happened in that room," he said. "Without ye feeling ye have tae get defensive."

"I'll get those biscuits," Vicki said with traces of anger still in her tone. She hurried to get them and returned to the table in a flash.

After careful consideration, and without being sure if he really valued my opinion or if he was hoping to lead me down a path of self-incrimination by letting me talk myself into a corner, I responded. "Bear with me for a moment and consider this possibility," I suggested, breathing deeply to calm down. "I wonder if whoever set it didn't want to actually harm me or anyone else staying at the inn. If that were the case, the person responsible wouldn't have left the window open for the smoke to escape."

"Ye mean it wasn't ye who left it open?" the inspector asked, clearly surprised.

I shook my head. "When I went to bed, the window was closed."

"Did you remember latching the window before bed?" Vicki asked.

"No, but I didn't notice whether it was locked or not, either."

"Must o' been unlocked," the inspector said. "There was no evidence of a forced entry."

I continued. "What if the Whistling Inn was the target? Maybe the arsonist wanted to shut it down for some reason, at least temporarily. Since I only just arrived, and no one in all of Scotland could possibly have a grudge against me, I'm going to guess that my room was chosen at random. Maybe my window just happened to be unlocked."

While I wasn't sure I believed my own theory, it did have some merit. And if there was a way to get the inspector to look for the real culprit, I'd give him as many theories as he could process.

"Or," Vicki added, "it was an inside job. Whoever cleans

the rooms might have left the window unlocked for an accomplice."

"Whatever the case," the inspector said, "I'm afraid that the smoke damage won't be cleaned up anytime too soon. Which reminds me, I have yer bags in my Honda. I put them there as soon as the fire brigade told me it was safe tae go up. Wouldn't want anybody rummaging through yer personal belongings."

He read the look on my face, and added, "Anybody who isn't conducting official business, is wha' I meant tae say."

"Well, thanks," I said. I still wasn't happy he'd gone through them, but I was grateful he'd brought them over.

A few moments passed while we all savored Vicki's biscuits and sipped our tea. Then the inspector glanced out the window. He let out a heavy sigh, and said, "Bugger. The fool managed to track me down."

I followed his gaze to where volunteer police officer Sean Stevens was hurrying up the walkway.

"Ye will never guess what I've just found out!" Sean fairly shouted when Vicki let him inside out of the rain, after stopping briefly to shake himself like a wet dog.

"I'm not in the mood fer games," the inspector roared at him.

"Most o' the blood on the floor wasn't belongin' tae the sheep shearer after all," Sean told us with great excitement. "The results came back while ye were out and aboot, Inspector."

The inspector looked pained. "If this is official business," he said to his trainee, "ye best be keepin' it between the two o' us and not go shouting it from the rooftops."

But the newbie cop was too excited to contain himself. "It weren't Gavin Mitchell's blood on the floor o' the cottage," Sean announced.

"Stop!" The inspector was on his feet.

But it was too late. "It was pig's blood, cannae ye believe it?"

Inspector Jamieson looked about to explode. He practically hauled Sean off by the scruff of his neck.

The last thing we heard from Sean as he was whisked outside was, "Wha's the matter? Wha'?"

"Ye have a big mouth, is wha'!"

The inspector came back with my bags, his face set and grim as he placed them on the floor, then whirled around and stalked out without another word.

Then they drove off separately, the inspector gunning it down the lane, the special constable attempting to keep pace.

CHAPTER 12

"Well, my dear authoress," Vicki said when we were alone again, "what do you make of all that?"

I shook my head, remembering how much blood had been spilled at the scene of the crime. "Pig's blood on the floor around the body? I don't know what to think. Other than that I'm completely confused." And disgusted.

"Do you think some sort of werewolf thing got Gavin?"

I glanced at Vicki, who looked perfectly serious.

"You're kidding, right?" I said.

"Not a bit. But instead of being part wolf, his attacker would have been part pig, part human?"

I spotted the hint of a smile on Vicki's face at the absurdity of this new direction, so I teased her by saying, "What I think is that you lived in California too long."

"Don't laugh at me, or I won't give you any more biscuits."

I rearranged my face into a more somber expression, because her biscuits were delicious. "There, is this better?"

"Much." Vicki rose to clear the table, and I pitched in. "I'm sorry to be making light of such a grim situation, but if I don't, I think I'll begin crying and never stop."

I gave her a hug. "I understand perfectly," I said.

"What are you up to today?"

"I have something to take care of regarding a certain vehicle."

My first project of the day would be to get over my fear of the rental car.

"I think I'll stay indoors and tend to my knitting," Vicki said.

After happily discovering that the clothing inside my luggage still smelled fresh, and even more happily accounting for everything else—passport, cash, bank cards, etc.—I scooped the car keys out of the vase near the door and tackled the issue of the rental car.

Except it wouldn't start. Wouldn't even turn over. I tried every gear, every possible combination. Nothing.

Vicki came out and joined me wearing a rain jacket, the hood up over her head. "I called the car hire for you and told them to pick up this sad sack."

What a friend! I smiled. "Are they bringing me an automatic?"

She shook her head. "Even better. I have one of my da's cars for you to use, same as I am. No sense wasting your hard-earned money."

I followed her to the barn, where she threw open the massive doors. There, beside the blue Citroën I'd ridden in last night, stood what I gathered was the offered transportation.

"What is it?" I asked as we moved inside to take shelter from the rain.

"An old Peugeot that's been here since I was a bairn,"

she told me, beaming. "She's seen much of the land in these parts, I'm guessing. And with the keys in her ignition, all set to go."

"Automatic?" I said, ever hopeful.

"Afraid not, but you'll manage."

"Does it run?" I said, not wishing to appear ungrateful, but hoping it wouldn't.

"I couldn't get it to turn over, but that doesn't mean much. She might just need a battery charge. We'll soon find out. Leith will be here anytime now to put the tools to her."

I couldn't think of a single tactful way out. "I can't let you do this," I said weakly. "You've already done so much for me. How could I ever repay you?"

She waved me off, ignored my protests, and went back to the house.

After all my determination not to rely on a man for help, here I was waiting for one to help me. And the same one again to boot. Well, when it came to vehicles, I guess I'd just have to accept any help I could get.

A few minutes later, Leith's Land Rover pulled up next to the barn.

He hopped out, his border collie, Kelly, right behind him. My heart gave a little involuntary flutter, not a reaction I had expected—but neither had I expected to see Leith climb out of his car wearing a kilt. Not the whole formal getup, like I'd seen on the MacBrides at the funeral or on the occasional bagpiper; Leith wore his kilt paired with a black T-shirt and laced-up boots. A manly look I could definitely get used to.

He headed for shelter from the rain and grinned when he came up beside me, then whispered, his mouth close to my ear. "I see ye staring at my kilt, and I bet yer wondering what's worn under it."

I felt my face heating up. Were my thoughts that transparent? Because in a flash I *had* recalled Ami's airport comment about finding out what was under those Scottish kilts.

"Well, are ye?" he pressed.

I shrugged, willing the color in my cheeks to return to normal.

"Nothin's worn under my kilt," he said with a naughty twinkle in his eyes. "'Tis all in working order." Then he winked and burst out laughing at the expression on my face.

I felt myself continue to blush through the involuntary smile on my lips. He'd rattled me, which I was pretty sure had been his intention.

Thankfully, at that moment Kelly came up to me, and I quickly bent to greet her, hoping to hide my schoolgirl reaction to Leith's double entendre.

"What's the occasion?" I asked Leith when I recovered, seeing that he'd opened the Peugeot's hood and had turned his attention to wires and mechanical parts. "Why the kilt?"

"I promised my girl I'd wear it fer her. I'm on my way tae see her next."

"Ah," I said, my stomach dropping involuntarily. But I quickly regrouped. Not only was I not interested in the man—or any man, I scolded myself—but I'd also suspected Leith was taken from the very beginning. I guess the flirting had made me forget.

Feeling embarrassed, I took advantage of a pause in the rain to leave Leith puttering under the hood while I wandered down to Sheepish Expressions.

And, once again, soon found everything spinning in a new direction.

CHAPTER 13

It was still morning, and Sheepish Expressions could only have been open for a short time. The parking lot was completely empty on this rainy Saturday, but a tour bus pulled in just as I arrived.

Upon exiting the bus, a woman turned to her male traveling companion, and said, "The Loch Ness Monster is only a legend. Just another tourist attraction, if you ask me."

The bus driver heard her, and piped up, saying, "Oh no, it's real for sure. Enough o' us have seen Nessie tae confirm her existence. And bones of another huge sea serpent were recently found in Russia, a cousin to our famous girl, their researchers say."

The woman harrumphed her disbelief. I figured the bus driver had a good line; whether or not the tourists believed in the giant lake dweller or not, they sure were showing up in one busload after another hoping for a sighting.

I stepped inside the shop behind the skeptic and took a sharp turn away from the counter. I slunk amongst the fine woolen clothing, enjoying the textures of all the lovely apparel. July hardly seemed the right time of the year to buy woolen products, but that wasn't stopping these shoppers. The woman next to me picked out an armful of brightly patterned cashmere scarves. When she noticed my interest, she said, "I know it's still July, but Christmas will be here before we know it. My friends and family will love these!"

After making a mental note to do some holiday shopping myself before flying back to Chicago, I ducked into the attached knitting room, where I pored over binders and magazines filled with patterns. They could have been Greek for all that I understood of the directions, but the photos of the finished products again lured me into thoughts of retrying my hand at knitting.

When I returned to earth from a dreamworld of possibilities, the knitting room was empty. So was the shop, judging by the lack of voices. Presumably the previous tour bus had departed for its next destination, and the next one hadn't arrived yet.

I heard a male voice call out, "Anybody left inside the shop?" and before I could figure out my plan of action, a female voice responded, "They're all gone, John. Next bus arrives in about five minutes."

John. That must be John Derry, Kirstine MacBride's husband, the one who tended the farm's sheep, the same one who had egged on his wife when she verbally attacked Vicki in the pub. I couldn't see him at the moment, but I had a visual in my head of the big, brash bully. I'd been about to declare myself, but now I only wanted to hide. I ducked down on the other side of the wall.

"Can I have a word with ye, Kirstine?" I heard him say to his wife. My ear had adjusted to the local accent enough to recognize that John's was different—somewhat similar, but not exactly the same. Nor did it sound like the rest of the MacBrides'.

I panicked, hearing their voices coming closer. Hiding had been a stupidly rash move on my part. It's one thing to be discovered alone in a back room, paging through magazines, blissfully unaware of your surroundings. It's another to be caught hunkered down, listening like a Peeping Tomette.

But that's exactly what had happened.

I'd hunkered.

And I was about to be busted with no good explanation to offer.

"The inn had ta close," John said from way too close, right on the other side of the wall. "And now the nosy American is here at the farm, those two gettin' tight like herrings in the salt."

Were they talking about me? Of course they were. Nobody else fit that description. And my current dilemma went a long way in proving the nosy part.

"The plan is in place," Kirstine said. "She could ruin it for us."

"I'll take care oof it. We want what's rightfully due us, is all."

"Turner should've warned the rest of the family," Kirstine said, "before it was too late. He's supposed to be the loyal family solicitor, but after this, I can't be so sure."

"Your stepsister killed Gavin Mitchell, then, that's the story we continue ta tell?"

"Who else would have done such a thing?"

"Handle both busybodies at once, is me thinkin'."

"That's my thought exactly."

If I was interpreting this pair's meaning correctly, and I was pretty sure I was, they were dangerous to my health. And to Vicki's. If they came around the corner into the room and saw me, I'd be in very real danger. The next bus of shoppers couldn't arrive fast enough.

I held my breath, my heart pounding so loudly that I thought the sound of it would give me away. But a bell tinkled in the front of the shop, and I heard the husband-and-wife conspirators move off.

They said they had a plan. What plan? And how did they think I could ruin it? There had been so many scary implications of ill will toward Vicki and me in that conversation. John had sounded disappointed that I was safe.

The purpose of the fire might have been to shut down the inn, but John had just presented another, one that concerned me decidedly more. Had he set it himself to scare me away?

Just as I was about to give up, I heard a miracle—voices at the front of the shop. As more voices joined in, I rose up on shaky legs and leaned against the wall until I felt strong enough to make a hasty retreat, hopefully unseen.

A fine mist was falling, but I hardly noticed as I hurried back to the barn. On the way, I really began second-guessing the meaning of the conversation I'd overheard.

Never trust a writer for an accurate, unbiased account of any situation she can infuse with additional drama. My vivid imagination tended to take over, making the smallest, most insignificant detail a major point of concern. Were John and Kirstine really responsible for the fire *and* for Gavin's death *and* guilty of planning to add Vicki and me to their pile of corpses?

I slowed my pace, let a little rain fall on my face, and came back from the edge of reason.

By the time I returned, a very sexy and very unavailable Leith Cameron was able to proudly proclaim the Peugeot to be in fine working order, and I had pretty much convinced myself that I'd read way more into their meaning than I should have.

But part of me wouldn't let the idea die. I decided to share my concerns with the inspector.

CHAPTER 14

Once Leith went off to see his girl, I drove myself to Glen-killen behind the wheel of the Peugeot for the first time. I coaxed the car through the roundabouts, staying well below the speed limit, and still managed to scare myself silly.

After parking and taking a moment to compose myself, I found Inspector Jamieson standing in front of the Whistling Inn, intently studying the exterior of the building as if clues to the fire would appear if he stared long enough. What did I know? Maybe they would.

"Excuse me," I said, "but I'd like a word with you."

"Ah, it's yerself again. Very well, let's find a quiet place tae talk. How about inside the pub? Will that do?"

"Yes, thank you."

A chalk billboard on the sidewalk outside the Kilt & Thistle announced *Pub Fayre!,* a new advertisement addition since last I'd been here, and even in my agitated state I managed to find some humor in that small slice of local color. Inside, we wound between occupied tables and found one tucked back in a corner, where we both decided on hot tea. The inspector also placed an order for food, and we made small talk until the tea arrived.

Over tea, I related to him what I'd overheard inside Sheepish Expressions—skipping over the part where I'd hidden on the floor, a detail too personally embarrassing to share, but the rest I laid out on the table, so to speak—as close to verbatim as I could possibly remember.

Inspector Jamieson listened without interrupting. When I finished, he said, "Based on my previous association with MacBride family members, I'm o' the personal opinion that they would have no qualms about using ye tae their own advantage. Kirstine and John probably knew ye were within earshot and were playing ye like a fiddle. That's why they had such a conversation right where ye couldn't help but overhear."

"I don't believe that," I said, although there was some logic to his explanation, one much less threatening to my future good health. If scaring me had been their intent, they'd succeeded.

The inspector went on with his assessment of the family. "John Derry has a hot temper, but it's all bluster, it is. His brother-in-law, Alec, tries to keep him in line but he's a hopeless case. John's already been spreading rumors aboot ye and Vicki, suggesting you two are in cahoots."

In the big city, for better or worse, nobody cared what anybody else said or did. Our lives were busy with long commutes into work, and afterward with families to tend to. Who had time for all this speculation and gossipmongering? Small-town ways were going to take some getting used to.

"Cahoots?" I echoed.

"Aye. According tae John, he wouldn't be surprised if ye'd been caught robbing Gavin Mitchell and one o' you killed him."

So John and Kirstine were already putting their so-called plan into place. They intended to drive us away one way or the other. "Is there anything you can do to counter that outrageous claim?" But I knew the answer before he opened his mouth.

He shook his head. "I don't make a habit o' responding one way or the other tae local gossip. All that matters is that I know the truth, and the truth o' your statement has been confirmed as accurate."

My knee-jerk reaction was to be offended that he'd actually checked up on the details, but I reminded myself that it was his job not to take me at my word. I sighed and let it go.

"John Derry is causing trouble for ye, and it isn't right," the inspector went on. "But he won't continue tae be a problem."

"Easy for you to say," I said. "People will believe what they want to believe. I'm most concerned about the Mac-Brides' campaign to cast suspicion on Vicki regarding Gavin Mitchell's murder. At some point in the near future, I'll fly back home to Chicago, but Vicki will have to face these vicious rumors daily."

"The killing of Gavin Mitchell is aboot tae be cleared up anyway, thanks to an important tip from Dale Barrett and his wife Marg, the owners of this fine establishment."

Just then, said owner set a steaming plate in front of us. "Always willing to help put criminal elements away," Dale said, before heading off at full speed to serve his other customers.

"The Kilt and Thistle has the best Scotch eggs in all of the country," the inspector announced when he noticed me observing the contents of the plate he'd ordered for us. "A new experience for ye tae put intae that novel yer writing. Careful—they're hot out o' the fryer."

Chicago's Irish pubs might serve Scotch eggs, but if so, I'd never had them. "They aren't wrapped in haggis, are they?" I asked, suspiciously eyeing the items in question.

He smiled. "No, but that's a fine idea. I'll suggest Dale give it a go. But this batch has similar ingredients—these hard-boiled eggs are wrapped in sausage, then rolled in bread crumbs and deep-fried. That's hot mustard sauce in the bowl beside it. Well, what are ye waiting for?"

Then he helped himself. So I followed his example, cutting off a piece of the egg, dipping it into the tangy mustard sauce, and carefully taking a small bite. They certainly couldn't be classified as health food, what with the sausage and the frying involved, so of course they were delicious.

"What's this new tip about?" I asked after I'd devoured two eggs and wiped my greasy fingers on my napkin.

While we continued to eat Scotch eggs and drink our tea, the inspector told me about how Dale's tip had given the case a new direction, pointing toward a likely suspect and, hopefully, a solved murder case.

"A while back, Gavin Mitchell, God rest his soul, made a trip to shear sheep near Elgin," Inspector Jamieson began. "Afterwards, being a man o' routine, Gavin stopped at a local pub he frequented when he was on the road, tae have a wee dram before heading home. He'd barely had time tae park when he came upon a nasty fight between two boozers. One o' them smashed a glass bottle over the other's head, seriously injuring him, but the other fella went on kicking the man even as he lay on the ground.

"Gavin always was a peaceful type, but strong as they come. He got involved and managed tae keep the brute from escaping until the police arrived. The both of them were charged with violent disorder. The loser got a suspended sentence, mainly because he'd been pounded tae pulp and he didn't have any prior incidents in a police file. But the other—Samuel Kerr's his name—had a long record of arrests, mostly for assault. Kerr was incarcerated for nine months."

"Gavin Mitchell sounds like a good man."

"That he was. We all knew aboot Gavin's experience at the time. When he went tae court tae testify, the folks here at the Kilt and Thistle bought him a round for making sure justice was served. But then it became old news, and we all forgot aboot it. Turns out Kerr was released last week."

"And Dale's tip?" I prompted.

"Our Dale has a sharp eye, and he spotted something. Not right away, but after his mind had a chance to dwell on it for a few days. He remembered the boozer's face from the papers all those months ago. So he rung me up last night in the middle o' the night tae say he'd seen the same face in the bar just the week before. Dale's wife, Marg, vouches for it as well. They went on their computer and found this Kerr fella's likeness. Marg confirmed that it was the same man as was in the pub, sitting in a corner looking like he had a heart filled with hate."

"This was the week before Gavin was killed?"

"Aye."

"He might have hung around the area, waited for Gavin."

"We're tracking down this Samuel Kerr now."

"Revenge is a powerful motive," I said.

The inspector said sadly, "That was an unlucky day for Gavin. He was in the wrong place at the wrong time, and sure he saved the one bloke from more o' a beating, but he paid a steep price. He never did get that whisky for the road, and now he's dead, possibly at the hands o' that violent character."

"We can't know how our good deeds might affect our

lives," I said. Then a new thought occurred to me. "But how does that explain the pig's blood?" I asked.

Inspector Jamieson scowled, whether from the fact that animal blood had been left at the scene or over his unprofessional new partner's loose lips, I didn't know.

"Gavin was killed someplace else, according to the official finding," he said. "Murdered in the early hours of Tuesday morning in a different location."

"Really?" This was big news. Although nothing was adding up. "What was the point of moving the body, let alone mixing in animal blood?"

"It would take an individual with a very low IQ tae think he could fool Forensics with that ploy, but this jailbird doesn't strike me as a particularly smart individual."

"Have you searched near the pub?" I asked. "Maybe he followed Gavin and killed him on his way home."

"Aye, I have, and nothing came o' it. Someplace out there is the real crime scene, and I'll find it. Once we bring in Kerr, we'll have more answers."

If Inspector Jamieson was able to wrap up this case with charges against Samuel Kerr, that would change a few things in the public's eyes in favor of my new friend. Any more attempts by John Derry to sway public opinion in regard to Gavin's death would go up in smoke, along with his credibility. The locals would see right through him and not be so quick to accept his lies in the future. At least, so I hoped. But I couldn't get the conversation I'd overheard between the Derrys out of my head. Even with a new suspect in the inspector's sights, I worried that John and Kirstine were dangerous.

"I'm still afraid of what John Derry is capable of doing to Vicki or to me," I told him. "The man is an ogre."

But the inspector scoffed at my concerns again. "John Derry is a big blowhard. I still believe he knew ye were listening in. He must o' seen ye enter and knew ye didn't leave with the rest o' the customers. At most he was just talking tough. I've seen the man cry over one of his dogs when the poor thing had tae be put down. Does that sound like a man who would hurt anybody?"

The inspector looked up, and recognition crossed his face. I followed his line of sight as he said, "There's Alec MacBride. He just came in. See him ordering from Dale?"

"What is Alec MacBride's role in the family business? I haven't heard him mentioned much."

"Not even a wee bit of interest," the inspector answered, proving me right. "He's an accountant by trade, and the business coulda used his skills. But he chose tae go off and start his own practice."

"Was James MacBride disappointed that his son didn't pursue the family business? Did he consider him the black sheep of the family?"

The inspector smiled. "Ah, you noticed that black sheep on the hills aren't nearly as plentiful as the white. They're a particularly hardy lot. As tae James's opinion o' his son, that I couldn't tell ye. He kept his private affairs tae himself. But look now, Alec's spotted us and is coming our way."

Sure enough, Alec MacBride was winding his way from the bar toward our table, carrying a pint of ale. I continued my quick assessment as he stopped before us. Alec was shorter, stockier, and darker than his sister, his deep tan unusual amongst the classically pale Scots. And it was further set off by his crisp, spotless white polo shirt, cargo golf shorts, and white canvas shoes, worn with no socks. He sported an expensive watch but no other jewelry, and was clean-shaven. He'd clearly nicked himself this morning, though. A tiny flaw in his otherwise perfect appearance.

He nodded a greeting to the inspector, then gave me a warm and welcoming smile.

"Have ye two met?" the inspector asked.

"I haven't had the pleasure," Alec said.

The inspector performed introductions in perfect gentlemanly form, and I cringed inwardly when he said my name. Call me paranoid, but I expected the entire town to know that I'd participated in the discovery of the sheep shearer's body.

But Alec MacBride didn't have any reaction other than to offer his hand, which I took.

He practically bowed. A strong, confident grip, no calluses—Alec was a white-collar type through and through. Definitely not working class.

Inspector Jamieson rose, and said, "I'll be on my way. I've got a murder tae solve."

"You've answered my question then," Alec said. "That's the reason I came over, to inquire about the investigation."

"It's ongoing, is all I can tell ye." And with that, the inspector bid us a good day and walked off.

"Do you mind if I join you?" Alec asked me.

"Not at all."

As he took the inspector's vacated seat, I wondered if Alec knew that his half sister Vicki and I had hit it off and that I was currently rooming at the farm. If he did, he didn't give me any clues. But I vowed to stay alert for signs of manipulation, calling to mind the inspector's warning that the family would use me as a tool in their battle if I wasn't careful. Alec MacBride turned out to be one of those people you meet from time to time, the sort who spews personal information faster than a ruptured pipe gushes water. Within a very short amount of time I knew quite a bit about him, along with an assortment of his eclectic personal opinions on various subjects.

An avid golfer who lived in an apartment at his club, Alec told me that he was a financial advisor by trade who'd managed to escape the marriage trap multiple times—but, he was quick to reassure me, he certainly enjoyed a woman's company. This was accompanied by a big smile of appreciation to prove his point.

"I was at your father's gravesite," I said, "and then a little later at the pub. I'm sorry for your loss."

"Thank you," he said, but he barely paused before continuing to confide in me that his father's death had surprised him but not half as much as the contents of the will, which he didn't elaborate on, other than to mention that his sister was challenging it. But he had mixed feelings about her decision. As hurtful as his father's decision had been, why put his own selfish interests above his father's last wishes?

I didn't quite know what to make of Alec. He oozed overconfidence and self-absorption, never once directing a single personal question my way, yet I found myself relaxing and enjoying his company. He might have had an ego too large to contain, but he wasn't boring by any means. I suspected I was breathing easier around him *because* he wasn't putting me on the spot with questions I didn't care to answer. My role was easy: simply listening.

"Do you golf?" Alec asked, finally showing some interest in me.

"No, I've never tried it."

"We'll have to get you out on the golf course and give you a lesson. I learned at a very young age. From my father. Tell me, you said you were at the funeral—did you know my da?"

"No, I had just checked into my room at the inn, and I

followed the crowds. It's my first visit to Glenkillen. I'm sorry, I shouldn't have shown up." I'd been a funeral crasher. How inappropriate was that?

But Alec, like Leith when he'd first extended the invitation, thought nothing of it. "All were invited. Including a visitor to Glenkillen."

"I was there when your sister had the very public showdown with the new heiress," I said, hoping to broach the subject of his brother-in-law and the man's temper. "Thankfully, I saw you intervene and end it before it went spinning out of control."

"That was no place for such behavior," he said, shaking his head. "My stepsister should have known better."

"I met Vicki on my flight coming in and then again at the funeral," I told him, deciding it was better to get that information out in the open. "She doesn't strike me as the aggressive sort." That was my way of saying I thought the fault lay with Kirstine. "And your brother-in-law seemed to enjoy the spectacle."

"John might be gifted with the sheep and working dogs," Alec said with obvious distaste, "but he shouldn't be allowed out in public. He's like them, an animal."

Like a wolf, was my impression.

His opinion of John didn't make me feel one bit better regarding my safety or Vicki's. I'd have to warn her to be careful.

From now on, I'd be on guard and steer clear of John Derry.

CHAPTER 15

After Alec MacBride finished his pint, he took his leave, saying he had a tee time at the golf course. Once he'd gone, I pulled my laptop out of my bag and moved to a spot at a secluded table in the farthest reaches of the pub. The steady murmur of voices up front were white noise to me, which didn't interfere with my writing as long as it stayed in the background and didn't demand my attention by invading my personal space. It often even improved my concentration.

While Vicki might be filled with warmth and kindness, her lively personality was sure to intrude if I tried to write at her house. All I wanted and needed right now was some relative peace and quiet and room to do some work.

But first, I checked my e-mail. Nothing from Ami, but I shot one off into cyberspace to her. "I've found a perfect copy of my hero in the human form of Leith Cameron. And he wears a kilt well!"

There! That should keep her guessing.

The hands on the clock spun by and the pub activity around me ground to a halt as I entered the world I'd created, slipping into the elusive place every writer hopes to find when she sits down to write. It's completely indefinable, but once I get there, it reshapes my reality, taking me off this plane and depositing me onto a different one.

While I'm there, I'm not even aware of it. The keys on the computer seem to fly of their own accord and the story unfolds as though I'm just a bystander looking on. It's exhilarating and exhausting and oh-so-important to the writing process, much the same as the experience of a reader escaping into the pages of a great novel.

My subconscious took over while I was writing today's pivotal scene. I continued to share Gillian's current situation, which certainly wasn't a fulfilling one. She was about to meet "him"—Jack Ross, the man of her dreams. Her love interest had refused to materialize as a fully formed person until I'd arrived in Scotland and met Leith. Now, in my mind's eye I knew exactly how that would happen, how she would act, how he would respond. I worked on Gillian and Jack's first conversation. It sprang to life, and inwardly I grinned at their dialogue even as I wrote it. Jack's image came into sharp focus.

Who was he underneath the sexy skin, though? And what was there about him that spoke to her heart above all others? What did he have that set him apart? It had to be more than witty conversation.

Those were the questions I still needed to answer.

Eventually, I blinked back to awareness and realized I'd been writing for hours without a pause. *Nicely done, Eden,* I congratulated myself.

Even without all the romantic elements nailed down, it had been a great session. Lots of buildup to upcoming tension and conflict. *Hello, Calliope, goddess of inspiration. Who knew you thrived in Scottish pubs?*

What happened next might have been due to my imagination still being in high gear, but after I'd packed up and headed toward the door—calling good-bye to Dale, who was still behind the bar—I had the creepy feeling that every single head in the bar had turned my way and that the din had died while everybody's eyes followed me out.

It was unsettling to say the least. While I had told myself that I didn't care what anybody said about me, that if they wanted to believe vicious rumors spread by John Derry it wouldn't faze me in the least, now—faced with the possibility that the locals actually believed him—I had a spontaneous urge to made a public denial.

Listen, everyone: I am innocent of all wrongdoing! And so is Vicki MacBride!

Shakespeare popped into my head. *The lady doth protest too much, methinks.*

Don't do it, I told myself. *Don't feed the trolls.* I'd learned that lesson well from Ami, if not from *Hamlet.* My famous friend was a bestselling author, but she still got the occasional one-star review or snarky online comment—sometimes things so absurd that anyone reading the review would know that that person hadn't even read the book. But Ami never responded to negative criticism, allowing other readers to form their own opinions of the nasty review and the person behind it.

"People," she'd told me, "have short memories."

Besides, I had other immediate worries, more pressing and dangerous than mere rumors behind my back.

The borrowed car, for example.

Needing a few minutes to work up the nerve to once again take my life into my shaky hands and drive off in the Peugeot, I stalled by walking over to check on what was going on over at the Whistling Inn. I couldn't impose on Vicki's generosity indefinitely.

There was a Closed sign in the window, but when I tested the door I found it unlocked. Jeannie was tidying up in the reception area.

"Well if it isn't herself!" she sneered, all traces of hospitality gone from her voice.

Taken aback, I said, "I just stopped in to see whether you might reopen soon."

Jeannie snorted, causing her bull-like nose ring to quiver. "The other wing is ready fer guests today, once the fire marshal gives permission, which he promised would happen sharpish. But the other rooms will be vacant until next weekend, thanks tae yer carelessness."

"I didn't set the fire," I protested.

"It started in yer room." She had her hands on her hips now. "My da and I count on our livelihood from this inn. Ye've cost us a whole week o' losses."

"I'm very sorry about that, but like I said, I didn't have anything to do with what happened. Are there any rooms available in the other wing?"

"You're not thinking to move back in?" she said, frowning.

Here goes nothing. "Uh . . . well, as a matter of fact . . ."

"Well, don't even think it! The last thing we need is fer the whole bloody place tae go up in smoke! Just because I want tae get out o' toon, doesn't mean I wish bad luck on my da!"

"I. Didn't. Do. It." God, I sounded like a guilty kid. "Not only that: I've prepaid for two weeks."

"Are ye suggesting a refund? And after what ye did tae the inn?"

"I didn't start the fire!"

Jeannie wasn't buying it. "Off with ye," she snarled at me.

I beat a hasty retreat.

I was relieved to hear that at least the damage hadn't been severe enough to close the inn permanently, and that part of it would reopen shortly. I assumed Jeannie's father carried insurance. But would it cover lost income as well as smoke damage? I sure hoped that was the case. If it were, I'd feel so much better.

I walked back into the pub and down to the other end of the bar, where the owner was washing glasses. "Dale," I said. "Who owns the Whistling Inn next door?"

"Bill Morris," he said, adding steins to sudsy water. "But his daughter, Jeannie, mostly takes care o' the place on her own."

That I knew already. "Do you suppose they have insurance to cover the smoke damage?"

He shrugged. "I suppose they might."

"I'd like to speak with Mr. Morris. Do you know where I might find him?"

"Ye can speak to him, but it won't do ye much good, not today or tomorrow or any other day, I imagine."

"Why not?" Then I remembered Jeannie saying he was physically challenged. "Is he too incapacitated to even speak?"

Dale smiled. "I suppose ye could call it that, if ye were being kind aboot his affliction. See fer yerself. That's Bill himself over there in the corner."

I followed Dale's gaze and made out a still form in a darkened corner of the pub. As my eyes adjusted, I noticed something else. He was facedown on the table, snoring away.

Bill Morris was dead drunk.

Chapter 16

Unfortunately, I couldn't rouse the man. He was out cold.

Leaving Bill Morris to his drunken stupor, I climbed back into the Peugeot and drove back to the MacBride farm with only one near-fatal incident, which occurred when I entered a roundabout to the right instead of to the left. But Scottish drivers were a forgiving lot—not one single horn blast or obscenity was flung out an open window at me. Their reflexes were top-notch, too, the cars scattering like sheep running from a herding dog.

After that harrowing event, I'd pulled off for a few moments to recover at an overlook with enough space for a few cars to park.

The view was stunning, with a cloud forming like an umbrella over rugged peaks before me. I got out and stepped close to a sturdy railing near a craggy rock formation. Foothills below led to a deep, lush glen. A lone golden eagle soared above, and for that brief interlude, I felt at peace and at home in this beautiful land.

Then, reluctantly, I got back into the Peugeot and continued my terrifying drive.

Back at the farm, Vicki's terriers were playing on the grass, chasing each other in circles. My rental car was nowhere in sight, gone for good thanks to Vicki. I would've been happier if my current loaner hadn't had all the same unnecessary equipment, and was testing my ability to live just as its predecessor had. Vicki was sitting in one of two outdoor chairs next to the main door leading into the house, knitting needles flying and tears streaming down her face. Between her crying jags and those lungs, which could really belt out some terrifying screams, I was beginning to realize that my new friend was a bundle of powerful emotions, and she wore them close to her skin.

"What happened?" I asked, sitting down beside her.

She sniffed, reached into a bag at her feet, and withdrew a stack of brightly colored . . . um . . . I didn't know what they were.

"Potholders," she informed me. "I worked fer days on them, using various tartan colors, with the thought to sell them at Sheepish Expressions. Not that they'd make much money, but that wasn't the idea. Sort of a peace offering, ye might call it."

"And?" I encouraged, pretty sure of the outcome, considering the potholders were in the bag at her feet rather than on display in the shop. And Vicki's Scottish accent had become more pronounced, which only seemed to happen when she was upset.

"The queen bee told me to take my beginner's knitting efforts elsewhere and practically ran me out the door. And in front o' customers besides."

"Your potholders are beautiful," I said, meaning it. I love

Scottish plaids, the combinations and patterns. "It was Kirst-ine's behavior that was terrible."

Wait until Vicki found out what else the woman was up to.

Vicki went on. "I have a mind to visit Da's solicitor and have her removed from the property. He works fer me now, not them, so he'd have to carry through with my request."

Having her half sister removed *was* certainly within Vicki's rights, at least until the will was finally settled once and for all. It was a very bad call on Kirstine's part to tick off her half sister with an insult like that. What nerve!

I'd had every intention of telling Vicki about the conver-sation I'd overheard, but this wasn't the right time. My friend was beside herself already. I couldn't add to her misery, at least just yet.

Before Vicki moved forward with her threat to remove Kirstine, I thought I'd better mention consequences of that action. "But if you went that route, then John would leave, too, and who would run the shop and tend the sheep?"

I was worried about the man and his temper, but the consequences of him leaving without a backup plan could be disastrous for the farm. Besides, the inspector had a sus-pect in Gavin Mitchell's murder in his sights. Maybe once the real killer was caught, John and Kirstine would back off.

Vicki paused to wipe her eyes with a tissue she withdrew from a pocket. "The two o' us? We could run it all, right?" she said in a weak voice, then gave me a small grin, and said in a lighter tone, "Which o' the jobs do ye want? Tend-ing the shop, or working the dogs and moving the sheep from pasture to pasture?"

Romantic visions of spending my days in fields of heather with sheep and border collies, wearing a polka-dot dress with pockets deep enough to carry a notepad and pen for my writing, danced briefly through my head. "Uh, well," I began, "if I had to choose . . ."

But Vicki interrupted. "I can't stand waiting around, and fer what? A judge tae decide what should have been already decided by the will?"

"What does your attorney say about the other side's chances of invalidating it?"

"That it's a distinct possibility and I should prepare myself." Vicki's knitting needles were flying again as she spoke. "The will was made long ago, and no updated one was ever drafted that specifically excluded the others by name. That's the problem."

"You mean the will was drafted before they were born?"

"Aye. And Kirstine's claim also has strong merit, according to the solicitor, considering her efforts here on the farm," Vicki said.

Maybe I'm overly generous with other people's money (an easy place to be when you don't have anything of value to lose), but I wanted to suggest to Vicki that she consider sharing her inheritance with her stepbrother and sister. An offer like that would mend a lot of fences, wouldn't it? Did that sort of selfless generosity ever happen? Had I ever heard of a case where an heir had willingly given up a piece of the pie? Not that I recalled, though it must have happened.

But it wasn't my place or my business. The farm belonged to Vicki fair and square, and it would be presumptuous of me to make a recommendation like that. On the other hand, there was one person who could present it as an option—a trusted counselor, an advisor who had all the facts and was familiar with the situation.

"This solicitor, have you met him?" I asked. "Or just spoken on the phone?"

"On the phone."

"If you met him in person, he might feel more of a connection to you and work harder on your behalf." It was worth a shot. Also, his name had come up in the conversation I'd overheard. What had Kirstine said to her husband while I was hiding on the other side of the wall? Something like, the solicitor should have warned her before it was too late. She had most likely been alluding to the old will and the lost opportunity to update it. Vicki glanced up. "You're right, Eden. I'll call and make an appointment on Monday. Will you come along?"

"Me?"

"Please?" she begged. "I'm an emotional mess and I'm no good with lawyers. I need your common sense to guide me."

"I don't have any experience with inheritances or wills."

"It's a friend I'll be needing, not an expert."

"Of course, if that's the case, I'd be happy to go with you," I reassured her, my interest piqued.

With our trip to the attorney's office assured, Vicki changed the subject, and I heard her accent receding. "I see Leith got the car running for you."

"It's a sweet little car," I told her, meaning about half of what I said. It was little and it was a car. "I didn't expect him to show up in a kilt, but it suited him. What's not to like about a kilt?"

Vicki's eyes slid to meet mine, and they had a twinkle, and not from tears either. "I think you'd suit him yourself. You'd make an attractive couple," she said.

I snorted. What was going on? First Ami, now Vicki seemed intent on setting me up. "He has a girlfriend. I thought you'd know that."

Vicki's needles paused in mid-click as she processed that

information, then she shrugged, and said, "There are a lot more fish in the pond, don't you worry. I'll give it some stick."

She saw my confusion and laughed. "That means I'll put some energy into it."

"That won't be necessary," I told her. "I'd prefer to have my love affair with Scotland."

Just then I heard the sound of a car approaching, and soon after Special Constable Sean Stevens pulled up and hopped out. His uniform was immaculate, his attitude businesslike. "I was hoping the inspector would be here," he said, sounding disappointed.

"Lost him, did you?" Vicki said. She and I exchanged amused looks.

"The man's a regular disappearing act. What's a body tae do?"

"Any more leads on the Gavin Mitchell case?" I asked, remembering that Sean had pretty loose lips for a cop, a bad habit I planned to use to my advantage.

"I can't be speaking o' police business," he protested, but I could tell he was dying to show us how important he was.

"The inspector and I just had a meeting at the pub," I told him encouragingly. "He told me he's looking for a man by the name of Samuel Kerr, a habitual offender, to question in Gavin Mitchell's murder."

"Aye," Sean said. "An' he calls me the blabbermouth."

Vicki gave me a questioning stare, so I related the rest for her benefit—how the man might have had a vendetta against Gavin for testifying against him, and how Kerr had been seen in the pub prior to the sheep shearer's murder.

"It would be a big relief to have this over with," Vicki said. "I feel as though the inspector has been focusing a good share of his attention on me and my whereabouts."

"He gives us all that impression," I reassured her, then I turned to Sean. "You have pinpointed the time of death," making it more of a statement than a question.

Sean nodded. "Aye, we have. The good man had been dead since the wee hours o' Tuesday morn."

"Heavens," Vicki exclaimed. "I didn't get the idea that he was stiff from . . . What is that? My mind has gone completely blank."

"Rigor mortis?" I filled in for her.

"It was past that point," Sean told us. "That's how the coroner came tae his conclusion."

"I don't want any details." Vicki had paled considerably. "It's too gruesome."

"Okay, then. Anyhow, our suspect is a slippery bird." Then directly to me: "Don't go mentioning that I called the inspector a blabbermouth. He must hold ye in high regard if he's sharing our business."

"And he'd want you to treat me the same," I said, scheming without an ounce of remorse. "So where are we regarding the fire?"

"Ach, ye know as much as I do. Nothing new there."

So that was a dead end for now. I tried a new tack. "Tell me a little about the owner of the Whistling Inn. The father."

"Old Bill? He's been on a bash as long as I can remember. His daughter takes care o' the business."

"Do they carry insurance on the inn?"

"Sure, and why wouldn't they?"

At this point, Vicki picked up where she'd left off with her knitting, but I could tell she was listening intently.

"Jeannie is trapped by responsibility," I mentioned. "She wants to go explore the world. Instead she's stuck in Glenkillen with more than a young woman should have to handle."

"That's the truth, all right."

"Perhaps she started the fire to escape from the village."

Vicki looked up between stitches and added her two cents. "That's a twist I hadn't thought of. Or . . . her father could have done it for the money."

Sean thought about those possibilities. "It's certainly worth a look, but how would we ever know fer sure?"

"The first step," I advised him, "is to find out how much insurance they have. The second is to find out where her father was before and during the period of time when the smoke was discovered."

"And the whereaboots of Jeannie, too," Sean said.

"That's easy." I offered up part of the puzzle. "She was inside the inn, making sure her guests vacated the building. I was there, remember? I saw her."

"So," Vicki said, "our Eden's an eyewitness to that fact. Jeannie was there, which means she could easily have started the fire."

Sean came to attention. "I'll look intae it," he said. "Don't ye worry. If one o' them was involved, I'll arrest them faster than ye can say William Wallace."

With a new mission, the special constable took off.

I should have felt guilty for using the poor man, since absolving myself from blame was my only reason for sticking my nose into the fire investigation. But my advice to Sean to pursue that line of inquiry gave him a sense of purpose. Plus, occupying him would give the inspector a little breathing space.

And that's how to rationalize one's actions when one has digressed from the most honorable path.

Chapter 17

The barn door was wide open when Vicki and I walked past it. A tractor loaded with bales of hay backed its way slowly through the open doors, then came to a halt inside the barn. John Derry turned off the engine and jumped down. Jasper the cat peered down from the top of a set of stairs leading to a loft but darted out of sight with all the commotion.

"What are ye two starin' at?" John said rudely, solidifying his position at the bottom of the proverbial barrel when it came to my list of favorite people. "Well?" he demanded when we didn't reply.

Again, I noted slightly different stress patterns in his speech.

I didn't know how to respond, and Vicki must have felt the same way because she didn't answer, either.

"I have a grand idea," he went on with a smirk, his lips curling as he sized up each of us with eyes that shot daggers of anger. "Ye can work fer yer keep by moving these bales up ta the loft."

With that work order, he stalked off out the door. We watched him until he disappeared down the lane.

Then Vicki and I sidled a little farther into the barn and looked up toward the hayloft, the heights of which could only be reached by the narrow set of stairs off to one side.

"I have a bad back," Vicki informed me.

I scanned the contents of the barn, which were numerous as well as unidentifiable. I'm blessed with a gift for the written word, but I can't tell a whatchamacallit from a thingamabob. Add a bunch of steel and iron doohickeys and I'm completely lost.

"There must be a better way to get the bales up," I said, "than carting them up all those stairs."

"If there is, I don't see it. Must be at least thirty bales," Vicki muttered. "We could tell John no, since his intentions weren't a bit on the kind side." And in case I hadn't heard her worming her way out of actual physical labor, Vicki put one hand on the small of her back and leaned a bit to the side as though trying to find a comfortable position.

But what could I say in reply anyway? I was indebted to her, so I went with the obvious response: "Don't worry, I'll take care of it."

I used both hands to grab one of the bales by the twine encircling it, and hefted the hay to establish its weight. Not nearly as heavy as I would have guessed, although I'd have to tackle this project in stages. The first few trips up into the loft might not be too taxing, but the lifting and climbing would have a cumulative effect, and I knew I'd burn out fast if I didn't take it slow.

The cat came out from hiding and found a sunny spot right outside the barn door but kept a cautious distance. After determining that we weren't threats, he sat down and began cleaning himself.

"Jasper likes you," Vicki commented. "He's allowed me the honor of petting him a time or two, but I've watched from the window when John's around. Jasper won't have a thing to do with that man. He's a good judge of humans. And look how he's watching you, so calm and relaxed."

Jasper and Vicki both watched my first few trips up and down the stairs before Vicki decided she'd be more useful making us some tea. "A few more bales," she suggested, "then take a break and come inside."

I did as she advised, stopping after several more trips up. I passed by Jasper on my way out of the barn, and he actually let me run my hand over his head and scratch his ears. The muscles in my arms already ached and I could feel those in my calves tightening. Inactivity is a side effect of a writing lifestyle. I'd have to start hiking the countryside, spending more time taking care of my body and making it stronger.

True to her word, when I entered the house I saw that Vicki had laid out tea and more of her delicious almond biscuits. We chatted for a few minutes, then she disappeared to lie down and rest her poor aching back—a physical issue I hadn't heard a thing about until work presented itself. I went back to the barn, determined to make headway and show the MacBrides that "we" were made out of the right stuff. Never mind that Vicki had bailed on the bales. At least Jasper was sticking around.

Before starting up again, I sat on the tractor and spent a few minutes appreciating my surroundings.

The sweet smell of harvested hay and its rich golden color assaulted all my senses. I felt closer than ever to the pure natural world. Instead of returning to the task at hand, I got up and wandered up the lane in a new direction, away from Sheepish Expressions. The sheep in the pasture turned and watched me make my way along with what could only be described as keen interest. When I looked back over my shoulder, they were still watching.

Two border collies ran along a low ridge ahead. Birds soared overhead, a sparrow hawk and then several buzzards, circling high above, letting the wind catch their wings, riding the breeze.

I soon came to the top of a high ridge, which surprised me, since I hadn't been climbing upward at a steep angle, or at least it hadn't felt that way. But the drive from Glenkillen to the farm had enough hills to account for this ridge. The farm must be situated on a plateau of some sort.

I stood at the top, a good distance from the edge of the steep incline. I become uncomfortable and anxious in high, open places. Flying in a plane isn't an issue, but put me on the edge of a cliff without large boulders or trees or a solid railing to protect me and give me a sense of security—however false that security might be—and I start to panic. It's not vertigo that paralyzes me, but rather a gripping fear of falling, or more specifically that some part of my brain will misfire and I'll lose control and jump. Silly, I know, but very real inside my head.

So I stayed back at a safe distance, breathing the light and herblike aroma of heather with the wind churning my hair, sending it flying about my face.

At that moment, I wished I could stay in Glenkillen for the rest of my life.

Minus, of course, the drama I'd encountered in the few short days I'd been here.

But without that drama, to be able to get up every morning and walk this path, commune with nature, roam free anywhere and everywhere—that would be such a wonderful gift. What a dreamworld! I had to try to get a handle on this glorious setting and put it all into written words before I was back on an airplane looking out a window at my last glimpses of Scotland.

"Live in the moment" had to be my mantra. A wise one. I had to relish every day.

With that sound advice to myself, I made my way back to the barn, this time first seeking out a pair of work gloves. I'd been feeling the beginning of blisters along the palms of both hands. This city girl needed to get toughened up.

Again, Jasper came out to watch the activity, but he kept enough distance to make a getaway if he had to. He seemed semi-wild, and I suspected he would always be that way, coming and going as he pleased; he was no lap cat to play with.

This time when I lifted the very first bale of hay, it felt twice as heavy as the previous ones had, a sure sign that I'd already reached my pathetic limit. *Just a few more*, I told myself, pushing a little further than normal.

I began the climb up the stairs with the bale in front of me, resting it on each step as I continued upward, using every last ounce of strength I could muster, and determining that this would be my last for now. I was almost to the top, cheering because the floor of the loft was in sight above me—and the next second, I felt myself falling. By the time I realized what was happening, I'd landed. Hard.

The wind had been knocked out of me. I couldn't breathe. Which caused me to panic.

Lack of air. Gasping to find it.

As suddenly as the spasm began, it ended. I managed to gather in lifesaving oxygen, filling my lungs but not yet attempting to move, staying as still as possible while I accessed the damage.

I had landed on my side with my back against the bottom

step. There wasn't any pain—not yet, anyway. But my body might have been in shock.

Then the barn began to spin before my eyes, my ears rang, and everything around me went white. I closed my eyes quickly . . .

. . . and must have passed out, because the next thing I knew I'd awoken flat on my back. I felt myself being lifted up. A siren screamed close by, and I thought we should pull over, let it pass. It was so loud and piercing.

Somebody told me to take it easy, that we were almost there. "Where?" I thought I asked, but then wasn't sure, because no one would answer my question even though I continued to ask it. After a period of time I couldn't measure, I felt myself lifted again.

Fragments of conversations floated past.

"Concussion."

"Lucky."

A familiar voice next, the first that I recognized. "Will she know who I am when she wakes up? She won't have amnesia, will she?"

"Vicki?" I said or thought, attempting to reassure her. Then more time went by and more voices, fading in and out.

"CT scan."

"Overnight for observations."

All I wanted was to be left alone to sleep. So tired.

The next time I opened my eyes, sun was beaming in and a cheery nurse with a tray was elevating my bed and asking me if I could sit up to eat. "What happened?" I asked her, my thoughts all jumbled as I slowly sat up. "Where am I?"

"Yer at the Kirkwall Hospital."

"And where is that?"

"Right here in Glenkillen. Now eat yer porridge." She

placed the tray in front of me and left the room after showing me a button that I could press if I needed any assistance.

The last thing I cared about was porridge or eating anything at all. I racked my brain trying to remember what had happened. Why hadn't I questioned the nurse further? I lifted the sheet and peered below. I was in a hospital gown, but otherwise everything seemed as usual. No lost limbs, no sutures, no pain.

Memory of voices. The word "concussion." I touched my head. No bandages.

Then I heard a throat being cleared. A voice said, "Good mornin'." I glanced up to find Inspector Jamieson observing me from a chair in the corner.

"Oh, is it morning?" I said, relieved to see a familiar face, but finding out that I'd lost a significant chunk of time rattled me. "Ah, I suppose, since this is"—I glanced at the contents of the tray—"oatmeal. Or rather porridge."

"A brilliant deduction on yer part, considering yer precarious condition." He stood up.

"How long have you been there?"

"Not long." But I noticed he was a bit stiff, slightly bent, hesitant with the first few steps: all indications that he'd been in the chair longer than he cared to admit. "You gave us quite a scare. How's the head?"

"Doesn't hurt," I told him, pushing the tray away. "But I'm not hungry."

"No headache?" he asked, sounding surprised.

"No," I replied, just as surprised. Yes, I really was perfectly okay. A bump on the head. That was it.

"And do ye remember what happened?"

"I fell."

"Vicki found ye unconscious."

"Ah."

"And ye know who I am?"

"Of course I do. You are Special Constable Sean Stevens."

The inspector stared at me, not sure how to respond. "I better get the doctor," he said, but right then I burst out laughing, and he realized I'd been teasing.

"Don't bring up that dolt's name," he warned me, trying to hold back a grin. "He's out at the farm now, digging around fer clues."

"Ahhh, you gave him some busywork."

"It's the only way I can get anythin' accomplished." Then he grew serious, his face clouding over. "I should have taken yer concerns aboot John Derry more seriously. He left ye to think ye had to carry those heavy bales up tae the loft, when all along he had a pulley system set up to do the job fer him. He's the one responsible for yer fall as surely as if he'd pushed ye himself."

What a rotten excuse for a human being the man was! My instincts had been right all along. To pull such a stunt!

"Ye better eat your porridge before it gets cold," the inspector said. "It'll make ye strong and healthy. The doc will want to see ye now that yer awake, but he already said ye can probably go home after he pays ye a visit, though he cautioned that ye might have your brain affected for a while."

"That isn't anything new," I quipped, content to know I was being released soon.

"Ye took the words right out o' my mouth," he said, turning away. But he hadn't been fast enough. I saw the amused grin.

CHAPTER 18

Over the next few hours, while I waited for a doctor to come to my room, I had the opportunity to observe a Scottish hospital in action. I've spent many long hours in waiting rooms and at my mother's bedside while she struggled to overcome her debilitating disease, so hospital policies, procedures, and routines aren't anything new to me, and this one was very much like those back home. However, I'd never been the patient before. I learned right away that I wasn't a very good one. Polite? I tried. But willing? Absolutely not.

"Get me out of here!" was my most frequent internal refrain, my bruised and swollen brain clearly still in charge and not coping well.

I had time to consider my options once I was released. Part of me wanted to hurry out and change that return ticket home from December to tomorrow. From the minute I'd gotten in the driver's seat of that rental car, nothing had gone the way it was supposed to. Nothing. The other part of me rationalized: I had a brain injury, no matter how minor, and that could be clouding my judgment. Best to wait a few days before making any decisions.

Finally, after what seemed like forever, the doctor came along, and my moment of freedom arrived.

"Everything's going to be fine and dandy after all," Vicki said to me when I scooted into the Citroën. "I didn't know what to think when I found you unconscious in the barn. I thought you were dead!"

"I owe you again," I told her with sincere gratitude. "You're my guardian angel, appearing every time I'm in serious trouble."

"You'd better put a stop to that before you're the death of *me*."

Vicki kept up the chatter, mostly motherly concern for my well-being, until we arrived back at her farm entrance. We drove past Sheepish Expressions, where several cars and tour buses were parked outside. Glancing over at Vicki, I saw her jawline tense up and her knuckles whiten on the steering wheel. She had more than her fair share to cope with. "Don't you have anybody back in the States you should notify?" Vicki asked as we got out of the car. "You know, family? Loved ones?"

"Vicki, I'm perfectly fine," I insisted. "Why worry anyone else when it's over and done with?"

But then it struck me: I really *didn't* have any family to contact in case of an emergency. I had Ami. She was a loyal friend and could always be counted on, but as far as relatives—they were all gone.

My sense of isolation almost overcame me as I got out of the car, but I used sheer willpower to keep the tears from flowing. Where had this bout of self-pity come from? I chalked it up to the blow to my head I'd suffered. I usually embraced being solitary, the kind of freedom that was now mine. The depths of self-pity wasn't a place I cared to visit, now or ever. Life is what it is, and during struggles and hardships we do what we have to do. This was a new beginning, an unpredictable next stage in my life. I couldn't invent new family members, but I *could* make more lasting friendships like the one I had with Ami. I was committed to that. And no better time to begin than right now, with Vicki MacBride.

"Thank you, Vicki," I said. "For everything."

"You'd do the same for me," she said serenely, letting Coco and Pepper out of the house before heading for her favorite outdoor chair and sitting down. "But enough sentimental sap for now," she said, smiling. "Here comes Sean from the barn. Wonder what he's been up to. He looks like the cat that got the cream, doesn't he?"

Sean practically jogged up to us. Whatever he'd been doing, his uniform was still crisp and his shoes remarkably shiny. Wasn't today Sunday? Shouldn't he have been home with his family? Regardless, here he was, holding a piece of splintered wood that I was pretty sure was part of the staircase I'd fallen from.

"What've you got?" Vicki wanted to know.

"I have tae find the inspector," Sean fairly shouted, even though we were right next to him.

He seemed to notice me for the first time. "Yer fit and fine then? And having yer wits about ye?"

I wasn't sure about that, but I said, "Yes, I'm going to be just fine. What do you have there?"

"Ye see this?" He held up his discovery with undeniable pride and ran his finger along the smooth end before pointing out the other side. "It's been sawed clean off, and musta been glued back on just enough tae stay put until ye stepped down on it."

"Are you sure?" I asked, my stomach doing involuntary flip-flops.

"Right sure," he told me.

Vicki let out a shriek and then covered her mouth. She'd caught the implication at the same time as I had.

Someone had intentionally tampered with the stairs to cause a fall.

Had Vicki been the intended victim? If not for her bad back, she would have been the one on the loft stairs, not me. It made sense that she'd been the target.

Someone had been trying to hurt her, and I had literally taken the fall on her behalf.

I put my arm around Vicki and gave her a reassuring squeeze. "It's going to be okay," I told her, hoping I was right. Then: "Should you be handling the evidence?" I said to Sean, thinking about the possibility of the culprit's fingerprints.

"I've been trained tae deal properly with evidence," he said, but I saw the telltale signs of a big fat fib in his startled eyes. Then: "I need a plastic bag. Quick. And make it a big one while yer at it."

Vicki hurried inside and came back out with a trash bag. Sean carefully placed his forensic treasure inside and tied it up gently.

We all stared at it.

If Inspector Jamieson was a violent man, which I suspected he wasn't, he'd use the bagged stair piece to knock this volunteer cop's block off for his carelessness with potential evidence.

"I best be off," Sean said, breaking the silence and moving at supersonic speed toward his car. We watched him roar off.

"What do you make of that?" I asked Vicki.

"That volunteer policeman doesn't seem to be very competent, if you ask me," she said, taking my arm. "Come on, let's get you in the house and settled in a comfy chair."

"That might have been you on the steps."

"Don't go thinking the worst until we know all the facts. We best wait and see."

Back inside, I dozed on and off for the rest of the afternoon, then went to bed early. The blow to my head had taken a lot out of me, more than I'd originally thought. All things considered, today had been an uneventful day: no ladder mishaps or room fires, no scary road trips with me behind the wheel, not a single dead body showing up.

I didn't want to think about what tomorrow might bring.

CHAPTER 19

Monday morning arrived dark and dreary with thick fog. When I looked out the window, I couldn't see the ridges or rolling hills that had been visible the day before. I couldn't tell if the sheep were still grazing on them. Even Coco and Pepper didn't want to venture out, preferring to curl up together and doze by a crackling fire Vicki had started in the fireplace.

"Typical Scottish weather," Vicki remarked. "It's a good day to stay in and read a book."

That was a tempting suggestion, but my brain was functioning well enough to remind me that I needed to make more progress with my writing. Ami was bound to remind me that I should skip ahead and write a scorching love scene. I thought about pretending that I had, but what if she wanted me to send it to her? And why was I resisting anyway? Reading those scenes was one thing; writing one was going to be another. I had several paperbacks in my tote to reread—a few of Ami's hottest romances, which I hoped would fire up that section of my reluctant brain.

Was my own past coming back to haunt me? What I'd thought was love had come and gone. And the sex hadn't been what I'd expected and had tapered off over the years, the passion gone. If it had ever been there to begin with.

Was this something personal I had to work through?

"What are you thinking about?" Vicki asked, setting down a bowl of porridge for me. I was getting the distinct impression that every single Scot in the land was eating the exact same thing: porridge. The full Scottish breakfast must be reserved for tourists, which made sense, as a daily dose of eggs and several different meats would have killed off every one of the locals long ago. "You have an angry expression on your face."

"Just sorting a few things out."

"I'll get you some toast to go with your porridge."

Sex and love. What if I found that I couldn't write about true love because I'd never experienced it? Same with passionate lovemaking. I'd had a few boyfriends before my husband, but none of them had been as thoughtful as I'd imagined they could be.

Wasn't it time to have a little fun? What was I saving my passion for anyway? Did I even have a passionate side? If I did, it was buried deep. Maybe it was time to let loose a little. Ami would be thrilled for me.

"Did you take your medication yet?" Vicki asked.

"No. I will after breakfast."

Did I have to have more than distant memories of sexual encounters to write that scorching scene? If so, I better get to it right after I finished eating, find someone to fill the bill, like . . .

Wait! What was I thinking? Apparently, my brain was seriously swollen and affecting the libido part of my noggin. The faster I could bring down the swelling, the sooner I'd get back to my normal self. Because this kind of illogical reasoning was definitely out of character for me. "I'd better take my meds now rather than later," I said.

"They're right here." Vicki set the bottle down beside me. I swallowed one ASAP.

"The doctor said you might feel a little strange for a while," Vicki reminded me.

I didn't remember Vicki being there when the doctor came in to release me from the hospital and give me instructions regarding meds. "How do you know that?" I asked her. "You weren't there." Then: "Were you?"

"No. But Inspector Jamieson phoned earlier and mentioned it when he asked about you. Apparently the doctor told him to treat you gently for a while."

Fifteen minutes later, after the pill had time to work its magic, I felt much better, physically and mentally. I showered, dressed, grabbed my rain jacket and laptop, and headed for the door.

"You could write here, you know," Vicki suggested.

"Um . . . I'm not writing until later . . . but . . . uh . . . I like to have my notes with me in case inspiration strikes," I said. This was awkward. If I told the truth, that she was too much of a chatterbox for me to accomplish anything, I'd hurt her feelings. Without thinking things completely through, I added, "I thought I'd drive over to Loch Ness and catch a glimpse of Nessie."

And groaned mentally when I realized I should invite her along. "You're welcome to join me," I offered as cheerily as possible, considering my blunder.

"Next time, give me more notice and I'll come along." Vicki looked down at her nightgown and slippers, blonde hair jutting out in all directions. "Besides, this isn't the best weather for sightseeing. I'd much rather stay by the fire with Pepper and Coco."

I muttered an apology. Next time, we'd plan in advance. Later today, I could always say I'd had car problems and hadn't made it to the lake. That was totally believable coming from me.

Before heading for the door, I decided to follow up on the investigation.

"Any news on the murder investigation?" I asked. "Did they charge that Kerr guy?"

Vicki's face grew long. "It was a dead end. The bloke had an alibi—ironclad, the inspector told me. He couldn't have been more disappointed."

"Back to square one, then?"

"That's what it looks like."

I wondered about Sean's discovery in the barn. "What about the loft stairs? Had they been rigged to trigger a fall like Sean thought?"

"The inspector wouldn't say, but he's coming this way to discuss it with me. Go on now, and don't you worry about the outcome just yet. I'll keep you informed."

"Oh? When is Inspector Jamieson going to be here?" I asked, realizing his visit was the perfect excuse to put off worrying about that pesky love scene. Procrastination has killed off more than one wannabe author, but a few more minutes wouldn't hurt.

"He'll be round soon enough."

"I should hear what he has to say," I reasoned. "After all, I'm the one who fell."

Yes, a delay!

Not procrastination.

A delay.

That sounded so much better.

CHAPTER 20

"Sean Stevens's position is aboot tae become redundant!" Inspector Jamieson said as we stood in the barn.

"Redundant?" I asked.

"Terminated," Vicki answered for him.

Oh.

"He's outside sitting in his car," I pointed out.

"He's been following me like a lost puppy, waiting fer word tae come from headquarters," the inspector said, tapping the cell phone in a case on his belt. "Any minute now, I'll get the word, and then he'll go back where he came from. And good riddance!"

I felt bad for Sean. He'd had the best intentions as he traipsed around unsettling everything and everyone. Or rather upsetting the only one who really mattered—his boss. It's pretty bad when you get fired from a volunteer position, but Sean somehow had managed.

I'd found the concept of regular folks working as police officers strange in the first place. But ever since Sean had arrived on the scene, I'd been noticing advertisements in the newspaper calling for more just like him. Or rather, like him but with some degree of competence. I clearly was in a foreign country where different rules applied.

"With a little more training . . . ," I started to suggest on Sean's behalf, until the inspector turned his sharp eyes toward me and glared into mine. "Never mind," I said.

"He's a blockhead," Inspector Jamieson muttered while studying the broken part of the stairs leading to the loft and comparing it to the piece of wood that Sean had bagged yesterday. "Nothin' ye can do with the likes of him."

I nodded to be on the safe side.

"Do ye remember anything unusual before or during yer fall?" he asked me. "Anything at all out o' place?"

"Nothing," I said, after considering for a moment. I looked up and spotted a furry head. Jasper was in the loft, lying between two hay bales, his eyes following us. "No," I said, surer now. "Nothing comes to mind."

"The step was sawed all right," the inspector said. "Even a dolt like Stevens could see that. I doubt we'll get any fingerprints, but I'll have the team come out and give it a try." He glanced outside at Sean's car, then looked down at his silent cell phone. "Even if there were prints tae be found, our eager beaver would've destroyed them."

I couldn't help thinking that John Derry's fingerprints would be all over the place anyway, since he worked in the barn.

"Are you most upset because Sean didn't take precautions with evidence?" I asked.

"I have a long list o' complaints against him. That bit o' handiwork was only the last straw."

"He means well," Vicki added. I knew she was feeling sorry for Sean, too.

Inspector Jamieson shook his head in disgust, and said, "You know what they say about good intentions?"

"The road to hell is paved with them," I recited. "An old proverb."

"And true as they come. But right noo I'm most concerned about yer fall and the person behind it," the inspector said. "I have trouble believing that John Derry woulda carried things this far. But I'll have a word with him."

"A word? That's all?" I exclaimed. "I could have been killed!"

"It was attempted murder, if you ask me," Vicki agreed.

The inspector looked over at Vicki. "Did ye ever think, Vicki MacBride, that the fall was intended fer ye?"

Vicki, a shade paler than usual, nodded. I decided it was time to tell her about the conversation between John and Kirstine MacBride inside the shop when they thought they were alone.

"There's something else you should know," I said, beginning my tale. The inspector also listened intently, although he'd already heard about it. Neither interrupted.

"John called us busybodies," I said, wrapping up the story, "and said he was going to take care of us." I gestured toward the steps. "And it appears that he's already made an attempt."

"John Derry was the only one who possibly could have done this," Vicki said after a few moments of considering the new information. "As Eden and I told you, it was his idea that we cart the bales up to the loft."

"Whoever it was," said the inspector—noncommittal, which was frustrating—"would have had a very small window of opportunity, since ye'd been on those steps right before taking yer break."

I agreed. "John must have snuck back in and rigged the steps before I came back out from the house."

"He intended for me to be the one to fall," Vicki said. "If

I'd been killed, they wouldn't have to worry about their precious inheritance."

"It certainly looks that way to me," I said. John couldn't have known about Vicki's bad back and might have assumed it was her turn to pitch in. Had he been watching us the whole time? Had he been surprised when I went back to the barn instead of Vicki?

It was obvious that the inspector wasn't going to discuss my fall any longer, so I changed the subject. "Vicki said your suspect in the murder case didn't work out," I said. "That's too bad. He seemed like the perfect suspect."

"Samuel Kerr was in toon all right, but turns out he'd come tae apologize. He's a changed man, he says. He'd threatened Gavin in court, but while he was in prison he found his way intae a group o' recovering alcoholics and he was following the steps. He came tae apologize for his bad behavior."

"And did he?" I asked.

"Aye." The inspector nodded. "The week before Gavin was murdered. And he had witnesses outside the pub tae vouch fer him, and an airtight alibi fer the period of time surrounding the death."

"And what's his airtight alibi?" I asked.

"Kerr picked up a bit o' work as a deckhand on a prawn boat. They went tae sea on Sunday and didn't return until the day before last. The skipper confirmed his story."

"You must be following other leads, right?" Vicki asked. "Please don't tell us you're at a dead end."

"Don't worry, I'll get tae the bottom of this before long," the inspector told us. "But ye two need tae practice patience while I sort each o' these puzzles out one by one."

Moments after that reassurance, his cell phone rang. He answered it, moving off to where we couldn't overhear the conversation. While he was busy presumably getting permission to terminate the excitable volunteer policeman, along with Sean's dreams of a real position with the Highlands police, I wandered over to Sean's car, grateful that the rain and mist had finally taken a blessed break. His window was down.

"I'm trying tae keep my chin up," Sean said, sadly. "But it doesn't look good fer me."

What could I say? Nothing cheerful, that was for sure.

Then he brightened, and said, "I was right, though, aye? If it weren't fer me, they'd have assumed it was an accident and never caught on."

Which might actually have been true. If he hadn't been such a bungler, the inspector wouldn't have sent him off on a wild-goose chase that wasn't really as wild as he'd thought, and Sean wouldn't have found the golden egg (in this case, an incriminating sawed-through piece of wooden step). Sean may even have inadvertently saved our lives; thanks to him, we'd be much more cautious from here on in.

Vicki came over, and I left her with Sean while I hustled over to the inspector, who was wrapping up his phone conversation and looking pleased with himself. "Redundant?" I asked.

He nodded and turned toward Sean's car.

I grabbed his arm, which startled him. It startled me, too. I had no idea I could be so forceful. And with a police officer besides.

"I'd like to plead his case," I said. "Please bear with me for a moment."

Inspector Jamieson sighed. "As though I have a choice."

I began by highlighting Sean's commitment and enthusiasm, followed by his sense of justice, honesty, and his real concern for others. The inspector looked bored, but too polite to give me the brush-off. So I went on, stating Sean's role in finding out that I hadn't taken an accidental fall. "Sean's investigative methods are amateurish," I said, "but those skills can be learned. The rest—integrity and passion—are innate. You have them or you don't. And Sean has an extra dose."

"Ye make a good case," Jamieson finally said.

"Besides, you'll only be assigned another volunteer, right?"

The answer was apparent by his involuntary grimace.

"The next one might not have any more thorough training than Sean, but might be sullen and refuse to take orders."

"I hadn't thought o' that," the inspector said. "Nor do I care tae think o' it."

"I tell you what—I'll take Sean under my wing, find some online reference sites, and work with him to make sure he retains what he learns."

"Ye don't know a thing about our law enforcement."

"It's very much like in the States," I gambled. "Please give me a chance. And if he doesn't improve in a week, you can let him go. How does that sound? You don't have anything to lose. But Sean has so much."

The inspector looked resigned and gave an almost imperceptible nod. Despite that small victory, though, the inspector's final words on the subject were anything but positive.

"Like the blind leading the blind," he said.

CHAPTER 21

The fog had blown away with the northern breeze, and the sun temporarily poked through the clouds. I drove into Glenkillen without incident, parked near the Kilt & Thistle, and wandered the streets absorbing village life. Another procrastination from writing, perhaps, but I chalked it up to necessary local research. Never mind that pesky love scene I was avoiding like the plague.

The Whisky Stop was doing a brisk business, I noted as I walked through the aisles. I knew that Scotland was famous for its distilleries, both the large and the small, and after reading some labels, they were well represented on the shelves—Lagavulin, Glenlivet, Clynelish, Glenfiddich, Oban, and many, many more. I met the proprietor, Duff Ferguson, and learned that there was a huge difference between Scottish whisky and American whiskey.

"Fer one thing," he told me, "Scotch whisky is made from malted barley. American whiskey is mainly corn mixed with all kinds of other grains. Pure barley fer us. That's why ye see all the vast fields o' barley around here."

"Is that what all those tall fields of grass, are? I've seen them but didn't know what they were."

"And now ye do," he said kindly, before other customers called for his attention.

Next I popped into Glenkillen Books and browsed the shelves, intent on the unlikely possibility of finding something to help educate Sean on police procedures. I hadn't expected to find anything, and I didn't, but I was pleased to see Ami's latest book front and center in addition to several endcaps devoted to her other titles. Her entire backlist was found in the romance section and covered several long shelves. She'd said she was popular in the UK but I hadn't realized just how popular.

Finding my friend's novels so prominently displayed here brought me back to reality. If I wanted my name to appear on these same shelves, I'd better stop goofing off. For the first time in recent memory, I left a bookstore empty-handed.

Before I could make good on my determination to get back to writing, A Taste of Scotland's window display brought me to a standstill. I might have been able to resist, except the door was propped wide open, releasing scrumptious aromas!

"I recognize ye," a woman in an apron and wearing a scarf tied back behind her head said after I entered. "Yer the woman who found poor Gavin Mitchell, and ye also . . ." She hesitated, seeming uncomfortable.

"Have been accused of starting the inn fire," I finished for her, hoping that item was the extent of the rumors that had reached her ears. "But I swear I didn't have anything to do with it."

"Well, I'm Ginny Davis, the owner o' this establishment and 'tis a pleasure to meet you. Don't worry yerself none about local gossip. Before long somebody else will be in our sights."

I smiled at her kind words. I liked Ginny already. "Thanks. I'm Eden Elliott."

"I hear yer a romance writer."

I smiled. "Who told you that?"

She returned my smile. "Sean Stevens keeps me informed o' all the goings-on in Glenkillen. He's me cousin. So it's true? Ye write romances?"

"I'm making the effort, yes."

"Well, if ye run out of material, I could tell ye a story or two."

"I might take you up on that," I said with a laugh. "I've been having some writer's block, to be honest! I've been wandering about looking for some inspiration and local flavor. Speaking of local flavors, what's a Dundee cake?"

"Ooh, it's lovely," Ginny said, leading me to an attractive display farther inside the shop and pointing out a cake that looked exactly like an American fruitcake except for rings of almonds on top. "It's filled with currants," she told me, "and almonds and bits o' fruit. We have more orders than we can fill around the holidays. But our specialty is our shortbread."

We returned to the front of the store, where several varieties of shortbread dominated Ginny's displays: traditional and blueberry shortbreads, chai and Earl Grey shortbreads, mint tea and lemon-rosemary shortbreads. She even had one that was gluten free.

"It's the butter that gives shortbread that wonderful flavor and texture," she told me. "The secret is tae use unsalted butter—rich and pure. Ye take your time. I see customers needing a ring-up."

Finally, after a lot of delightful indecision, I opted for a package of traditional shortbread.

"Don't make yerself a stranger," Ginny said after making change for the ten-pound note I'd handed to her.

"I won't. And thank you for your kindness." Which I meant with genuine sincerity. It was immensely reassuring to make the acquaintance of this friendly business owner.

Outside, I opened the bag which turned out to be my downfall, since I wasn't able to stop at just one and continued to chow down while walking slowly back to the Kilt & Thistle.

This time, the inn owner was awake and alert in a corner of the crowded pub when I entered. Even though it was barely afternoon, he had a glass of beer in front of him. Who knows how many he'd already downed? If he didn't pass out cold again later, at least he wouldn't have far to go, since the inn was right next-door.

The pub owner's redheaded twin boys, Reece and Ross, ran past and out the door, noisy with devilish grins and mischief up their sleeves. No wonder the innkeeper was awake.

He squinted up at me when I presented myself at his table. Up close he had several days' growth on his face, red-rimmed eyes, and a bulbous nose. "Ye be the one who near burnt doon my inn," he snarled after I introduced myself.

"I had nothing to do with the fire," I said, instantly regretting my impulse to do a good deed for the man, but it was too late now. "But I'd like to talk to you about your insurance. It might pay for the smoke damage as well as your lost revenue."

"Goo away."

"I'm trying to help."

"Ye've done enough, thank ye very much."

"You *do* have insurance?" I asked.

"And plenty o' it, not that it's any o' yer business. Like I said, goo away, lass."

"That's a relief." I'd wanted to help, but it wasn't my fault that he wouldn't let me. At least I'd tried. I'd done what I felt I had to.

After that, I ordered tea at the bar, then hustled off with it to my new writing cave in the far reaches of the pub. The more I thought about whoever may have started that fire, the more convinced I became that either the inn's drunk of an owner or his daughter was behind it. Maybe both. She wanted out and he couldn't possibly run the place without her. Torching it was a simple solution. This was all speculation on my part, but I intended to mention it once again to Inspector Jamieson at the next opportunity.

With my computer powered up and the pages on the screen, I turned my attention back to my work in progress. I backtracked to the preceding chapter and began reading. Going back to a point in the past like this usually gives me a jump start into the next scene. When I come to the end of that last chapter, my fingers will be flying again.

This time I had the dreaded writer's block.

I forced a sentence, hoping for a few words that would convey the necessary sexual tension. Instead it just felt forced. *He gazed into her eyes and she felt as though he was touching her soul, reading her mind and her runaway emotions. She shivered with excitement.*

And then my mind went totally blank.

I did what I always do when I'm stumped, I took a break to check my e-mail. Nothing new from Ami, but I had plenty to write home to her about. I started with the abundant presence of her novels in the bookstore. After that, I told her about my fall and the brief stint in the hospital, and went on to reassure her that I was feeling perfectly fine. I decided to let my friend believe the fall had been an accident, at least for right now. No sense worrying her.

I'd barely shot that e-mail off, when a reply came back. "Sure is exciting in your part of the world compared to mine. Relieved that you weren't more seriously hurt. Please be more careful. I'd hate to have to come and pick up the pieces (only kidding). Now, tell me about the kilt guy."

"Nothing to tell. He's involved with someone."

"Darn! Doesn't it just figure? How's the book coming? How many sex scenes have you written?"

Um . . . "I'm writing one of those not-all-the-way scenes right now." There is something about lying to your best friend in an e-mail that is so much easier than lying to her face.

What was wrong with me? What was the holdup? Well, I did have excuses for my lack of focus—murder along with a fall instigated by an unknown attacker. Was it any wonder I couldn't write about love at the moment?

I waited a few minutes before a response came back.

"I have to sign off," she wrote, "but in the next day or so, I'll expect a full-blown sex scene attached to an e-mail from you!!!!"

Okay, then.

I picked up my tote, rifled through it, and removed several of Ami's novels. I tossed them on the table and stared at them.

A moment later, I heard close by, "What's that yer reading there?" I jumped about a foot before whipping my head around to find the owner of the pub peering over my shoulder.

"Dale, you startled me."

"I can see that," he said, his goateed face expressing amusement.

Why did I feel like I had to explain myself? But I did.

"You know I'm a romance writer, right?"

"Aye. The whole toon knows that."

"I'm struggling with some serious writer's block."

"Thought ye might like a top-up for your tea." He set a fresh teapot on the table and picked up my empty one.

"Maybe that'll clear out the cobwebs. Oh, and Vicki McBride called for ye."

"What?"

"She called and asked if ye were here. When I said aye, she said tae tell ye the appointment with the solicitor is at two o'clock."

"Uh, thanks. But I'm sorry she bothered you."

"No trouble at all."

"I haven't been making calls from my phone," I explained. "The cost is so high, so I've been doing all my communicating through e-mail."

"Ye can rent a temporary mobile, ye know. It's cheap and reliable."

"Yes, thank you, I should do that. And I will. Soon." *Especially if Vicki's going to track me down through the locals and make my business their business.*

On the other hand, I'd gained a certain freedom in ditching my phone. It was so rare these days to be unreachable for a while. Why was it that at home I'd taken the darn thing everywhere? It had become almost an addiction. Panic would set in if I realized I'd left it behind at home. How had the world managed before the invention of the cell phone?

"Let me know if ye will be needing anything else," Dale said before disappearing from sight. "And good luck with yer story."

I glanced at the clock on my laptop. The appointment with Vicki's attorney didn't give me very much time to write that love scene.

Oh darn.

CHAPTER 22

I recognized Vicki's solicitor, Paul Turner, from the service at the cemetery for James MacBride. He'd been standing slightly ahead of me, and he'd stood out in my memory where others hadn't because of the enormous walrus mustache he sported. He'd been with the woman who had pointed out the corbie.

Paul Turner's office was on a side street right off the main shopping area. Judging from its simple decor, the attorney's practice wasn't exactly thriving. I guessed his age to be mid to late seventies, so perhaps he wasn't taking on any new clients these days and so didn't feel a need to modernize his office.

He was properly attired for his role as defender of justice in a black blazer, white button-down shirt with a conservative tie, and gray slacks. But in the same vein as his messy hair and overgrown mustache, his clothes were wrinkled and worn threadbare.

"We have a battle before us," he told Vicki after we were seated at his cluttered desk. His accent wasn't as strong as that of others I'd encountered in Glenkillen, making me suspect he'd been educated elsewhere. "This could drag out for years if we aren't careful," he warned. Vicki was mute, simply staring across the marred wooden desk at the man on the other side.

When she didn't respond in any way, I jumped in on her behalf. "Have you been James MacBride's solicitor for long?" I asked. "And have you represented his children in the past?"

He frowned before glancing at Vicki, seeking her approval to address my questions. She nodded.

"James and I were childhood friends," he told us. "He trusted me with his personal affairs, and requested that I act as his executor-nominate. If you are suggesting a conflict of interest, the answer is a negative. I have not represented his offspring in the past."

"If I understand correctly," I said, addressing Vicki, "Gavin Mitchell was the one who called and broke the news to you of your father's death, not Mr. Turner."

"That's right," Vicki said in a timid voice, unlike the woman I'd come to know. What was wrong with her?

"Sadly, I was away on holiday when James passed on," Turner explained. "Gavin Mitchell was also a good friend of the MacBride family and took on the responsibility of notifying his heir in my absence. Fortunately, Kirstine located me and warned of her father's impending death. Sadly, I returned the next day to find I was too late to see him one last time."

I turned to Vicki. "Did Gavin tell you the terms of the will when he called you?"

She shook her head. "But he insisted I come immediately."

"It wasn't Gavin Mitchell's place to do so," Turner said to me, "even if he knew of the terms. I am the executor of the estate, and therefore the only one with that power. Ms.

MacBride and I met first thing on my arrival back in Glen-killen to discuss those details."

I had a meaty question, now that he had opened the door on the topic. "And is it true that Vicki's father hadn't updated his will since the birth of his other children?"

"You are an inquisitive young lady, but I believe I represent Ms. MacBride in this matter, not Eden Elliott." His mustache twitched with annoyance. "Now, if you will allow me to continue."

"My apologies. Please do." With that deserved scolding, I went into silent mode and listened, but it was clear from the start that Vicki didn't have enough experience in these matters to ask any questions at all. And she seemed pathologically intimidated by the attorney.

"The other side will present their case to a judge," Turner told her. "The date is set for the second Tuesday in August, three weeks from now. Because the opposing side wasn't specifically disinherited in the bequest, they have an excellent case and undoubtedly will be awarded the right to claim a share of their father's estate."

Vicki's solicitor looked pleased with his pronouncement. Paul Turner might be Vicki's attorney in theory, but his support was obviously with Kirstine and Alec. And why not? He'd lived in the same town where they were born and raised, had probably held them in his arms as babies, could even be a godparent to both for all I knew.

I wanted to snap at him, ask if he was counseling both sides and favoring the other. But I held my tongue.

"However," he continued with a trace of regret, "if they should win, their shares will be held in moveable property only."

"Meaning?" I asked, since Vicki continued to just sit there.

"Meaning that Ms. MacBride would be allowed to keep the land and buildings, but would have to divide up the more liquid assets, such as equities and cash positions. She would also be required to partner with her half siblings in regards to the business end of the estate."

That certainly carried some relief for Vicki if the suit against her bore fruit. Even if the other side won, Vicki couldn't be forced out of the house. She'd still own the shop building and a portion of any cash accounts. This didn't sound like the worst that could happen. More like the fair distribution I'd envisioned from the beginning.

So why were Kirstine and John so worked up? It appeared they were in a no-fail situation. So why all the subterfuge, all the plotting that I'd overheard in Sheepish Expressions? Why mastermind a serious injury in the barn?

There was only one logical explanation: One third of the estate wasn't enough for the couple. They wanted it all.

A glance Vicki's way told me she didn't seem upset with the possible outcome. Or maybe she didn't understand it. Even now, Vicki didn't ask any questions or express her opinion. No wonder she'd insisted that I attend this meeting! I had to be her voice. So I kept going. "Do you have experience contesting bequests? Litigation is a very specialized area of the law, at least it is in the States."

Turner addressed Vicki. "Ms. MacBride, really! Your friend has all the tact of"—here he glared at me—"an ugly American."

Vicki looked stricken.

"Vicki requested that I attend this meeting," I said, taking a deep breath. "I'm here as her representative, isn't that right, Vicki?"

She still couldn't speak, but at least she managed to nod in agreement.

I pressed on, "Do you have the proper experience to handle this case?"

Paul Turner's mustache twitched again, but he answered. "I've been the family's solicitor for more years than you've been alive. Do you think I haven't handled contentious issues before?"

I wasn't familiar with the court system in Scotland, and if it were anything like the law enforcement system I'd encountered, I didn't know what to expect. "And has the judge handled cases like this in the past?" I went on to ask.

"Of course," he said rather condescendingly. Then he stood up and addressed Vicki dismissively. "If you have any questions, Ms. MacBride, please feel free to contact me again."

Outside after the meeting, walking back to the pub, where we'd left our cars, I expressed my growing concern. "I don't believe Paul Turner has your best interests at heart."

I couldn't help feeling that he had something up his sleeve that he wasn't sharing with his client. What, I didn't know. When Vicki didn't reply, I studied her. "Are you all right?"

"It's just . . . lawyers and courts make me *so* nervous. I'm not used to handling conflict, and all I want to do is run away. And to think how far they'll go to get their own way!"

"At least they can't take your new home away from you."

"Why should I even want it? To have to get up every morning and be faced with nothing but hatred?"

She did have a point.

"Perhaps you can work out some sort of compromise with Kirstine and Alec without going into court," I suggested. "You know, sit down and extend an olive branch."

"Kirstine and her husband scare me."

They scared me, too, but I didn't want to make things worse, so I said, "At least think about it."

"All right, I will." Then she brightened. "Leith Cameron

rang to check on you. I think you may be giving his girl some competition."

I laughed. "Matchmaking, Vicki? Two can play that game. Let's see. How about fixing you up with Sean Stevens?"

She wrinkled her nose in distaste. "Too excitable for my taste."

"Inspector Jamieson?"

"Not excitable enough."

"Paul Turner?"

"Too old, hairy, and married. And he scares me speechless!"

"Speaking of 'married,' have you ever been?"

"Twice before," Vicki replied. "I'm about as good at marriage as my da was, and that's all I have to say about the subject."

"You simply haven't found the right man yet."

Vicki snorted.

"Let's see. There must be someone suited for you," I teased.

"Don't go suggesting that boozer of an innkeeper."

"So you know about his permanent address at the local watering hole??"

"I saw him at the pub during the funeral, and he hasn't changed one bit. The Morris family has owned that inn since the beginning of time, and every single one of them liked their liquor. I remember Bill from my summers here, and even then he was pished more than he was sober. Bill's a harmless old goat though."

I laughed along with her, agreeing that he was an old goat but not as sure of the harmless part.

CHAPTER 23

I tried to keep up with Vicki on the drive back to the farm, but like all the others drivers I'd encountered in Scotland, she drove as though the road were a racetrack. She quickly left me in her dust.

When I arrived at the farm, I saw Leith Cameron's Land Rover parked by the farmhouse and his dog Kelly trotting along the fence across the lane. Kelly watched the sheep with that intense border collie stare and visibly quivered with anticipation. The sheep watched her right back but without the calm they had exhibited while observing me. They stared in unison, seeming skittish, nervous—and no wonder. The sheep were expecting to be herded any moment.

Vicki and Leith had been chatting when I pulled up, but as soon as I exited the Peugeot, Vicki hurried away toward the house. "I have a few things to do inside," she claimed, but not before she gave me a conspiratorial wink behind Leith's back.

I did an internal head shake. The woman was absolutely tenacious when she set her mind to something.

"Eden Elliott, I heard ye took a fall. How are ye feeling?" He seemed genuinely concerned.

"Pretty much back to normal," I told him.

"That's good tae hear."

At Leith's call, the obedient border collie left the fence and trotted behind us as we entered the barn and approached the stairs leading to the loft. Meanwhile I explained about John Derry on his tractor, the bales of hay, and how he'd left us to haul them to the loft.

"Ye broke the step, ye did," Leith said.

"It turns out that someone tampered with it," I told him, explaining what had caused my fall and how Sean Stevens had found the sawed stair piece. "It's hard not to think that Vicki was the most likely target. And I believe it has something to do with the litigation started by her half siblings."

By Leith's darkening expression I knew he was becoming increasingly upset and angry as I shared what had happened. "Ye must be right about it being a MacBride up tae no good," he said. "Nobody else would have a reason tae do such a thing. But the inspector will have a tough time proving it."

He looked around for Kelly. "She was a fine herder in her day," Leith said proudly. "Not every dog o' her breed is born with the ability to herd sheep. Either they have it as pups, or they never have it. Herding isn't something that can be taught. Some o' the working dogs here at the MacBride farm are from one or another of her litters."

"How old is she?" I asked, surprised to learn that Kelly wasn't a youngster, and that she'd been a mom multiple times.

"Goin' on twelve," Leith told me. "She has a bit o' arthritis in her legs and the beginning of cataracts. Her herding days are behind her. Time tae turn the task over tae another generation, but as ye can see, she's still got plenty o' spunk even in retirement."

"You'll have to find another job for her to do," I suggested.

"She has a good nose. Maybe she can sniff out truffles and help me dig them up. She'd give those trained pigs a run fer their money. Come over here, Kelly. What are ye up tae over there?"

I followed his line of sight over to the far side of the barn, on the other side of a tractor, where the canine's head was in view. She was digging away. Small stones and pieces of hay flew in the air, pinging against the tractor body.

"Quit that!" Leith called out. Kelly stopped and gazed at her owner, head cocked as though trying to understand what the fuss was all about. "Don't know what's gotten intae her," Leith said to me. "She isn't usually a digger."

Vicki came into the barn then, and with a wily smile said, "I just got off the phone with Alec."

"You don't seem upset," I said, studying my friend, who appeared unusually calm. "Did he suggest a peaceful resolution?"

"Nothing like that. No business at all. He was actually polite. And he asked after you."

Really? Although, he *had* suggested a golf outing. But I'd thought he was just being polite.

"He offered to take you golfing tomorrow morning and I accepted for you. I told him you'd be ready at nine o'clock sharp," Vicki told me.

"But I don't know how to golf!" I cried.

"If anyone is qualified tae teach ye it's Alec," Leith said, apparently not fazed in the least by this announcement. So much for Vicki's matchmaking efforts. "It's easy tae learn," he went on. "And Scotland is the best place tae try it out. The sport was invented here, after all."

"You should be the one to teach her," Vicki said, not giving up.

Before Leith had a chance to respond, he glanced sharply in the direction of the tractor, where the border collie was digging again. "Kelly!" he called out loudly. This time she ignored him completely, too intent on her task to notice. Leith walked toward her, giving Vicki an opportunity to whisper to me, "A little competition will do our neighbor some good. He'll take another look at you now that some other man is showing interest."

"He's with someone, Vicki," I hissed back, "and I'm not going to try to steal him."

"It can't be anything serious," she answered. "He'll come round. Failing means you're playing!" At my confused expression, she translated for me, "That means at least you're trying."

Just then Leith called out, "Vicki, you'd better take a look at this."

Kelly had found a new job all right, and it was somewhat on the lines of sniffing out truffles.

Only she hadn't found buried delicacies.

She'd unearthed something hidden under a layer of hay that had been roughly scattered to conceal what was beneath.

Some had soaked into the straw.

Some had seeped down into the crushed-stone flooring.

And even though it wasn't fresh—not bright, but rather rusty in color—it couldn't have been mistaken for anything else.

"Blood," I said.

"And lots of it," Leith added.

As for Vicki, true to character, she started screaming.

CHAPTER 24

Inspector Jamieson arrived first. Next came Sean Stevens, and within the hour a whole contingency of forensic specialists were combing the barn for evidence.

Sheepish Expressions hadn't yet closed for the day, so there were still customers coming and going from the parking lot, where they couldn't help noticing the commotion up the lane. Some of them had formed a group on the perimeter, where a police officer kept spectators out of the way.

"I don't need tae wait for lab reports tae know whose blood is all over inside this barn," I overheard the inspector say to Sean. "It's Gavin Mitchell's, I'll bet you, and it's safe tae say we've found the scene o' the crime." Then he gave Sean strict orders, "Ye stay out o' the barn and don't touch anythin'. Keep track o' the witnesses and make sure they dinnae wander off. Do ye think you can handle that? Keeping tabs on them?"

Sean nodded and scurried off right past me, one of those witnesses in his charge. So much for keeping tabs.

Kelly, who had discovered one of the most important

missing pieces in the investigation, had been confined to
Leith's Land Rover. Inspector Jamieson wasn't taking any
chances with the crime scene. The border collie didn't care
in the least that she'd been banished, thanks to the rawhide
bone Leith had presented to her for a job well done. The
treat kept her busy for a while, then she took a nap, perfectly
content to be out of the loop.

Vicki, conversely, was inconsolable. And I didn't blame
her. Since her arrival in Glenkillen, she'd been on the receiv-
ing end of plenty of hostility and suspicion. Not only had
she taken possession of a local family's inheritance, but then
she'd found a popular resident's dead body in his cottage.
Now the community was about to learn that he'd been killed
in her own barn. And they'd learn this latest fact sooner
rather than later, with shop customers hanging around
eagerly waiting for the latest gossip.

Any hopes I'd had that the sheep shearer's murder had
been the result of an interrupted burglary and that the per-
petrator had been passing through Glenkillen flew out the
proverbial window with Kelly's big discovery. I really hadn't
had much to base that theory on anyway, other than a box
moved from the top of the television and flung down beside
the body.

A MacBride or someone close to the family must have
murdered Gavin Mitchell. John and Kirstine? Derry's name
came to the forefront every time something new came to
the surface. And his wife had to be an accomplice. But
somehow Vicki was in the hot seat.

"John Derry had nothing tae do with tamperin' with the
stairs," the inspector told me when I inquired during a lull
in the action, after Leith, Vicki, and I had written out our
statements and while the forensic team was still going about
their business. "He had plenty o' witnesses who saw him in

town, from the time he left ye with the hay until well after ye were taken to hospital by ambulance."

Well, wasn't that convenient? He would have had to leave the tractor and instantly drive to Glenkillen. "How can these witnesses be so specific as to the time?" I argued. "Surely he could have squeezed in a little sawing."

Inspector Jamieson was grim but certain. "He was attending a local business association meeting. That bunch is always hatching up one scheme or the other tae bring more visitors intae the village. I compared the times ye gave me, and no way could John Derry have rigged those stairs unless he did it right before ye started hauling bales up, and . . ."

I interrupted and finished the sentence for him. "And since I had made multiple trips up and down before going into the house for a break, he didn't have the opportunity."

"Ye took the words right out o' my mouth. It's becoming a habit with ye."

Either John's business buddies had covered for him, or his wife had been involved.

"What about Kirstine?" I asked. "Where was she at the time?"

"Ye need tae let me do my job the way I see fit," the inspector said. Then he turned to Vicki. "I suppose ye don't have anybody tae vouch for yer whereaboots?"

"And what specific period of time should I be concerned with?" she asked him, her voice strong, but I could tell she was rattled by his line of questioning. I know I'd have been.

"Ye can write out a detailed time line fer me later, including your travel schedules back and forth between here and London with a list of those who can vouch for ye. Right now I'd like a brief accounting o' yer movements from the time ye learned o' yer father's death until ye discovered Gavin Mitchell's body."

"I need to account for several days? Every second?" She paled. "How am I supposed to do that?"

At least I could help a little. "We were at the cemetery and then the pub and together until we went to the cottage and found the body. And we were on the same flight from London. We sat next to each other."

"How about we just worry right now aboot the day of and the day before ye met with Paul Turner regarding the will," the inspector said. "I'm well aware that Gavin was the one who phoned ye with the news of James MacBride's death. What else did he say?"

"That I should come immediately," Vicki said.

"Did he tell ye why?"

"No, I had no idea. I tried to get more information, but all he would say was that I needed to get to Glenkillen as soon as possible. So I caught a flight and arrived that same evening. I stayed at the inn."

"And that's the last ye heard from him?"

Still pale, she nodded, well aware that the investigation had taken a turn in her direction. "He was friendly on the phone, said he remembered me fondly from my childhood and imagined I'd grown into a fine woman." With that, Vicki broke down and wept.

I'd had limited experience with murder, and knew of only a handful of motives: fear, love, revenge, greed.

Fear seemed unlikely—I couldn't image anyone being so afraid of the sheep shearer that they'd felt they had to eliminate him to preserve their own skin. From all his acquaintances' comments, everybody had liked Gavin. As for love, people were known to do crazy things for it, but no one had mentioned any romantic interests in Gavin's life. If there had been one, that person would be high on the inspector's list of suspects, yet I hadn't heard any gossip of that sort. And based on the mess in the dead man's cottage, he didn't have anyone helping him with upkeep or anyone he was looking to impress. It looked every inch a confirmed bachelor's pad.

Revenge maybe? Although, the only person I knew of with a motive was Samuel Kerr, the jailbird who had been released from his cage, had been following the twelve steps, and had apologized for what he'd done. Not only that, but according to the inspector, Kerr had an ironclad alibi.

The most likely and strongest motive, then, was personal gain.

Was the box that had been moved from the television a clue? Had it contained something that the killer was searching for inside the cottage? Had it been found? And what in the world could it have been? While Inspector Jamieson attempted to question the sobbing Vicki, I noticed Kirstine and her husband had joined the group of spectators, but, oddly, they didn't come forward to find out what was happening. If this were my farm, I'd be demanding answers. It made me wonder if they already knew what we'd found.

Leith noticed the couple as well and went to join them, the three moving away from the others milling about, their heads bent together. Leith appeared comfortable with them, relaxed. The guy didn't ruffle easily, even in the barn when we'd realized what Kelly had discovered. The only time I'd seen him react strongly was when he'd found out the reason I'd fallen from the loft steps.

Eventually Inspector Jamieson looked out their way, noticed them, and waved them over as he walked along the side of the barn. Leith came back and stood next to Vicki and me. From our position, I could see that John Derry was questioning the inspector rather than the other way around, but I couldn't hear what he was saying. John directed several hostile glares our way, as did his wife.

Suddenly, Kirstine raised her voice in anger. "She was seen, she was!"

"Who?" the inspector asked, bewildered.

Vicki blanched as white as one of the sheep in the pasture. Kirstine was pointing directly at her. "Vicki MacBride and Gavin Mitchell," she spat. "They were together on the beach, 'twas late that night, but Bill Morris could tell it was them. Right near Gavin's cottage. She must have lured him out to our barn and stabbed him to death."

Vicki, crying out, turned and ran for the house.

"Get her!" John Derry yelled. "She killed Gavin Mitchell!"

"Hold on, now," Inspector Jamieson's voice was raised just as loud. "I can't go arresting people on yer say-so. Or Bill's either. And keep yer voices down."

But it was too late. The shop's customers hadn't missed a thing. Before long, everybody in Glenkillen would have heard it through the grapevine.

It took a few moments for the full realization of Kirstine's accusation to strike me.

If Vicki really had been seen with Gavin Mitchell, what about Vicki's claim that she'd only talked to the man on the phone? If what Kirstine had said was true, Vicki had lied. To me. To the inspector. To everyone.

I didn't believe the accusation. Either Bill had lied, or it was Kirstine who was lying.

Wasn't it?

CHAPTER 25

Despite my attempts to talk to Vicki that night, I'd been unable to persuade her to unlock her bedroom door and let me in, and I'd eventually given up. The next morning, the sky was the darkest it had been since I'd arrived in Scotland. The only upside to the dismal weather was a temporary reprieve from my golf outing with Alec MacBride. He'd called the house early to express his disappointment. Somehow I was able to conceal the joy I was feeling. We rescheduled for the next day.

Vicki refused to get out of bed even as the morning slowly wore on. She pleaded illness when I tried to coax her to rise and face the day . . . and to answer a number of questions I was curious about, though I didn't say that.

In Vicki's absence, I turned my attention to the other house dwellers, Coco and Pepper. I let them outside to do their business and then back in, filled their bowls with fresh water, and served them breakfast.

Shortly afterward, Inspector Jamieson phoned and asked me to meet him at the beach near Gavin Mitchell's cottage.

I told him I'd need an hour to get ready. My mood threatened to become as dark as the day.

I showered, dressed in shorts and a T-shirt, and told Vicki through her bedroom door that I was heading out despite the gloomy weather.

Driving today was yet another new adventure. I drove through and over the moors and hills, encountering fog patches that blinded me from the road ahead. Rocky slopes began at the side of the narrow road and were abruptly swallowed up in the murk. High beams, I found out quickly, made visibility even worse. I slowed way down and crept along, nervously navigating the roundabouts.

A few tiny rays of sunlight peeked out here and there, but did little to illuminate my other issue—the writer's block I still suffered from. No way would I be able to write a single decent sentence until the Gavin Mitchell murder case was solved. Ami hadn't known what she was wishing for when she suggested I immerse myself in Scottish culture!

Well, I certainly hadn't stuck a hesitant toe in to test the water. I'd dived right in without even finding out how deep the water was. It's not like I was going to make the brume dissipate until my head was clear and my mind focused. And how would that be possible with all the drama going on around me?

I resolved to assist the inspector in closing this case as quickly as possible so life could return to normal—not only mine, but Vicki's and Inspector Jamieson's, and the lives of everybody else caught up in this mess.

So when the inspector had called and requested my presence in Glenkillen, I'd been more than happy to accommodate him, even though he'd refused to divulge his reason for our meeting.

It didn't take long to find out what he wanted.

"Please explain this system to me," I said after I parked on the street next to the beach and joined him. By this time, the rain had begun to fall, our umbrellas only protecting us so much against the wind and mist sweeping across the sand from the far reaches of the ocean.

"CCTV," he said, appearing more rumpled than usual, indicating he'd had a night as long as mine had been. "Closed-circuit television."

"Ah."

"We've been using it in the big cities fer years," the inspector informed me. "Especially in areas that need monitoring, such as banks, airports, car parks. The use o' them has increased over time due tae the fact that they decrease our crime significantly, sometimes cutting it clear in half, percentage-wise. These days, every city center in Scotland has a system in place, even the smaller villages like Glenkillen."

The light mist turned to heavy rain pouring in streams off the edges of our umbrellas. I adjusted the angle of mine to find a little relief from the spray. "And those cameras are here at the beach?"

"Aye," he answered, pointing at a light pole. As much as I tried, I couldn't see anything other than the post and its light fixture. The surveillance camera must have been up inside the light housing. "This car park is monitored mainly against theft," he continued. "We had a rash o' auto break-ins at the beginning o' the summer so we installed them here after that. We didn't catch the thieves, but they stopped their handiwork. See the sign?"

Sure enough, at the entrance to the parking lot a big, bold sign warned of the use of television cameras. *Looking Out For You* it read. I hadn't noticed it previously when Vicki and I had walked onto the beach, but it had been growing dark that night.

Big Brother and thoughtcrime. I couldn't help thinking of poor, betrayed Winston Smith in *Nineteen Eighty-Four.* It seemed that America wasn't the only place that was losing the battle for individual privacy. Would future generations even know enough to miss it? Almost certainly not. I shivered, whether from thoughts about the world we live in or the chilly dampness, I didn't know. But I was grateful that the path Vicki and I had taken that night hadn't crossed the parking lot. The thought of cameras following our every move was unnerving, even though we'd done nothing to be ashamed of or to have been concealed from prying eyes.

"Kirstine MacBride has some nerve," I said, still upset over her unfounded accusation against my friend, "making an outrageous claim like that against Vicki. If she had known you could check on her, she might have held her tongue. And going so far as to involve Bill Morris in her scheme."

There was a slight pause before Inspector Jamieson asked, "Ye and Vicki have become good friends, then?"

Something in his tone sent a warning to me to tread softly. "I haven't known her long enough to categorize her as a *good* friend," I answered, suddenly realizing I barely knew the woman.

"Are ye absolutely sure ye don't have anything to add to the investigation? Anything at all?"

We locked gazes. And then I knew.

"You already viewed the recording from this camera, didn't you?" I said. "And you *do* have Vicki on the video, don't you? Kirstine was telling the truth. Bill did see her."

He could have nodded, but he didn't have to. The answer was in those penetrating eyes.

I felt physically ill. *Vicki* had been the one who'd lied.

She'd lied to me as well as to the inspector about never having met with the sheep shearer.

She'd meant to deceive us. Yes, she certainly had spoken to Gavin on the phone. The part she'd left out was that they had met right here on the beach, a short distance from his cottage right before he died.

"Why didn't Bill come forward earlier with this information?" I asked.

"Bill never would have on his own. He's usually drunk as a lord."

"But he told Kirstine?"

The inspector nodded grimly. "She ran intae him on the street yesterday while doing a bit o' shopping. And when she got back tae the farm and found out that Gavin had been murdered right on the MacBride farm, she couldn't wait tae tell me what she knew."

This wasn't going well.

"That recording only proves that Vicky met with Gavin," I reasoned, more to convince myself than the inspector. "Withholding pertinent facts doesn't make her a killer. Meeting him in a parking lot is a long way from stabbing him to death in a barn. Besides, she has no motive."

"A person's motive fer murder isn't always readily apparent," the inspector said. "Rather, it seldom is."

My thoughts went back to the night we'd found Gavin's body, the box beside it, a telltale dustless square on a dusty old television. My belief that his cottage had been searched. "What was inside the box beside Gavin Mitchell's body?" I asked.

"Important papers," he said. "Deed tae the cottage, insurance policies, bank statements."

"And he kept them in a box on top of the television?"

"Ye sound surprised. It's not uncommon as all that. We're a simple folk."

Simple? That remained to be seen. I very much doubted that the inspector was uncomplicated. "Anything obviously missing?"

"Nothing out o' the ordinary, no. His life was pretty much accounted fer."

I stared out at the crashing waves of the firth.

"How did Gavin Mitchell find out that James MacBride had died?" I asked the inspector.

"MacBride slipped intae a coma at the end. His daughter, Kirstine, had just arrived and Gavin was at his bedside when he passed. Herself was in a very bad condition, and so Gavin offered tae call all the family members and tried tae reach the solicitor. When Paul Turner couldnae be found at home, Gavin began making arrangements. Luckily, Turner was notified and returned the next morning."

This fit with what the solicitor had told us.

I wanted to ask if the inspector had confirmed Paul Turner's whereabouts during that period of time, but I didn't want to appear to be trying to cast suspicion away from Vicki without just cause. Besides, after Vicki's deception, I had to face the facts: She could very well have murdered the man. At minimum, she wasn't as innocent as she'd led us to believe.

Had she used me as a pawn in an evil game, actually leading me along to "discover" the murder scene with her? Inspector Jamieson had been onto her from the very beginning, asking all those questions. Me? I'd bristled at his implications and been blinded by her kindness just as surely as I'd been blinded by this morning's fog.

"Vicki did it, didn't she?" I asked, weakly.

"Best not tae be jumping tae conclusions," the inspector

advised as I jumped from one to another. "In an ugly business like this, we'll come tae the best type o' conclusion tae the case with facts we can substantiate. It looks bad fer her, though. That I will admit."

"What are your personal thoughts?" I decided to ask him.

"My own," he answered somewhat coolly.

Overnight, it felt, our relationship had changed. Until now, I'd shared a certain camaraderie with the inspector, which I have to admit I enjoyed. After this reserved comment, I sensed him taking a step back from me. I had been friendly with the suspect, taking her up on her offer of a roof over my head. With Vicki in his sights, Jamieson wasn't going to trust me any more than he did the suspect.

"Ye aren't planning on leaving Glenkillen anytime soon?" he asked, official and all business.

"No. I'm staying a little longer." That had slipped out. I wasn't even sure it was true or that I wanted to. But the expression on the inspector's face was a warning.

"I'll hold ye tae that," he said. "When will ye be able to move back tae the inn?"

"Not anytime soon, I'm afraid. Jeannie Morris is convinced I started the fire."

He seemed to think about that for a moment, but all he said was, "Keep a sharp eye out fer trouble and don't go making any."

I watched him walk away. Even with his back to me and his collar pulled up, his posture and the faded umbrella gave him an unmistakable aura of a man with a heavy burden to bear.

CHAPTER 26

By the time I reached the Kilt & Thistle, the heavy rain and howling wind was making my umbrella more of a handicap than any actual protection from the elements. Sean Stevens and I banged into each other in our rush to escape the weather, our inverted umbrellas tangling, and by the time we made it through the doors of the pub, I was drenched. Somehow Sean made it inside in much better shape than I did.

"So sorry," Sean repeated over and over. "Let me buy ye a pint for yer troubles."

"You're drinking? Does that mean you're off duty?"

"I'm always on duty, but that doesn't have anything tae do with a sip here and there."

"I think I'll stick to tea, thanks."

"Suit yerself. Mind if I join ye at a table?"

"No, not at all."

Most of the tables closest to the bar were taken. I spotted the drunken innkeeper at his favorite table, a pint in front of him. He tracked me with narrowed eyes. Vicki had believed Bill Morris was harmless, but he might very well be her downfall. The man was more alert than I'd given him credit for.

Heads turned our way and eyes followed our movements; one table of two patrons were whispering, one's hand held up to another's ear, cupped to muffle sound. Paranoia tried to run rampant, but I beat it back with threats to its life.

Let them talk. It didn't affect me in the least.

Dale's wife, Marg, came over once Sean and I sat down, and after exchanging complaints about the weather, Sean asked her, "Have you a good Cullen skink today?"

"Came in with this morning's catch. Couldn't be any fresher than that."

Sometimes I forgot I was in an English-speaking country. "Cullen skink?" I asked.

"Smoked haddock in a rich stew," Marg explained. "The recipe hails from Cullen, a town not too far away along the coast."

"It comes with mashed potatoes," Sean said.

"And a few secret ingredients tae call it the pub's own," Marg added.

For the first time, I realized how hungry I was, remembering that I'd fed the terriers this morning but hadn't taken time to eat anything myself. "And two cups of tea," I finished.

"What tea?" Sean said, glancing from me to Marg. "I don't think so."

"If you're on duty, you shouldn't be drinking alcohol," I insisted, sounding more churlish than I wanted.

"That might be true where ye come from, but over here is a different matter," he protested.

"Two cuppas, it is," Marg said, hurrying away in spite of Sean's continued protests.

"Yer awfully high and mighty today," Sean said, annoyed. "A real do-gooder."

"If you remember correctly, I saved you from redundancy. It's time you got serious about your career."

He bristled. "I take my job serious enough."

I wasn't about to forget my pact with Inspector Jamieson. I'd promised to help the volunteer. "Didn't you receive training when you were first offered the position?"

"I was."

"In the form of?"

"A training manual."

"And did you read it?"

Sean looked at the ceiling and rolled his eyeballs around in his head, so I was pretty sure he hadn't.

"I was aboot tae start it soon," he murmured.

"Read the first twenty pages tonight, and we'll discuss them tomorrow."

Sean's face was reddening with barely suppressed emotion. "Wha' are you? My ma? I don't take kindly tae your meddling in me affairs."

I let silence hang between us. He began to squirm. The truth came out soon after.

"I'm dyslexic, if ye must know," he told me. "Reading anything is hard fer me. Even so mooch as a scrap o' paper takes me ferever. I couldnae read a whole training manual."

Ah, that explained a few things. "Should I see if the inspector can round up a video instead?" I asked.

"Ye better not tell him aboot my problem. That would give him more reason tae make me redundant fer good."

True. "Maybe we could just discuss some of those pesky law enforcement procedures," I suggested. "Starting with no drinking on the job."

Marg arrived with two steaming bowls of hearty haddock chowder, which turned out to be wonderfully flavorful and was even better when I followed Sean's example and dipped crusty bread into the thick, rich broth.

Silence stretched as we enjoyed our meal. Sean, I noted, was serious about his food, focusing entirely on the meal before him.

"How's the fire investigation going?" I asked when we were scraping the bottoms of our bowls.

"Nowhere." Sean had downed his soup as though he'd been rescued from starvation, but now he paused to scowl at his glass of water before elaborating. "Security cameras in the street and lobby didn't pick up any unusual activity," he said. "That tells us the arsonist either knew where the cameras were placed and avoided them, or it was an inside job."

His lack of prejudice against me made me like him a little better.

"What about the owners?" I suggested, leading the newbie along by his nose.

"Jeannie and old Bill?" At the mention of the innkeeper's name, Sean glanced over at Bill's table, although it was impossible for him to overhear Sean from that distance, especially with all the other conversations going on around us. "Why would himself do such a thing?"

"Maybe they're tired of running it. Jeannie mentioned how much she'd like to see the world and get away from the village. And her father . . . well, he doesn't seem fit to take over."

"No reason fer them tae try tae burn up their own place, though."

Did I have to spell out the entire thing for him? "Jeannie's father told me the inn is insured. That's a good financial reason if I ever heard one."

Sean scoffed at that. "Leave it tae Bill tae make ye think he's better than he is." He shook his head in disbelief. "And the man is starting tae go dotty, with all the booze and old age."

"What do you mean?"

"They dinnae have a bit o' insurance."

What? No insurance? But that was what I was basing all my accusations on. Owners trying to cash in—one in particular who wanted to escape this village. "That can't be true," I said, flabbergasted.

"'Tis. Old Bill let coverage lapse over a year ago."

"Does his daughter know that?"

"Aye, she's the one who told me. I confirmed it with the insurance company. They're runnin' bare as a newborn's bottom."

Sean had been more thorough in his investigation of the fire than I'd have ever given him credit for. Maybe he would make it as a cop after all.

But there went another one of my promising theories, flying out the window, cackling as it went. Surely Jeannie wouldn't burn down an uninsured building. If she really wanted out, she would put the inn up for sale. If she and her father didn't have a motive for starting a fire, then who did?

CHAPTER 27

Jasper the barn cat was grooming himself in the open barn door when I parked and got out of the car, slamming the door harder than necessary. I was damp, chilled, and ornery, with a dull, nagging headache, which I suspected was due to more than my head injury. I needed to remember to take my meds. The cat froze and watched me but didn't run away when I walked over to stand just inside the barn.

The tractor partially blocked the area where Gavin Mitchell had met his death. The police had finished collecting evidence and had gone away as though they'd never been there. The inn fire hardly mattered in the light of a man's death. That was merely an annoyance to the guests and a brief financial setback to the owners. No one had suffered loss of life or belongings, nor had anyone had to be hospitalized for carbon dioxide poisoning.

It shouldn't have been worth more than a fleeting consideration in comparison to a man's murder.

So why did I have such a strong feeling that everything that had happened so far was connected? That the fire wasn't an isolated incident. Neither, I believed, was my fall from the barn stairs. I should be able to connect the dots, but I couldn't. At least not yet.

Vicki's car was gone, making me wonder if the police had ordered her to appear for questioning. Was Inspector Jamieson interrogating her at this very moment, demanding to know if she was guilty and trying to cover up a terrible crime?

My brain had so many questions but not a single answer, only suppositions.

I wanted desperately to blame someone other than Vicki for my fall. Would Kirstine have had time to run down from the shop? Would she have left it unattended? How prompt were the tour buses? Could she have had a gap between one bus departing and another arriving? But how would she have known when I would take a break? Or even if I would?

John had an alibi, but that didn't have to mean as much as one might think. Friends have been known to lie for friends.

As hard as I tried to cast blame elsewhere, it boomeranged back to Vicki. Had she been the one who'd sawed the steps leading to the loft? Had she intended to injure me? Or worse? I thought back and remembered going into the house for tea—Vicki *had* excused herself from the kitchen briefly. Had it been enough time for her to make sure I fell when I went back to work?

But why would she hurt me?

She'd gone over and above the call of duty when she'd rescued me the night of the fire. She'd given me a bed in the middle of the night and treated me like a welcome guest.

Yet, there might be an explanation for her to orchestrate my fall. It was devious; that was for sure.

Maybe she wanted John Derry to appear guilty. He'd been

a verbal and threatening adversary. She couldn't have known that he'd have an alibi that would be supported by several village businesspeople. It's possible that the idea of using me to get to him occurred to her after she took me in and was concocted on the spot when John ordered us to stack the hay. A convenient opportunity that she took advantage of.

The more I turned the incident over in my mind, the more suspicious Vicki's actions became. If she'd done this, she could have killed me.

The more I thought about my fall, the angrier I became.

Sometimes we see what we want to see. I'd been a sucker from the moment I boarded that plane in London, desperately searching for a friendly face in an unfamiliar country. And then Vicki sat down next to me, and she hooked me in. Never mind the warning signs that she wasn't exactly perfect. Shouldn't a few red flags have gone up?

After all, Vicki MacBride had walked off with an inheritance that should in all fairness have been split three ways. Even if the one-sided bequest had been her father's intent, shouldn't she have made an effort to reach out to the other side? Worked to find a way to compensate them?

I rubbed my head to relieve some of the pressure. So much for first impressions. I considered kicking one of the Peugeot's tires a few times to work off some steam. Instead I stared at the tractor, remembering how Vicki had screamed when we'd found the sheep shearer, and again when Kelly had discovered the scene of the crime. Her reactions had seemed so genuine.

Once I calmed down a little, the rational part of me still had the strength to counter some of those damning claims. So Vicki had been unwilling to compromise with the others; but had they even given her a chance? And wasn't her reaction to their hostility perfectly normal?

Disputes like this happened all the time, and sometimes reaching out wasn't an option with so much emotion involved. Famous television personalities, film stars, and many others in the public limelight have died and left survivors to duke it out over their assets. And families don't have to be divided like the MacBrides to disagree and go to battle.

What was the expression?

Where there's a will, there's a war.

Wasn't that the truth? I was getting to witness a very nasty one with my very own eyes. Lucky me.

So I decided not to pass judgment on Vicki based on the way she handled the rest of her family. She and I had bigger issues to address, and I really wanted to give her a chance to explain, to reassure me that she'd had nothing to do with my fall or with Gavin Mitchell's murder. I would give her that much.

If only the surveillance cameras hadn't caught her in such a terribly incriminating lie!

Jasper mewed, bringing me back to the present.

I turned slowly and squatted down a few feet away from him, motionless while we made some serious eye contact. He stared right back, unflinching but alert to any sudden movements for me. Then he came forward several steps, slowly, until he was close enough to rub against my knee. Which, to my amazement, he proceeded to do. On his third pass against my leg, his tail straight up in the air, his back arched, his eyes at half-mast, he began purring.

"So you aren't the big bad tom that you like us all to think you are," I said to him, smiling, feeling the headache receding as my body relaxed. We all could learn a thing or two from cats. They sure know how to de-stress.

While Jasper and I became friends, the rain clouds

moved off into the distance and the sun made an effort to appear. It failed, but at least the dark gloom lifted. I was starting to get used to the volatile weather patterns, how one minute the sky could be perfectly clear and the next it would pour buckets. It was because of these torrential rains that the Highlands are such a lush, visual delight. This place was growing on me daily.

If only the people were doing the same!

Cautiously and slowly, I picked up Jasper in my arms. His purring missed a beat while he assessed the risk, but then his motor started up again. He was larger and heavier than I'd expected, and when I examined his claws, they were well honed. Jasper had an amazing built-in defense system. It would take a formidable animal to win a physical confrontation with him. Maybe they sensed that and kept a safe distance, because Jasper had a perfect shape and coat. No torn ears or burrs.

A few minutes more of cuddling, then Jasper's ears perked up. He quickly swung his head toward the lane, alerting me before I heard the approaching vehicle. He began wiggling in an attempt to flee, and I quickly put him down before he could unsheathe his claws. I watched him disappear from sight, an old pro at finding hiding holes inside the barn.

Leith Cameron's Land Rover pulled up next to my car, and I took back a little of my criticism about the people I'd met not being as wonderful as the land. This guy was one of the exceptions. In my anger I'd forgotten that, and I appreciated this reminder.

He got out of the Land Rover, went around to the other side, and opened the passenger door. Kelly bounded out. I expected one of his lazy grins, but he didn't gift me with one of those lopsided smiles. There was a distinct air of seriousness about him today.

"Have ye seen her?" he asked without any sort of greeting.

"Who? Vicki?"

He nodded.

"Is she missing?" I asked uneasily.

"It appears so. I was having a chat with Sean Stevens when the inspector came along asking questions about where she might be. Jamieson is rounding up volunteers tae search fer her. Hope nothing's happened."

"I'm sure she's fine," I said with a sense of foreboding.

"Some o' the roads along these hills can be tricky," Leith said.

I'd traveled some of those roads Leith was talking about and, yes, they could be treacherous. And if a car went off one of the steep cliffs and landed in heavy brush, it might not be seen from the road, might not be discovered for days or even weeks.

"It's more likely that she's on the run," I said, more certain of that happening than a car accident. If anyone was at risk of taking a dive off a cliff, I was a more likely candidate than she was. I'd seen her drive. She was a pro at navigating the Highland roads.

Leith frowned, puzzled. "Why would she run?"

"As of this morning or late last night, she's the prime suspect in Gavin Mitchell's murder."

"What?" Leith had been a witness to Kirstine's accusation, but he hadn't heard about the surveillance camera video that backed up Kirstine's claim. I quickly filled him in, ending with, "The surveillance camera footage means Vicki's in a heap of trouble. Actually, I'm surprised the inspector is going to all this trouble to search the hills when he should be putting up roadblocks."

For the first time since I'd come back from town, I heard

the terriers barking from the direction of the house. Which surprised me. I thought they'd be with Vicki, wherever she was.

Leith glanced toward the house. "The inspector told me he came by here, found the dogs alone, and no sign o' Vicki on the farm or in the village. Do ye have any idea where she might have gone?"

I shook my head. "I haven't seen her since this morning. I just returned from town myself a few minutes ago."

Leith and I walked to the house and let the dogs out. Coco and Pepper loped off to play with Kelly.

"Vicki wouldn't leave town without her dogs," I said.

"She loves those wee dogs," Leith agreed. "But if she is hiding out, it would be hard enough alone without two noisy West Highland terriers tae deal with."

Which also was true.

"I'm worried about Vicki," he went on. "But I was even more concerned when I realized ye could o' been with her and something might have happened to ye, too."

I smiled. "You were thinking of me?"

"Aye," he said with that grin I'd hoped for earlier. Leith had enough confidence for both of us. He continued to grin. I'm sure I blushed as I turned away, uncomfortable with the attention but loving it just the same.

After a good run, Coco and Pepper collapsed on the wet grass, their tongues hanging on the ground and their eyes popping out of their sockets. Despite being considerably their elder, Kelly looked like she could have gone on playing forever.

"Kelly and I are going tae help in the search," Leith said. "Why don't ye join us?"

I gazed up from the panting dogs and studied him. Leith was wickedly good looking in the filtered sunlight streaking through the clouds above. Tall and strong, as though he could easily throw me over his shoulder and make off with me . . . have his way with me. . . . Oh my gosh! What was I thinking?

"Uh, okay. But I need to take my medication before we go," I stammered, hurrying toward the house. "For my head . . . uh . . . and I better leave Coco and Pepper here. I'll be right back."

The dogs must have found their second wind, because they were right on my heels.

CHAPTER 28

"We're probably wasting our time," I muttered from the passenger seat of Leith's Land Rover. Kelly had relinquished the position without any fuss and was happily sitting on her haunches in the backseat, enjoying the ride as only a dog can.

I really *did* hope we were wasting our time. I hated to think of the alternative. I might be angry with Vicki, and disappointed and hurt, but I didn't want this to end badly. If she'd had an accident, she could be seriously injured. Or worse. Whereas if she'd taken off rather than face certain accusations, that at least meant she was safe. And alive.

I saw Inspector Jamieson's police vehicle approach us from the direction of Glenkillen. We stopped and he came alongside, his window sliding down. The inspector gave me an official nod, then said to Leith, "Anything?"

"Nothing yet."

The inspector addressed me. "Do ye have any information regarding Vicki MacBride's whereaboots?"

I shook my head. "She was at the farmhouse when I left this morning to meet you in town."

The inspector looked off ahead, and said, "It's impossible tae see over some o' the drop-offs from inside a car. That's a problem, but we can't search all the hillsides on foot. It would take the rest o' our bloody lives."

"Aye. But I think we'll pull over when we can and walk a bit all the same," Leith told the inspector, who nodded, then drove off.

A little farther down the narrow, twisty road we found enough room on the side to park.

"Up fer a bit o' hillwalking?" Leith asked as we got out. To Kelly, who had jumped out and was watching Leith for a command, he said, "Stay near."

I swung my eyes up to the vertical heights, the rocky slopes and peaks. "We're going up there?" I tried not to squeak.

"We will be able to see much more from above," he said, glancing up at the sky. "At least the sun is cooperating fer the moment."

"But we're climbing straight up?"

"We'll find an easier path than directly up," he assured me, looping a pair of binoculars over my head and adjusting the strap. "Ye can be in charge of these. Come on, Kelly."

So Kelly and I followed our leader as he began the ascent.

Even though I was used to walking extensively in the big city, this hike up into the hills was challenging for me, and I felt myself tiring quickly. And I'm sure my recent fall didn't help either. I hid it the best I could, not wanting to look wimpy. Leith, having lived in this mountainous terrain all his life, didn't break a sweat, and, of course, Kelly was born for running.

Waist-high evergreen bushes dominated the landscape, thriving in the dry, rocky soil and displaying a profusion of small yellow flowers.

"Gorse," Leith informed me when I asked what it was. "Extremely invasive. We haven't been able tae control it. Watch out fer the thorns. They're as sharp as any cactus needles."

Naturally, I soon found out the hard way just how dangerous they were. I stepped wrong and turned my ankle. Upon realizing that I was falling, I instinctively grabbed for something to break my descent, which happened to be a handful of those thorny leaves.

"Ouch! Yowwww!"

I let go quickly and keeled over, remembering at the last moment to protect the binoculars around my neck. I closed my arms around them like they were a newborn baby.

Leith rushed over.

"Are ye all right?" he asked, squatting down beside me.

"The binoculars are okay," I said after a quick examination. "I'm not so sure about me."

"Ferget the binoculars."

"I turned my ankle. But it doesn't hurt nearly as much as my hands do." I sat up with my legs out straight. My hand wasn't the only place I'd taken a few stabs and jabs. There were several long scratches along the shin of my right leg where the gorse had ripped through the skin. My shin stung, my hands stung, the ankle . . . well, that remained to be seen.

Leith ran his hands over my ankle, his hands gently prodding. "It isn't swelling. That's a good sign. Let's see if we can get ye on yer feet."

With Kelly looking on from the sidelines, Leith helped me up, and I tested the ankle. It seemed all right.

"Yer lucky ye didn't fall into the very thick o' it," he said. "It would have entangled ye, and we'd have had a hard time gettin' ye out."

"It's like a hedge filled with small but razor-sharp

swords," I complained, readjusting the binoculars while imagining myself totally surrounded by the stuff.

"Didn't I warn ye?" he said with a soft chuckle.

"I like to discover things on my own," I quipped.

"Let's go back tae the rover and doctor you up," Leith suggested. "I've a first aid kit with me."

"No, really, I'm perfectly fine."

"Ye don't look so fine."

"We've had this same conversation before," I said, starting to laugh.

"When ye were kicking the snot out o' your rental car? Aye, I remember," he laughed along with me.

Kelly had left us and now stood on a ledge slightly above, her eyes partly closed in the light breeze, as though she were soaking in the sensations and enjoying them as much as we were. A light scent of . . . coconut? . . . wafted through the air. I'd smelled it throughout our walk but hadn't been able to place its source until my fall. I'd been more interested in escaping from it to concentrate on its fragrance, but now, bending close to a gorse bush brimming with yellow blossoms, I discovered that the sweet tropical smell really did originate from the gorse. Every rose has a thorn.

I commented on the flowers on the hills. "Your gorse might be prickly, but it's so fragrant and pretty when it blooms."

"It's always blooming. We even have a saying about that in these parts."

"Oh, really? What's that?"

Leith grinned, and said, 'When gorse is out o' blossom, kissing's out o' fashion.' "

What could I possibly say in response? My mind went blank, which was becoming a familiar state these days. The moment was about to turn awkward between us. Then I thought of a reply. "I'll have to use that line in my book."

I raised the binoculars to my eyes and focused my attention on something less uncomfortable—the landscape surrounding me.

"Ready tae go?" Leith asked. "I'll call Kelly down if ye feel ye can walk."

As we turned our attention to the border collie, her head swung sharply away from us. Her ears perked up. I swept my eyes over the rocky slopes in the same direction, and saw something . . . a flash of blue? Up here in the hills, the color yellow dominated the landscape, along with every hue of green imaginable. But blue?

I adjusted the focus on the binoculars. My heart took a running leap and jumped up into my throat. I pulled the binoculars from my neck and handed them to Leith wordlessly, not wanting to accept what I'd seen.

Because I'd been looking at an overturned car.

A blue Citroën.

Exactly like the one Vicki MacBride drove.

CHAPTER 29

"She was on her way toward toon," the inspector said from our position at the side of the road, where he was investigating angles of trajectory based on tire marks he'd found near the cliff directly above the overturned, severely damaged car.

By the time help had arrived, I'd dismissed all prior charges, suspicions, and accusations against my friend. All the betrayal I'd felt toward Vicki MacBride had vanished.

"No one could survive a fall like that," I said, speaking my fears aloud for the first time.

"Let's not give up hope yet," Leith advised me, putting a comforting arm over my shoulders and giving them a squeeze.

Two more rescue works hurried past us with a stretcher and began tying ropes to secure it for the descent. All were total professionals who I imagined had experience with these kinds of accidents since the Highland terrain is anything but flat. Emergency workers were busy preparing to traverse the steep slope while the rest of us waited anxiously for the frontline team to start down. When they finally disappeared over the side with medical supplies, I tried to follow along to be right there when they assessed Vicki's condition. But a sharply barked order from Inspector Jamieson to stay out of the way brought me back to my senses.

What had I been thinking? The climb up the hill with Leith and Kelly and then back down again (just as difficult as going up), had been child's play compared to what these rescuers were about to attempt. The first responders had to literally rappel down the side of the cliff. Given that my lack of coordination had already led me to take a dive into a stand of gorse, I'd have only given those trying to help Vicki another accident victim to deal with.

"It will be a while before the mountain rescue team can extricate her," the inspector said more gently. "I suggest ye go back to the farm and wait fer word. We'll make sure yer the first tae know."

That certainly had an ominous tone to it. I sensed that Inspector Jamieson expected the worst-case scenario too and was trying to protect me from any potential gory details.

"Go on noo, lass."

I shook my head, emphatically. I wasn't going anywhere.

I might not be much, but I was all Vicki had at the moment. Who did she have in her life besides me? Was there family other than two hostile half siblings? Vicki's father was gone. So was her mother. Was there anybody else? Friends in California and London probably; Vicki was so outgoing, someone who drew others to her. But I didn't have contact information for anyone.

I knew so little about Vicki MacBride.

And who would take care of Coco and Pepper? Would they find a new home someplace safe where they could be

together? Or would they end up in a shelter? Then eutha-
nized? God, I was getting morbid.

What a fair-weather friend I'd turned out to be! Whatever
happened to the sense of justice that is supposed to be the
American way—that everyone is innocent until proven
guilty? Vicki may not have been entirely honest with me,
but who amongst us hasn't told a few fibs at one time or
another? I hadn't even given her the benefit of the doubt,
hadn't confronted her with what I knew, hadn't demanded
a reasonable explanation. True, most of us would probably
classify our own transgressions as minor compared to hers.
Most of us haven't dug our own graves by withholding
important information from law enforcement officials per-
taining to a murder investigation. But still.

Time dragged on at a crawl. Thankfully, Leith was also
determined to stay for the outcome. We stayed close together,
silent, each immersed in our own thoughts.

I crept forward a bit closer to the sheer drop, coming side
by side with several members of the rescue team; I had to
see what was happening. I ignored the familiar signs of my
height phobia: sweat forming on my forehead and a nauseous
feeling in the pit of my stomach—and forced myself to look
down. The first responders had arrived at the scene of the
accident below, investigating the underbelly of the Citroën.
I couldn't make out their expressions or hear their conversations from my position, but I watched as one of them
wormed his way under the crushed vehicle.

A stretcher had arrived on the scene, ready for use.

Anticipation was torturing me slowly. Knots of tension
pulsed in my head, reminding me of the blow I'd taken,
realizing how much worse this was than anything that had
happened to me. The same question haunted me: How could
Vicki possibly have survived a fall like this?

That could have been me down there. I was such a rotten driver. But Vicki was a native, familiar with the hills and valleys, the roads so narrow that it was a miracle two cars could even pass each other.

What had happened to cause her accident?

I wanted to scream with frustration as more rescuers near me adjusted lines while we waited, getting ready to bring up whatever still remained of my friend.

"Can't they give us some kind of preliminary report?" I said, turning on the inspector, understanding that I was taking my tension out on him but unable to stop myself.

"Ye aren't their first concern right now," he answered, clipped and concise. And so true.

As if my demand had been heard, however, the inspector's phone rang. He frowned my way and walked off, the phone to his ear and his voice low.

Leith put an arm around my shoulders again and gave me another reassuring squeeze. "We'll know soon enough," he said. "Let's move back and give them more room tae work."

The inspector disappeared from view as we left our position.

Dead or alive. Which?

The team that had remained above was peering over the side, leveraging the ropes, having rigged a pulley of some sort, and they were working the lines, lifting up something heavy. I had enough sense to follow Leith a little farther still, well back from the rescuers.

Finally, the stretcher came into view and cleared the top of the rise. Capable hands grabbed hold of the sides of the stretcher, helped it swing over.

Oh my God. I gasped in dismay at the awful sight of Vicki's pale face, closed eyes, and slack mouth.

Another rescue worker climbed over the side and stood up, looking grim. "Let's get moving!" he barked to the rest of the team. "She's alive," he told us. "But barely."

Alive? Alive! Hope surged through me finally.

Barely alive was far better than the alternative.

Before, while we waited for news, time had played out one painstaking second at a time. Now, it spun past faster than a speeding locomotive. Faster than the ambulance whose running lights and wailing siren gave me a glimmer of hope. There I was, standing next to Leith, listening to the sirens fade like they were the finale to a musical performance by the Chicago Symphony Orchestra.

And I wanted to give them a standing ovation.

CHAPTER 30

Throughout the rest of the evening, I continued to phone the hospital, trying to get information regarding Vicki's condition but without any degree of luck.

Coco and Pepper slept with me all night, curling up around my feet, one on each side. In the morning I let them outside first thing to sniff around and relieve themselves, and while they were busy with that, I put fresh water and kibble into their bowls.

They seemed to enjoy my attention, apparently having decided that I was a fun doggy-sitter, whose job it was to entertain them for a short while until their mom returned. If only they knew the truth about their human companion.

Finally, Inspector Jamieson called. Vicki had suffered two broken legs, and there was concern about potential internal bleeding. Her doctors were cautious and watchful.

Vicki MacBride, I realized, was important to me, and if she would only stay alive, we'd sort through this gorselike tangled web of deceit and hidden agendas and deal with whatever came our way.

I wanted more than anything to communicate with Ami, to share with my friend, but I was afraid to leave the house in case a call came in regarding Vicki. For the first time, I missed Internet service at the farmhouse.

As the morning progressed without any new news, my hackles began to rise when no one representing the Mac-Bride family had bothered to show up at the farmhouse door to inquire about Vicki. John stayed out in the fields, where I spotted him occasionally working with the border collies to drive the sheep to greener pastures. Kirstine didn't come around either, but I was sure she had opened the shop and was conducting business as usual.

They couldn't use the excuse that they hadn't been informed, because I knew for a fact that the inspector had made calls to both of them explaining Vicki's accident and that she'd been transported to Kirkwall Hospital.

For the MacBrides it must have been a day of rejoicing. I was beginning to think that the MacBride clan was filled with noxious weeds and bad seeds.

And then, perhaps to prove me wrong on some accounts, Alec MacBride arrived. I was sitting outside on a bench, slathering an antiseptic on yesterday's worst gorse thorn wounds, applying a final coating to the hand I'd been foolish enough to use to stop my fall, when he walked down the lane from the direction of Sheepish Expressions wearing—*Oh no*—golfing attire. Did he really think I felt like playing golf?

"What happened here?" he asked when he saw the red, inflamed scratches I was tending to. "Did that pesky barn cat take his claws to you?"

"Nothing like that," I said. "I had a run-in with a wicked bush, something called gorse, while out searching for Vicki yesterday. It turned out to be a very unpleasant experience."

"Ah, that stuff is bad news. In fact"—Alec held up his

right arm, where I saw several bandages—"the exact same thing happened to me."

I barely managed to mask my surprise. "You were searching for Vicki?" I asked, a little incredulous.

"Indeed. I was looking around near the hills on the other side of Glenkillen."

"Isn't the ocean on the other side?" I asked, still doubtful and trying to trip him up.

"Along the coastline and to the south," he explained. "I was still out there when I heard that you and Leith Cameron found her. If not for you, we'd be planning a funeral."

"I'm not so sure we won't be planning one, anyway."

"Probably what she intended, after what came out about her."

I frowned. "What she intended? You mean you think she wanted to run off that cliff?"

"Either she was running from taking responsibility for her crime against Gavin, which is the most likely. Or the game was up, she realized that she couldn't escape, and was ending it all. Either way, it doesn't make a whit of difference in the outcome. She can't profit from an inheritance if she earned it by spilling a man's blood. That's the law."

"What are you talking about?" My voice became clipped.

He didn't seem to notice my reaction. "It's perfectly obvious that Gavin Mitchell knew something important enough to my half sister that she killed him to keep him quiet, to keep the secret safe. And that could only concern my father's will and the distribution of our inheritance."

"You are so wrong about everything." I found myself getting steamed. "First of all, her beloved terriers were still at the house, an indication that she was not running away from anything. She'd never leave them behind, certainly not without making arrangements for their care. She would have left a note or something, which she didn't. Besides, simply meeting with the sheep shearer doesn't make her a murderess."

Alec made some kind of huffing sound with his breath to indicate disbelief.

Then I went a step further, thanks to my growing irritation with the whole MacBride family. "I'll even go so far as to say that Vicki is innocent of *any* wrongdoing whatsoever," I said, unable to stop the cascade of words in her support, "And it's horrible the way she's been treated by you and your family."

"That woman is no relative of mine after all the trouble she's caused." He gave me an assessing look. "You really believe she didn't kill Gavin Mitchell?"

Well, to be honest I was still on the fence about that one, but I couldn't let him see my doubt. Any indecision on my part and he might attempt to sway me to the other side, and I wasn't about to become a pawn in this game.

I dug my heels in further by saying, "Yes, she is innocent. And I'm going to prove it."

"I doubt that's possible. She's guilty as sin."

"I'm going to make you eat your words," I told Alec with a little threat in my voice.

"Easy, luv," he said. "No need to get worked up. Everything will become clear when she wakes up and Inspector Jamieson has a chance to interrogate her."

"Interrogate? You mean interview!"

He still wouldn't let it go. "Why don't you face the truth? She was seen with Gavin right before he was murdered," he went on to say. "We have Bill Morris and Kirstine to thank for that bit of evidence, which might never have been uncovered if it weren't for my sister."

Which I didn't believe for one second. Inspector Jamieson would have gotten around to those cameras in time.

Alec continued, "And then the silly cow made the

mistake of trying to cover up that fact. May I point out that Gavin was a longtime friend of the family, and we don't take kindly to strangers intruding in our affairs—or stabbing our friends to death! Especially on *our* property."

Okay, there certainly wasn't going to be any friendly golf outing today. I'd taken my side. Alec had stated his. He wasn't as cool and calm as he had appeared previously when we'd discussed his family. I'd brought his loyalty to the surface.

We glared at each other, at an impasse. But then in the blink of an eye, his expression cleared and he smiled. "Let's not allow our differences to come between us. I do believe I owe you a round of golf, and I'm looking forward to a delightful afternoon on the course."

"Today won't work," I said, not letting go of my anger as easily as he had. "Vicki is battling for her life. The last thing I'm going to do is go play a game."

He shrugged. "Another time, then."

As he walked toward the lane, I remembered to call out a piece of advice I'd thought of earlier. "I suggest you remove the bandages from your arm. Your wounds need air to heal."

He raised a hand in acknowledgement without glancing back.

What I really wanted to do was remove those bandages myself, as painfully and as slowly as possible, ripping out each hair one by one. Or better yet, I could whistle for Kelly to round up a herd of sheep and run him down.

That would really mess up his expensive golf outfit.

CHAPTER 31

I hadn't a clue how to convince people of Vicki's innocence, but one thing I knew for sure—I was going to have to make it persuasive.

I'm a writer. This is what I do—I create believable story-lines. Which was exactly what I planned to do now.

I decided to start by finding out where the pig's blood someone had splashed around Gavin Mitchell's cottage had come from originally. Yes, that was a good place to begin. Someone *had* poured animal blood around the body. So where had that blood come from and why on earth had the killer left it there?

You'd have to have been raised in a cave to be unaware of modern-day forensics. That swapped-blood ploy might have worked in the eighteenth century but not in this one.

I needed to find the inspector. He was a thorough inves-tigator. He might even have some answers regarding the how and why of the animal blood. Then I remembered our last conversation and how cold he'd become toward me.

What I really needed to do was find that blabby volunteer cop.

I drove through Glenkillen in search of Sean Stevens with no luck, then headed for Kirkwall Hospital to check on Vicki. The hospital was a nondescript, two-story beige building with two ambulance bays on one end. Small, but at least Glenkillen *had* a hospital. I was grateful for its existence when I needed medical attention and especially now for Vicki's sake.

When I stopped in the lobby waiting room to check on Vicki's progress at the information desk, there was Sean, watching television and looking extremely bored.

"Nothin' has changed with Vicki MacBride's medical status," Sean informed me. "Don't exactly know why I'm sitting here doin' nothing but waiting fer her eyes tae peek open when I could be out patrolling the streets tae keep them safe." Sean sighed heavily at his significant cross to bear. "But the inspector says it's important that I be here."

Could his assignment have anything to do with the inspector trying to keep the rookie out of his hair? Apparently Sean hadn't figured that out yet, and I wasn't about to be the bearer of bad news.

"Where were you yesterday during her rescue?" I asked him. "It's not like you to miss that sort of action."

"Our dear inspector failed to inform me o' the situation, sayin' it slipped his mind in the rush o' things. So there I be, nappin' like a babe when all the important law wheels they were a-turnin' without me."

"Well, you're doing important work now," I assured him. "Once Vicki wakes up, you can be the first to inform the inspector, and hopefully we'll have some answers."

"If she doesn't get that solicitor bloke involved tae put a lid on her lips."

I hadn't considered that, but it might be a good idea for me to contact Paul Turner, especially if charges were pending against her. Although, then he'd get involved, possibly suggesting he was qualified to handle the case, and I was positively sure he wasn't.

"Did you get a chance to look at that video taken near the beach?" I asked Sean, helping myself to a cup of tea from a self-service station.

"I saw it, all right. It was herself fer sure with the sheep shearer, blathering away. The very same woman as now lies in a room on the east wing o' the second floor, no mistakin' it."

I did an internal headshake at Sean's unique gift for disbursing more information than he should. The hospital staff had refused to release Vicki's room number when I'd called to request it, claiming that the nurse in charge had ordered a ban on visitors because of Vicki's condition. Now, Sean had just unwittingly supplied me with enough information to get close enough to find her on my own.

"Anything else significant about the recording?" I asked. "Was anybody else there with them? Could you make out what they were saying?"

Sean shook his head. "They were deep in conversation, that's fer sure, and neither o' them looked one bit happy. Too bad we don't have any sound tae find oot what they were discussin'. Speaking o' videos, did ye ask the inspector about a training video instead o' that manual, and did ye keep the reason we need it tae yerself?"

"I promised you I wouldn't tell him about your dyslexia and I won't. Um . . . as for the video . . . he doesn't have time to check for one right now," I punted, falling easily into one of those permissible fibs I'd recently ascribed to those of us who weren't covering up crimes against humanity.

Although, in defense of justification, what I'd told Sean

was true. The inspector really was busy with a murder investigation, so why bother him with trivia? Sean would have plenty of time to learn police procedures *after* the sheep shearer's murder was solved.

On second thought, the man was a gem, a diamond in the rough, a fountain of private police information. I paused to wonder why I was planning to help him improve his basic police knowledge when the more he learned proper protocol, the more he'd clam up and become useless to me.

Sean and I sat quietly for a while. He went back to watching the television program and I moved to a more private corner and pulled my laptop out of my tote, powering it up.

"Tell me about the inspector," Ami had written in an e-mail. "What's he like? Any interest there?"

I took a moment to assess Inspector Jamieson's qualities.

"Intelligent, intense, startling blue eyes, handsome. A widower. His wife died from cancer. Reserved, private . . ."

Private. Yes, I guess that made him mysterious. Anything else? Was I interested on a more personal level? I wasn't sure. I enjoyed his conversation, but a murder investigation was hardly conducive to romantic inclinations.

"But enough of that," I wrote, then went on to tell her about Vicki's accident and how Leith and I had found her. "I'm at the hospital right now," I added, "waiting for word."

"Tea?" I asked Sean after a bit.

"Not right noo." He looked tired out.

"Did the inspector pursue the source of the pig's blood?" I asked him, moving across the room and sitting down beside him.

"Wha' you think we are? Incompetent bumblers?"

Okay, that had been a dim-witted question. Of course, they had. "And?"

"And I'm not aboot to divulge important police business regarding an ongoing investigation tae a civilian."

What? Had Sean been studying police protocol on his own after all? "Since when do you know that?"

"Since watching some copper films last night. I'm going tae start watching on a regular basis and take some tips. Don't know when I'm supposed tae get any sleep."

"You can give me a hint, though, right? If I happen to guess . . . ?"

There was a pause while he considered my suggestion, then said, "Okay, that should be all right. Let's see . . . ye want to know if we chased down the source o' that blood. . . . That's the question ye asked?"

I nodded.

Sean would have made a terrible poker player. He wore his emotions too close to the surface of his uniform sleeve. Right now he was lighting up like a spotlight. "I know what will help ye. . . . Yer using the wrong tense o' the word." He beamed.

I frowned. "Which word?"

" 'Did' is the word I'm speaking o'. Ye know . . . past instead o' . . ." He waited on the other end.

Did they look into it? That could imply some sort of conclusion. *Had* they looked into it? Same thing. How about *would* they look into it? Meaning they hadn't started on that line of inquiry yet? It wasn't like the inspector to leave loose ends dangling, and Sean had confirmed that they had, so that wasn't the answer. Past tense? What was he talking about?

If I imagined I were him—God forbid—what would I mean?

I had it.

"You *are* looking into it," I said.

"Yer good at this."

Disappointment set in. He'd made me jump through hoops only to learn they *were* still looking into it. That only meant they hadn't found a connection yet. So it wasn't a local purchase, making it much harder to track down. In essence, nothing was new on that front.

"We're at a dead stop on that one," Sean added, confirming my own thoughts.

I changed subjects, expressing my anxiety over my friend. "Why aren't we getting more updates on Vicki's condition?"

"She'll come around. That one is tough as nails."

She certainly was. Vicki would have won the grand prize as a survival reality show contestant. I'd seen what was left of her car. Nobody should have made it out alive. The woman was blessed with nine lives.

"What room number did you say Vicki was in?" I asked Sean, getting up.

"Ye know I can't divulge classified information," he said, puffing up with pride and self-importance. "Strict orders from headquarters."

"Wonderful," I said, then headed off to find an elevator that would take me to the east wing of the second floor. A nurse was stationed at a circular desk behind a visitor station at the entrance to the east wing. I decided that, instead of stopping to inquire about visiting, I'd have better luck if I breezed past her as though I knew exactly where I was going. If I acted confused or hesitated for one second, the nurse would sense my indecision like a shark would sense fresh blood.

It worked like a charm. I smiled smugly to myself. This was easier than I'd ever imagined.

Reasoning that the staff probably put their most critical patients closest to the station, I poked my head into a few rooms and found Vicki in the third one. Not only that, she was awake—or semi-awake; her eyes were at half-mast—but she recognized me immediately and produced a weak smile.

"Am I in heaven?" she asked.

I laughed quietly so as not to alert anyone out in the hall. "You'll have to wait a little longer for that. How are you doing?"

"I feel pretty good."

She had to be under some pretty heavy sedation, because as I moved close, I could see that she looked awful. Black and blue, cuts and scrapes, both legs in casts, hooked up to lots of bells and whistles.

"What happened?" she wanted to know.

"You had a car accident."

"Are the terriers okay? They weren't hurt, were they?"

Was I this out of it after my accident? Remembering back, yes, I definitely had been. "They weren't with you in the car," I assured her. "I'm taking care of them. Don't worry."

"I'm really sleepy."

"Don't go to sleep yet. I have a few things to ask first."

But her eyes closed.

I really wanted to find out why she'd met with Gavin and what they had talked about. Her answers were important and might shed some light that could clear her from suspicion.

"Vicki?"

I checked the monitor to make sure she hadn't flatlined. The waves continued bopping along without a glitch. I bent down to listen to her breathing and found more reassurance in the lifting and falling of her chest. Vicki was okay, at least for now. But she wasn't going to be any help in exonerating herself. The entire thing was dumped in my lap. Unintentionally, perhaps, but unavoidably, it was now all up to me.

CHAPTER 32

From the hospital, I drove over to Leith Cameron's home. The approach was neatly fenced with earth-colored stonework. I could see sheep up on the hillsides to the south in the direction of the MacBride farm, and I remembered Leith mentioning that the sheep were marked because the hills were shared.

The wind was gently blowing, causing grain fields on both sides of the road to wave their long spikes in the breeze. Nestled behind the fields, Leith's comfortable-looking brown stone cottage reminded me of something out of a children's fairy tale.

The scene before me put a smile on my face as I parked beside his white Land Rover. Or was it discovering that he was home that gave my step the extra oomph?

I got out of the Peugeot and walked toward the house, where I spotted Leith standing inside, watching me through a half door. The bottom half was closed, the top open. He grinned.

Was that a tingle? And what kind was it? Excitement? *Darn! Get a grip on yourself, Eden. The guy is taken in*

spite of his playful flirting. And you aren't interested any-
way, so stop it.

"Well, if it isn't Eden Elliott," he quipped. "A sight fer sore eyes."

I couldn't help returning his big, goofy grin as he swung open the lower half of the door and came outside, but it slid away as soon as I told him that I'd come bearing news.

"About Vicki?" he asked. "Have you been tae hospital?"

I nodded. "I saw her for a few moments. She doesn't look so good."

"She'll be well cared fer at Kirkwall, just as ye were. Don't let its small size fool ye. It has a good reputation. How are the scratches?" he asked, taking my hand and studying my palm. Was it my imagination or was he taking his sweet time assessing my wounds?

"Fine, thanks," I said when he released me, doing my awkward thing by turning away and changing the subject. "Is that barley growing in the fields?"

"Aye," he said. "Also commonly known as bere in these hills. Mine will most likely be ready to harvest next week if the weather cooperates."

Kelly rounded the corner of the house at full speed and put on her brakes as she thundered up to us. She wagged her tail as I stroked the top of her head. What a life she had, with all the freedom of the great outdoors.

"We were just heading out fer a fishing expedition," Leith said.

"That's right, Vicki told me you're a fishing guide."

"This wee bit o' barley ye see isn't enough tae make a decent living. Sometimes I take fishermen out tae the rivers tae fly-fish for trout and salmon. Today I've been hired tae take a group out on the North Sea, but if the weather doesn't cooperate we'll stay within the bay."

"And Kelly is your crew?"

"Someone has tae make sure none of my paid customers fall overboard when I'm not looking."

No wonder Leith was so calm and relaxed all the time. He fished for a living. And his was not the uncertain life of the commercial fisherman, who goes out for days on end in every kind of weather imaginable in hopes of filling his hold with enough fish to sell to make a meager living.

If I got to spend my day casting a rod, I'd be eternally on an even keel, too. Not that I've had any experience fishing, but I could just imagine how easy life would be.

"I'll only keep you a minute then," I said, watching him open the back of his Land Rover and rearrange the fishing equipment inside. "I'm looking for a local source of pig's blood."

He straightened and gave me a quizzical look. "And ye were thinking I might have some?"

"No, but I thought you might know the name of a source."

"Yer going to make blood sausage, are ye? That's getting intae the Scottish spirit of things. A little black pudding will spice up yer life."

For some reason my brain hadn't made the connection between the pig's blood found at the scene of the crime and the traditional Scottish breakfast item. Actually, I hadn't given any thought to the type of blood used in making pudding. I guess it did have to come from somewhere, but my brain couldn't help thinking, *Gross, gross, gross.*

"Can I purchase pig's blood in a regular store?" I asked, persevering, hoping it wasn't a commonplace grocery staple, like eggs or bread. If it was available in the grocery stores, my chances of tracing it to the killer were slim to none.

So I was disappointed when he said, "Sure ye can."

"How much would I need to make a batch?"

"About four hundred and fifty grams fer a standard rec-ipe," he said with an amused chuckle. Why, I wasn't sure, unless it was the expression of distaste I was having trouble keeping from my face. "Let me know when ye make it so I can stop by and watch, take a picture or two fer yer Scottish scrapbook." Was he laughing at me?

I did a quick calculation, and roughly estimated four hundred and fifty grams to be a little less than two cups. Not enough. "What if I wanted a big bucketful?" The back of his Land Rover was still open. A bait pail caught my eye. I pointed to it as a comparison. "Like that much."

His smile faded. "What are ye up tae?"

I decided I'd better explain myself before he carted me off to an insane asylum. Besides, I didn't have to worry about breaking police confidentiality. Sean had been the one who'd announced the blood source, and while the inspector had been livid at the volunteer, he'd never asked *me* to keep anything to myself.

"The killer poured pig's blood around the body to make it look like Gavin had been killed in his cottage," I explained. "When in actuality . . . well, you know where he was really murdered; you were there when Kelly discovered it."

"It would take a real brainbox to do a thing like that."

Brainbox? I caught his meaning, pleased that I was adapt-ing to the Scotman's unique manner of speaking. Must be that Scottish heritage on my bum of a father's side.

"Killers are rarely known to be clever outside of books and movies," I said. "From my understanding, they're more likely to do all kinds of stupid things, like running off through the snow and leaving tracks that lead right to them."

"Or boozing it up at the pub and announcing the crime tae the rest o' the customers," Leith added. "That's happened a time or two in these parts."

"Or falling asleep in the victim's home and waking up surrounded by police."

"People can be right foolish."

We grinned at each other.

"Anyway, that's what I thought at first," I said, "that the killer had a rather low IQ. But our man—or woman—went to a lot of trouble to get all that pig's blood. I'm starting to wonder if there was another reason for it."

Leith shook his head. "Some dolt thought he could fool the coppers, that's the amount o' it."

"I can't explain it any better at the moment," I admitted. "It might have been a dolt, as you suggest, but I still want to know where the blood was purchased."

Leith thought about that. "It could still have been bought at the grocer's," he decided.

I disagreed. "The killer wouldn't have wanted to draw too much attention by buying buckets of blood."

By the look on his face, Leith thought otherwise. "Pig's blood comes dried in a sack."

Well, how was I supposed to know that? "Dried? Then it's mixed with water?"

Leith nodded. "If I remember correctly, it's one part blood tae six or seven parts water, or thereaboots."

"Oh."

I felt my initial excitement about the blood source as a possible avenue of exploration draining away. If the killer hadn't had to lug around gallon jars of blood and could have whipped up a batch right at Gavin's cottage without anyone noticing, what chance did I have of tracking down the killer from that angle? It had probably been wishful thinking, but I'd really hoped for limited sources, maybe one or two places to obtain pig's blood, and a short list of customers to sort through as potential suspects.

The inspector would have already checked with local outlets anyway. I hated starting from scratch when he probably had a huge lead on me. A smart woman would bow out gracefully, let the police do their jobs, and concentrate on writing the best book she could. But how could I focus on fiction with all this real-life intrigue going on around me?

"Don't be discouraged," Leith said, walking me to my car. "Everything will work out in the end."

I really hoped he was right. As he opened the Land Rover's door, I thought of something. "Leith, you've known the MacBrides a long time. How did the father get along with Kirstine and Alec?"

"James MacBride was a private man. He was difficult tae read, but there were never any outward signs o' problems. Most likely they had their share, working together as they did, but nothing unusual."

"He approved of Kirstine's handling of the shop, and of John's tending to the farm?"

"They do a fine job. It's prospered under their care."

I smiled, and said, "Well, thank you for answering all my questions, and enjoy your fishing trip."

We both got into our cars, Leith with Kelly in the passenger seat, and me following behind. Before I turned into the MacBride driveway, Leith stuck his arm out the open window and waved a farewell as he headed for the open sea.

As I drove past Sheepish Expressions, it dawned on me that I had taken a stance firmly in support of Vicki, and I hadn't had a single doubt about her today. A good sign that I'd successfully weathered her deception over her meeting with the sheep shearer and had come out still cheering for her. She'd saved me. Now it was my turn to try to save her.

I just hoped, in my eagerness, that I didn't end up pounding in a few of Vicki's coffin nails instead.

CHAPTER 33

When I checked on Coco and Pepper, they were thrilled to see me, reacting as though I'd been away for weeks and weeks instead of a couple of hours. I took a moment to bask in the glory of their admiration. Then, while they ran around outside, I plopped down in the same outdoor chair Vicki favored.

Putting my frustrating efforts to follow the trail of blood on the back burner, I turned my full attention to pondering the motive for Gavin Mitchell's murder. Love, money, revenge: they all sounded good in theory. But they were only words. Without some proof, they didn't mean a thing.

And just because Vicki and Gavin had been seen together the day before his death didn't mean she'd killed him. Vicki had opportunity and means, but so did a whole lot of other people. Since the sheep shearer had been such a likeable guy and his craft had taken him out and about, he'd probably had many interactions in the days preceding his death. Those shears could have been picked up and used by nearly anyone.

So it really boiled down to finding the right motive.

The inspector would have to prove beyond a reasonable doubt that Vicki MacBride had committed murder. Until then, he couldn't charge her. At least, I thought he couldn't. Truthfully, all my knowledge of police work came from crime shows on TV, but at least the British ones seemed similar enough to ours in that regard.

I still couldn't understand why James MacBride would bequest his entire estate to only one of his three children. And to the one who wasn't an active participant in the workings of the farm, who didn't even live in Scotland. What father would do that? And why? Especially since there was no outward conflict between the father and the other children. It didn't make sense that he'd intended to cut his other children out; either there was a missing new will, or— possibly—he'd just never gotten around to updating it. But if that were the case, and one or several family members were plotting to eliminate the heiress, shouldn't *Vicki* be the person dead?

Could Gavin have gotten wind of their intent, overheard them making their plans in the same way I had listened to that disturbing conversation between Kirstine and John inside Sheepish Expressions? Only, unlike me, who'd managed to escape unseen, had he been found out? Maybe so— which meant that they'd had to change their plan. They'd stabbed Gavin to death, and efforts were put into motion to frame Vicki for his murder, which had been working out just fine until she "accidentally" lost control of her car and plunged over a cliff. Had someone become impatient?

I placed the potential suspects in an imaginary lineup:

Kirstine had a strong motive to eliminate Vicki. Her livelihood and childhood home were on the line. I could have chalked up her behavior in the pub to duress, as she'd buried her father the same day and learning about the will couldn't have been easy—if only I hadn't later overheard her plotting with her husband. She wasn't on my list of likeable characters. Although, I had a difficult time imagining her thrusting the shears into Gavin's body.

I shuddered and pulled my sweater tightly around my torso.

My thoughts turned next to John Derry. In the short time I'd known him, I could tell that he was seriously rough around the edges and thought nothing of spreading rumors and threatening whoever got in his way. I could easily picture him plunging the shears into Gavin Mitchell's body. And he was a strong man. Moving Gavin would have been easy for him. And motive? He had the same one Kirstine did: His livelihood was in the balance, thanks to an outsider who didn't belong.

Alec was next in the lineup. In theory, he could have had the same motive as his sister—protecting his financial future. But only if he were personally involved in the business, which he wasn't. He had his own source of income as a private accountant, and so had no cause to suffer nearly as much as his sister by being excluded from the will. And from our first meeting and subsequent conversations, he *had* sympathized with his sister and suspected Vicki of murdering Gavin Mitchell, but he hadn't expressed any interest in the operation of the farm or any inheritance. Flirting and selecting the proper golf club were his top priorities as far as I could tell. It must be great to be that financially secure.

So there we had it. If this was the only will, and I had no proof otherwise, then John and Kirstine Derry had killed the sheep shearer because he'd overheard them plotting to kill Vicki, then changed their plan to frame Vicki for his murder instead.

I'd love to connect Paul Turner to that bunch. I didn't like the man on a personal level and found his professionalism and ethics seriously on the dicey side. Turner was in the other side's corner. That was obvious.

Only, the sticky part was going to be how to prove any of this.

Before I had time to ponder another scene—in which there had been a second will and some kind of cover-up, which would have had to involve Vicki—Kirstine's husband, John, the man who never seemed to move from the top of my suspect list, walked past, heading toward the shop with a sheep following behind on a short rope. The ewe was limping. Part of me wanted to hustle back inside until he was well past. From my brief association with him, he was a despicable character—not to mention a potential killer— and he might have nearly killed me with that fall. The other part decided to approach him anyway.

In spite of my bravado, I was immensely relieved to see some Sheepish Expressions customers milling about outside the shop. They were a distance from us but within shouting range. Knowing they were there gave me some extra reassurance that I was safe from any sort of attack by John. I walked in his direction.

The man really was an imposing figure up close. Tall, rugged, hairy, and gruff—exactly the caricature of an old billy goat. Only a *gigantic* old goat. I'd really only ever seen him from a distance, and even then he'd seemed more immense than any of the other locals.

"Whereto is the woman?" he asked as I came alongside and joined him. "Still in hospital?" He had a different accent, too, which I'd noticed earlier, with even more rolled "R"s, stretched vowels, and songlike sentences than the lovely Scottish accent. It seemed contrary coming from so much mass.

"Still in the hospital," I answered, matching his steps since he hadn't paused, and feeling I didn't owe him much of an explanation. "You aren't from around here, are you?"

"Southern Wales." I'd watched rugby tournaments between the European countries. All the players on rival teams were huge, but the spectators from Wales were just as large as their countrymen playing the sport. They were all big boys in Wales, I'd gathered. That explained his size.

After the first glance, John hadn't given me another look, had kept his eyes straight ahead.

"What's wrong with the sheep?"

"Must oof turned a leg."

"What will happen to it?"

Now his eyes slid over to me, so he had to notice mine were glued to him, watching for reactions. "What's it ta you?"

"Just concerned. I'm an animal lover and hope the poor thing isn't going to end up on someone's dinner plate."

"We don't make meals oof our sheep on this farm," he said, somewhat more gently, which reminded me of the inspector's earlier observation about how sensitive John was to animals. If only he showed the same courtesy to his own species. "But she'll produce a mighty fine carpet," he added.

What? "You're going to make her into a carpet? How could you!" This was an outrage. The beast was going to make her into a sheepskin floor covering?

He stopped then and his face crinkled up. I wasn't sure what was about to happen. Was he going to blow his top, show his stripes? Instead, he burst out laughing. "Our sheep's *wool* makes fine carpets as well as tweeds," he sputtered still chuckling. "As for the ewe, she'll be as good as new by tomorrow. The MacBride sheep are good milkers as well, so she could always turn to that if the injury doesn't heal well, but there's no good reason it won't. Now it's my turn ta ask questions. What are you still doing on our land?"

"Our" land? In a matter of seconds, his expression had gone from merriment at my expense to shades of anger boiling right below the surface. "Vicki invited me to stay with her after my room at the inn caught on fire," I explained, sure that he already knew about that. "And since she's in the hospital, I'm taking care of her dogs."

He fell silent and continued on his way with me still keeping pace, not much of an effort, since he was taking it slow in consideration of the sheep.

"I could have been killed on the loft steps," I said. "And I've learned that they were tampered with. Who would have done such a thing?"

John didn't look over at me, but his face reddened and his eyes narrowed. "You've been properly warned," he said in that musical Welsh lilt. "Stay out oof our affairs," he said softly, which struck me as more threatening than if he'd raised his voice. "And ta help you with that, I'll give you twenty-four hours to clear out, you and the wee barking beasts."

I stopped and stood in the middle of the lane, watching him continue on.

Could he do that? Throw me out?

I picked up my jaw, which had fallen close to the ground, and stomped back to the house.

Where I called Paul Turner and told him about John's threat to throw me out. Turner may have been in another camp, but he still had to pretend to ethically abide by the laws of the land. Besides, he was my only option at the moment.

"He can't force you to leave as long as Vicki is fit to make responsible decisions and tells you you can stay," the solicitor told me. "But right now that's debatable. It's within Kirstine MacBride's rights to go into court and request a temporary order to manage the farm's affairs. She will be required to prove her stepsister has been incapacitated by the car accident and that her request is in the best interest of all concerned."

"Vicki opened her eyes and spoke to me, and she was perfectly coherent," I told Turner with a rush of relief and confidence that she would be perfectly capable of handling her own affairs just fine without any outside help from the others.

"Perhaps you don't see the situation in the proper light."

"Have they started those legal proceedings?" I asked next, suspicious now. And for good reason. He was advising them; I was sure of it.

"Kirstine," he informed me after a noticeable pause, "has been in touch with the courts. A hearing has been set for Friday morning. Kirstine appealed for a timely court date due to the condition of the hospital patient. As Vicki Mac-Bride's solicitor, I've been duly and appropriately advised."

"And when were you going to tell us?" I felt the heat of anger rising.

"I wasn't aware that I owed you anything at all, Ms. Elliott. I'll be speaking with my client as soon as the police and hospital staff clear me. Until then, I will handle the situation as I see fit on Friday."

This wasn't even going to be a fair hearing. The Mac-Brides were going to railroad their agenda through. It didn't look good for our side. "Please," I said, taking as much disgust out of my voice as possible. "Vicki needs you, and she's asked me to get as much information as I can and relay it to her. I've been able to come and go from her room."

Not exactly the truth, but I didn't care at this point.

"Very well. Please let her know that I will be there, representing her best interests."

Yeah, right! "What are Kirstine's chances of success?"

"Very good. She and her husband have been managing the farm for years. If you were a judge, how would you rule?"

He was right. Kirstine would certainly win the temporary order. "And the hearing to decide the bequest?" I asked next. "Will that be postponed due to Vicki's condition?"

"That date is set and will be heard in a few weeks regardless. Kirstine is determined. The will maker would have felt that he had a moral duty to his other children, and his daughter is in great financial need."

Paul Turner was actually gloating. I could hear it in his tone. "You seem pleased," I couldn't help saying.

"And you seem unable to accept facts," he replied. "As the saying goes, one eats an elephant by starting to nibble at its toes." Then he hung up.

I sat with the dogs for a long time, churning over every detail of the conversation, hoping for a hole in the opposing side's argument.

Big bad John couldn't boot me out in twenty-four hours like he'd threatened, but he might be able to in a few days. I wasn't too concerned about myself—I would find someplace else to stay—in Inverness, if nowhere else—but for Vicki, this would be yet another uphill battle. If she didn't recover quickly and dodge the murder charges, the rest of the family would get exactly what they'd wanted all along.

But how in the world could they be stopped?

CHAPTER 34

After I hung up, I went to steep a pot of tea in the kitchen. I decided that my one hope for any kind of reprieve on Vicki's behalf was through an appeal to Alec MacBride. He didn't have nearly as much at stake as his sister. Although I had little information on his personal or professional life—other than that he had an accounting background and, in his words, had managed to dodge the marriage bullet—he seemed free from the responsibilities that go along with a family-run business. And he hadn't been hostile toward me. More importantly, he'd been respectful with Vicki the time he'd called the house for me and spoken with her on the phone.

Of course, that was before the crime scene had turned out to be in the MacBride barn and Vicki had been caught on camera with the victim right before he was murdered. After that had come to light, Alec's attitude toward her had cooled significantly.

That had led to a heated discussion about her involvement in Gavin Mitchell's death. He was convinced she'd murdered his father. I had made it perfectly clear that I didn't agree. But we'd parted on better terms, or at least he'd made the effort to patch up our differences. In hindsight, I should have accepted his olive branch.

Another plus for Alec: He'd brought the unpleasant scene in the pub the night of the funeral to an end instead of escalating it, and until recently he'd seemed okay with the terms of the will. It wasn't until more information came out that he'd formed a more cynical view. Could I blame him? It did look bad for Vicki.

To me, he came across as a commonsense kind of guy, and he wasn't a hothead like his brother-in-law.

At least I might be able to convince him to speak with his sister, to ask Kirstine to hold off a little longer until Vicki was well enough to defend herself. If Vicki had even another week or so to recover, I was convinced Kirstine wouldn't get her way. And if the real killer was arrested soon, this whole new attack on Vicki would be a moot point.

Time was in short supply. Today was Wednesday. The preliminary hearing was Friday. Vicki was hospitalized, and she wouldn't be able to represent herself that soon. I was convinced that Paul Turner wouldn't give it his best shot. Were there other, more competent solicitors in Glenkillen? And time to bring one of them up to speed? Probably not.

If she didn't catch a break soon, Vicki was going to lose.

Just then, my train of thought was interrupted by a sharp knock at the door, belatedly followed by Coco and Pepper announcing a visitor.

"You two are supposed to warn me before, not after," I told them, moving from the kitchen to the entryway with the two terriers racing to beat me. "What good is it after the knock comes?"

Peering through the pane, I saw Inspector Jamieson on the other side of the door.

I paused for a moment to seriously consider refusing him entry, but then I put myself in Vicki's shoes. She would have greeted him with a warm welcome and a hot cup of tea.

"Vicki's okay?" I asked after opening the door. "You aren't here because . . . ?"

He shook his head. "Nothin' o' the sort. No, she's improving by the hour. She be a strong lass, that one."

"Oh, good. That's a relief."

I let him inside—never mind that he was the enemy until proven otherwise—offered him a chair at the table, and put on the kettle.

I'd learned several tricks to making proper tea by observing Vicki. First, I made sure that the water was boiling before pouring a small amount into the teapot and swishing it around to warm the pot. Then I discarded that water. Next, I placed small round teabags inside the pot, remembering Vicki's instruction to add one bag per cup and an extra one for the pot. Once the tea started to steep, I covered the pot with a tea cozy, selecting Vicki's favorite, one with an embroidered lavender motif.

The trickiest part for me was knowing the perfect length of time to let it steep. I'd noticed that tea in Scotland was stronger than in the States, but whether that was from stronger tea or longer steeps, I wasn't sure. I hadn't thought to time Vicki. "Well?" I asked after the inspector had taken a sip of tea, without any ensuing facial or verbal complaints. "To what do I owe the pleasure of your company?"

"Ye want tae know why I've come round, then, do ye?"

Of course, I did, but I gave a little shrug as if to say it didn't matter to me and took a sip of tea. But the china clinked against the saucer a little too loudly when I put it down. His gaze was as intense as always.

Occasionally I can get downright snippy and snarky. Like when I'm off my writing schedule. Or when I've been told to vacate my current premises. Or when the local inn owners have made it clear they won't take me back. Or when my new friend is the prime suspect in a murder investigation, and the man about to charge her is sitting across from me.

Ornery, crabby—yep, that was my mood at the moment. "Let me guess." I smirked. "You're about to tell me that you have proof that Vicki had been run off the road."

The inspector looked surprised, whether at my witchiness or my charge that Vicki had had a little help over the edge, I didn't know. Or care.

I was on a roll. "How convenient that Kirstine MacBride just happened to run into Bill Morris, who just happened to have seen Vicki and Gavin together shortly before his murder."

Inspector Jamieson opened his mouth. Then he closed it, realizing I was like a runaway train on a steep incline without brakes.

"Or"—I couldn't stop myself—"maybe you stopped by because you have evidence to suggest that the killer intentionally let the victim bleed out in the barn before moving the body, then used animal blood to send the police off to look for the real crime scene. Kelly beat you to the punch and uncovered enough evidence to cast another dark cloud over Vicki's head. One more reason to suspect the heiress, the outsider who doesn't belong. All the duckies are falling into a row."

If the inspector wanted to comment, he didn't get a chance. I kept going. "The police weren't moving fast enough with charges, so the killer became really impatient and changed the plan. Why not run her off the road? Take her completely out of the picture. What if Vicki had died? Wouldn't that have solved a whole lot of problems for this horrible family? It's so obvious. Why haven't you arrested them?"

Finally, I crossed my arms and glared across the table. The inspector took his sweet time responding. He blew on his tea, took a sip, set it down, then looked at me, and said, "Things aren't always wha' they seem."

I shook my head in frustration. Even so, something about my big theory was niggling at the back of my mind. Something was off.

After another period of silence, the inspector said, "Aren't we chipper today?"

Which just riled me more. My tone was sickeningly sweet as I replied, "The only thing missing at the moment are her fingerprints on the murder weapon!"

The inspector calmly and irritatingly watched me in silence, waiting for me to run down.

But I couldn't shut up. All my pent-up frustration spilled out. "Please don't tell me you have her fingerprints on the murder weapon!" I said, a little frightened that he might actually have them, although pulling that off would have been a real trick. The killer would have to be a magician.

"No fingerprints . . ." he managed to say before I cut him off.

"And I imagine you're sitting at this table accepting my hospitality while getting ready to arrest me as an accomplice!"

He stood up, looking resigned. "Perhaps I'll return another day, when yer less agitated."

The man seemed totally bewildered by my outburst. With that, all my anger drained away. I jumped up, instantly regretting my harsh words. "I apologize for blowing up. It's just that everything has been so stressful."

"It's frustrating, I know. Ye can't control the situation like ye can in one o' yer stories," he said.

Wasn't that the truth! I'd love to change this ending to suit myself.

"Why did you really stop by?"

He hesitated, then said, "I didn't come tae argie-bargie with ye, that's fer sure."

If the situation hadn't been so serious, I would have been amused by that phrase. "Argie-bargie," I assumed, meant quarrel.

He went on. "I was hoping ye hadn't had lunch yet and would allow me tae buy ye a rather late one at the pub. I'll even drive ye."

Well, didn't I feel like the fool? I hadn't thought about food at all, but now that he mentioned it, I was starving. I didn't understand the man at all. One minute he was cold and calculating, the next he was inviting me to lunch. One day he was distant and withdrawn, the next he was asking for my opinion.

Maybe his confusing behavior was a side effect of his solitary lifestyle. That took its toll over time, making people eccentric. Add the responsibilities of law enforcement, and I could imagine how truly quirky one could get.

But who was I to be calling the inspector weird? *I'd* been the one acting bizarre this time around.

Inspector Jamieson was still waiting for an answer.

"I'd like very much to have lunch with you," I said.

CHAPTER 35

"What are you trying to get me to eat now?" I asked, surveying a plate between us on the bar. We'd decided to sit at the bar on stools rather than at a table. The boozer innkeeper wasn't in his regular spot for a change, and the pub was quieter than usual, given the time of day, sandwiched between lunchtime and cocktail hour.

"Haggis," announced the inspector, with what I suspected was his version of glee. Was this payback time for my earlier behavior? "A Scottish delicacy that it's time ye tasted."

I'm pretty sure I grimaced.

"A little heart." He went on. "Lungs, liver, suet. Eat up, lass."

Behind the bar, Dale was watching and listening to our exchange. "The inspector ordered ye the vegetarian haggis," he called out. "He's pullin' yer leg."

"Thanks fer spoilin' my fun," the inspector called to him.

"I don't believe there is such a thing as vegetarian haggis," I shot back to both of them, pretty confident that vegetarian haggis was a contradiction in terms.

"There most certainly is," Dale insisted. "All 'tis is onions, carrots, lentils, beans, a few peanuts, rolled oats, and secret spices, and the lot served with a nice whisky sauce."

"And what's that?" I asked as Dale brought over another dish.

"Neeps and tatties," he answered.

The inspector interpreted for me. "Turnips and potatoes."

Dale went off to help another customer, calling over his shoulder: "Ye wouldn't catch Rob Roy eating that wimpy version o' haggis, that's fer sure. Nor William Wallace."

I inspected the plates cautiously while the inspector placed a little of everything on a smaller plate for me.

Regardless of what those Scottish ancestors would think, I found the vegetarian haggis delicious. The haggis owed most of its flavor to a whisky sauce, which was wonderful. And the neeps and tatties reminded me of home, of days long gone when my mother would prepare a boiled winter-time dinner with ham, potatoes, and turnips. Comfort food.

While we ate, Inspector Jamieson and I talked of simple things, of the beautiful hillsides and the weather, which had been every bit as unpredictable as I'd heard it would be.

"Aye," he commented. "It's fickle."

When we were through eating, he said, "I'm not the monster ye envision."

"It's been a rough few days for all of us. Please accept my sincere apology. I'm just so frustrated."

"Yer apology is accepted and already forgotten. I appreciate yer point of view, I really do. But I have a question fer ye: Why would our killer go tae all the trouble and risk to kill Gavin Mitchell simply tae frame Vicki MacBride? Why not take her out first thing and be done with it?"

Which, I realized, was exactly what had been bothering me, too.

The inspector continued. "Now, I have tae suspect a stronger motive fer murdering the man."

"To keep him quiet?"

"Aye, most likely."

"He was with James MacBride at his deathbed."

"I know yer thinking about that will, but if the father had drafted an updated one, none o' the other family members would have had a motive. They certainly would have benefited. Leaving . . ."

"Yes, the most likely suspect in that case: Vicki."

That was the reason I hated the idea of an updated will. "We're missing something, a key piece of information. What about the box on the floor of the cottage?"

"It might have been knocked off the telly when the killer was bringing in the body, fer all we know."

Granted, the room was small, the television not far from Gavin's body.

I decided to change topics, since we were at an impasse.

"How are things working out with Sean?"

"He's still a heather goose," the inspector said, then clarified when he saw my confused expression. "A ninny," he explained. "But I've learned how tae handle the nuisance."

I smiled. "By sending him off with busywork?"

"Shrewd as ever, ye are."

We sat in comfortable silence for a short while. Most people dread a lull in conversation and will fill it with any noise just to be making sound. But the inspector was perfectly fine with it, and so was I.

A few minutes later, I brought up Alec MacBride by saying, "He's an interesting man, and successful it appears. His business must be thriving, since he has time to golf on weekdays."

The inspector paused in thought before saying, "The man seems tae set his own hours and throw his money around plenty. He's known tae be somewhat of a lady's man, so be aware o' his smooth talk."

"You don't have to worry about me," I said, remembering only too well my last conversation with Alec and the note it had ended on. If I wanted his help in stalling his sister, I'd have to make amends first.

"So ye think Vicki MacBride was run off the road?" the inspector asked, his intense eyes watching me again.

I squirmed, regretting that accusation. I had absolutely no basis for it. "It was only one theory, and not a very good one, spoken in a moment of extreme frustration. I shouldn't have suggested it."

"There's no evidence tae support such a claim. Vicki is the only one who can answer that question, and she hasn't remembered anythin' at all regarding the accident in the few short times she's been awake fer questioning. And when I try tae solicit an answer regarding her exchange with Gavin Mitchell, all she'll say is that she doesn't remember." He paused. "Her doctor says that's common after psychological trauma, and she certainly had plenty o' that. I'm anxious tae question her further, but those nurses are a difficult lot tae get past."

"Did you know Kirstine MacBride and that husband of hers have scheduled a court hearing for Friday to try to take over the farm? They'll get it back if Vicki can't manage it. Not only that: John ordered me off of their property."

"He's a hothead," was all the inspector would say.

"So I've been told repeatedly. Doesn't his temper trigger alarm bells for you? And that lawyer! He's a piece of work."

Jamieson didn't respond right away, giving me time to

feel bad about allowing more of my sarcasm and frustration to come between us.

What was wrong with me today?

"Sorry," I said, deciding it was my day for apologies by the boatload.

"I'm following every lead," he said calmly, "and eliminating most o' them along the way. That's my method, and it's proven tae be effective fer me. In the end, it's the pieces left in my hand, the ones that don't fit intae the puzzle, that matter."

A wise and true observation.

"Are you about to charge Vicki?" I asked.

"Would I bring charges against a woman recovering from a car accident while she's still in hospital?"

"I'd hope not, and especially not without a motive."

"Don't ye have a story ye should be writing?" he replied instead. "Instead o' worrying aboot my competence?"

"I have absolute faith in your ability to solve this case," I said with a friendly smile.

After the inspector departed, I set up in a back corner, hoping to get something done on the story, no matter how small. But first, I had an e-mail from Ami.

"I could feel your attraction to this inspector coming through cyberspace! If your writing reflects the same for Gillian and Jack, you're going to have a bestseller on your hands. By the way, where is that scene you are supposed to be sending?"

Oh, please. I'd simply described the man. It wasn't like I'd told her he was a sexual magnet or anything. Granted, the inspector had many good qualities, but that didn't have to mean I was interested. Ami should have been in theater. I didn't bother responding.

I tried to write; I really did. I gave Gillian and Jack a few special gazes into each other's eyes and some internal dialogue to go with the eye locks, but my thoughts kept going back to the conversation I'd had with Inspector Jamieson regarding Vicki.

I couldn't help thinking that he had locked onto Vicki with jaws as tenacious and powerful as a pit bull's.

CHAPTER 36

After that, I returned to the farmhouse, gave Coco and Pepper a little exercise, then put my plan to make amends with Alec MacBride into play by phoning him with a request for a golf lesson the next morning. But first, I needed to apologize, even though I wasn't sorry at all that I'd defended Vicki.

"You simply expressed your opinion," Alec said graciously. "We don't have to see eye-to-eye on the family drama. I was in a bit of a snit myself, I must admit, and said more than I should have. But that's behind us."

"So you'll give me a golf lesson? Maybe tomorrow?"

"Come to the club now," he said, expressing pleasure. "Or better yet, I'll pick you up."

"It's almost eight o'clock," I said, mulling over the best way to ask for his help regarding his sister's latest plot. "Isn't that too late?"

"Not at all. As long as we have a wee bit of daylight, I can show you a few swings. My club's dress code is casual.

No jeans, though, and certainly no collarless shirts. Oh, and
a set of waterproofs if you have them."

I resisted his offer to pick me up, got directions to the golf
course, and dressed accordingly, aside from the waterproofs,
which I was pretty sure meant a pair of rain boots. It hadn't
started raining yet, but the overhead clouds were threatening
to unleash a torrent. There was a certain eeriness to the atmosphere, the sort that descends right before a storm. I wished
it a speedy arrival and a quick exit from the greens.

I headed out, deciding I could get used to these long summer
days, except they were balanced out by short winter hours
of daylight, which would depress me for certain. I couldn't
imagine surviving on less than seven hours of sunlight. But
summer, with its extended daylight and twilight following
slowly behind, suited me just fine.

"You're in for a treat," Alec explained with obvious pride
after meeting me in the parking lot. "Golf originated here
in Scotland during the Middle Ages, then it spread to the
rest of the United Kingdom and on to the US, so visiting
golfers are keen as mustard to play the greens here."

Yeah, right. I sure hoped it would be a once-in-a-lifetime
event, though I meant it in a different context than Alec
would have. The absolutely only reason I was going to suffer
through a game of golf was for Vicki's sake.

This coastal golf course wasn't like any I'd seen in the
States. It was what Alec called a links course. There were
no trees to circumvent, little water other than the deep blue
sea far across the course, and all the sand dunes were covered with fragrant heather (and its wicked companion, gorse,
which I identified immediately and planned to stay far away
from).

We teed off. And teed off again. And again.

Even without rain, at this rate we wouldn't see another hole before night closed in on us and forced us to quit. In spite of the sweet refreshing smell of salt air and the light breeze stirring my hair, I was annoyed with myself and majorly frustrated.

Alec was charming, though, and if he was frustrated with me, it didn't show. As the inspector had warned me, Alec was quite the lady's man. He was intensely focused on me and my every need, and I allowed myself to be pampered and appreciated, in spite of the game I knew he was playing. A little attention never hurt a girl's ego. And these Scottish men really knew how to flirt. It was harmless and fun.

But surprisingly, I didn't feel any attraction to him. Maybe it was his charm. He had a lot of it. So had my ex-husband.

"Like this," Alec said, coming up behind me, wrapping his arms around my arms and putting his hands on top of my hands, which were tense as I white-knuckled a golf club. He guided me through the various parts of the swing once again.

"Keep your eyes on the ball. Don't let them drift. Swing"—our arms went up into the air together—"and follow through." His arms lingered around me for a few seconds longer than necessary. Then he broke away. "Now, you try."

There were too many instructions to remember all at once—keep your feet planted this way, knees slightly bent, arms stiff, shoulders relaxed; tilt a wee bit to the right, elbows locked, head down, eyes on the ball. My head was spinning with information overload.

Alec stepped clear. I held my breath, forced my eyeballs to stare at the ground, and swung through, connecting with

the ball for the first time. I peered into the distance to follow
its trajectory over the fairway, really praying that it traveled
straight and true like an arrow, like a bird, like a . . .

Where had it gone?

Alec moved quickly, lunging forward. He reached up
over my head, catching the ball as it shot down from directly
above. It would have bopped me right on the top of my head.
I gave him an embarrassed but grateful smile of thanks.

"My hand and eye coordination is awful," I murmured
unnecessarily after he'd saved me from my next almost self-
inflicted injury.

"No one is perfect when they start out," he said at one
point, with white teeth contrasting against his tan skin. "But
a woman with a few flaws is much sexier anyway." He
winked.

"It's going to rain any minute," Alec finally announced
at the second hole to my great relief. "Why don't we wrap
it up for now and have a whisky in the clubhouse."

I agreed quickly.

Once inside the club, a bald man with an angry expression on his thin, pinched face approached Alec.

"I need a word," he said, addressing Alec.

"Not now, Warren," Alec replied with hostility in his
voice. "As you can see, I have a guest."

The man backed away, his face flushed, and we continued
into the bar area.

The members of the club wore blatant symbols of
wealth—in the style of their haircuts, in the fine jewelry
they had on display, in their casual yet pricey golf attire.
Even the walls of the clubhouse dripped with elegance.

I felt less than comfortable in this place, immensely preferring my humble table in the back of the Kilt & Thistle

surrounded by my writing tools. But I was here on a mission, and that was more important than my comfort level.

Alec's eyes didn't wander to the other women in the club- house. I was sure of that because I watched him carefully. He might be a player, wooing many women without ever making any kind of commitment, but he was a considerate one. And obviously well-heeled.

While we sipped a locally produced whisky, I made my appeal, not claiming it on Vicki's behalf, but rather on my own, where I felt I had a better chance of success. First, I went into how his sister and brother-in-law were going after control of the farm in court on Friday, including my assess- ment of the solicitor's lack of concern for his client's best interests. I suspected that Alec probably already knew most of this, but he didn't let on if he did.

"John Derry has ordered me to leave the farm," I said next. "And Paul Turner is sure that they will win in court on Friday and have the authority to make that happen. I don't have any place to go. If only Kirstine would give me a little more time."

Alec's expression had given nothing away while I pre- sented my case. When I finished, he said, "Kirstine and I didn't—and still don't—see eye-to-eye on the best way to handle the situation after my father's will spelled out those unfortunate terms. And John is an instigator through and through. His mouth opens before he knows what's going to come out, but I'm sure he will give you time to find suitable accommodations."

Not exactly what I'd hoped for. "Finding out about your father's will must have been a horrible shock for all of you," I said.

He shrugged as though it hadn't been that bad, but I

noticed that his voice was tight as he responded. "Life is full of surprises."

"If only your father had thought to update his will before he passed. I'm sorry for all the complications your family has had to deal with."

"Things have a way of righting themselves. The disposition of the family property and business, for example. A short while ago, we thought we'd lost all claim to our family's estate. Now it looks like the problem will be solved for us. At great personal cost to a family friend, I must remind you. Gavin Mitchell shouldn't have lost his life in the process. But in the end, justice will prevail."

I'd expected him to take his family's side to some extent, but I'd hoped he'd consider intervening for my sake if not for his stepsister's, but his response dashed my hope.

Alec smiled as he raised his glass to his lips, took a sip, and said, "Vicki will pay for her crime." He must have seen the distress on my face, because he quickly added, "But let's not discuss that. Otherwise, we'll be back where we were earlier, at a standoff. And I hate to see you upset."

"I just wish Kirstine would wait a little longer," I said, "and not try to take advantage of Vicki while she's a hospital patient, at least give her a chance to defend herself. And I'm not sure where I would stay if John followed through with his threat."

Alec still wasn't picking up on my plea, or if he was, he wasn't rushing in to offer his services. Besides, his sister and her husband seemed to be calling all the shots. Alec was way too busy sporting around.

Shortly after, I made my escape. The skies had opened up while we'd been inside, but I'd refused his offer to get my car for me. As much as I hated driving—and although driving on the left after dark was a new experience, one that scared me—I was glad to have my own transportation. I wasn't about to get trapped in a confined space with an overly testosteroned male like Alec.

Back at the farmhouse, alone with the two Westies but safely inside with the doors securely locked, I watched the storm rage outside the bedroom window. At some point I must have dozed off. Then some sound startled me awake. I wasn't sure what it was.

The sound came again, like nails scraping on a window. Or chalk screeching across a chalkboard. Pepper and Coco rose up on the bed, hearing the unfamiliar sound, too. They began barking, their little bodies trembling with fright.

Just a tree branch scraping against a windowpane, I told myself.

"Shhhh," I said to the dogs, petting them until they quieted.

Outside, the wind howled.

It was pitch-dark. I turned the switch on the lamp beside my bed. Nothing happened. The farm had lost electricity. The scratching sound came again, and I decided to investigate to reassure myself that there was nothing to worry about.

The canines didn't follow, content to let me handle any monsters under the bed or in the other room.

After feeling my way along the wall, I paused outside the bedroom when a gush of outside air blew at me. Wind? What was going on? Something clanged to the floor. My eyes began to adjust to the darkness.

Vicki's knitting needles had fallen from an end table. They'd make a decent weapon if it came to that, so I scooped them up as I rushed to an open window, where the curtains were billowing. I hadn't left it open; I was sure of it.

A flash of lightning struck close by, framing me in the

window, exposing my position to a would-be attacker. I wanted to duck and hide, but instead I held the knitting needles high, gripped like a knife, hoping I looked scary rather than just plain scared. Then I quickly slammed the window shut and locked it in place.

Holding out for a rational and harmless explanation, I roamed the house quietly in the dark, but didn't find any tree branches close enough to any of the windows to produce the sound I'd heard. And it never came again. If someone had been trying to frighten me, they'd done a good job of it. But if they were trying to scare me away, they didn't know me well. I was more determined than ever.

Eventually, after making sure all the windows were bolted, I attempted to go back to sleep.

But it was a long night.

CHAPTER 37

The sun rose in a big ball of glory on Thursday morning. Sheep grazed on the hills outside and birds flittered about singing happy songs. A pair of bullfinches called to each other in a thin, piping whistle. And, best of all, the electricity was back on.

Last night had been like a bad dream. Had it really happened? Had someone really been trying to spook me, or had I left the window open without realizing it?

I stood in the open doorway enjoying the scenery when a rugged but muddy Jeep four-by-four pulled up, and a tall young woman wearing jeans, a thick braid down her back, and strange footwear jumped out.

"Charlotte Penn," she said, walking up, and extending a hand. "I'm Gavin Mitchell's apprentice sheep shearer. Or . . . rather . . . was his apprentice. Ye must be Vicki."

I took her offered hand and found that she had a firm grip. "I'm Vicki's friend, Eden Elliott."

Charlotte looked past me into the house. "Is Vicki home?"

"I'm sorry, no. She's in the hospital."

My visitor looked surprised. "I ran intae Alec MacBride in Inverness on Tuesday," Charlotte said. "He told me that she had inherited his father's farmhouse and was living here, but he didn't mention any medical issues."

"Would you like to come inside and have some tea while I explain what happened?" I asked, wondering whether to go into specifics of all the drama surrounding Vicki or simply skim the surface. Skimming sounded best. Perhaps she already knew some of it anyway. "Or there's coffee, if you prefer?"

She shook her head. "Nothing fer me, thanks. I really just stopped by tae introduce myself. I've been all over the countryside in the last few days since Gavin's death, breaking the bad news tae the outlying farmers and shearing their sheep."

So she hadn't heard about Vicki. If her Jeep's condition was any indication she really had been all over the Highlands.

"Hey, Jasper!" Charlotte had turned toward the barn and, sure enough, Jasper was venturing out farther than I'd ever seen him. He was heading right for her. She met him half-way and scooped the big tomcat into her arms.

"You're a natural with animals," I told her, smiling and walking over to join them. "Jasper isn't the friendliest cat I've ever met, but he sure likes you, I can tell."

"Jasper and I are good friends."

"He was wild at some point, right?"

The big guy started purring as she worked her hands over his fur. "Jasper wasnae a heather cat," she said. "If that's what ye thought. This guy gets his wary nature because he was mistreated in his first home. James MacBride rescued him from a life o' torment."

So that explained Jasper's cautious behavior.

I was studying Charlotte's footwear, which seemed to be some sort of moccasins. When I looked up, she smiled.

I explained my curiosity. "You're the first person in Scotland I've seen wearing moccasins."

"They're made o' felt. I always wear them when I'm shearing so I don't slip, which is easy tae do with all that oily wool underfoot. Moccasins make moving around much safer. I made several pairs o' them myself, including these."

Which I could sort of tell. "They look comfortable."

"Aye. I wear them most o' the time."

Charlotte flipped Jasper onto his back, cradled him like a baby, and stroked his chest. The big feline could have been a rag doll cat; he was that easygoing and mellow with her.

"How long have you been helping Gavin shear sheep?" I asked.

"I've been his assistant for several summers . . . or had been . . ." Charlotte teared up. "There aren't many taking up sheep shearing these days, so I'm the only one around fer now. Gavin does . . . did . . . about sixty farms, and I'm not sure I can keep up by myself. We'd worked our way through many o' the farms fer this year, but next is going to be difficult."

Sixty farms! And if each of them had as many sheep as this one! For the first time, I considered the scope of the shearing business. "How many sheep would you say are in the Highlands?"

She put the big cat down and swiped at her eyes with her fingertips. "Counting all the lambs, yearlings, rams, and ewes," she sniffed, "I'd say several million at least."

"Amazing!" It really was.

"Nobody knows fer sure," she said, with a weak smile. "Whenever we get tae counting, we fall asleep."

We both laughed, and I realized I wanted to get to know this woman better, so I extended an invitation one more time. "Are you sure you don't want tea?"

"Okay, sure. That would be nice."

Inside, I put the kettle on, and while the water heated I put out all the trimmings—milk, sugar, and a plate of almond biscuits. While that was going on, I asked Charlotte more about her work, and she went on to explain how important the shearing was for the sheep's health. "Besides finding the wool useful, a good, close trim keeps flies and maggots away from them."

"And keeps them cooler in the hot summers?"

"If ye can call our summers hot." Charlotte grinned.

"You should be in Chicago about now," I told her, vividly remembering July in the city. "The sidewalks practically sizzle. So count yourself lucky. Especially since you work outdoors."

As we stirred our tea, I also told Charlotte a little bit about Vicki's accident, that she must have lost control and gone off the road, and had suffered injuries, but that she would heal with time.

Charlotte would hear the other details of the sordid mess soon enough, I was sure, since the accident was recent local news. "She's pretty beat-up and both her legs are broken," I finished, then to stay optimistic, added, "It could have been worse."

"That's awful! The poor woman! But there is a very nice rehab facility inside the hospital. She'll have the best care."

Somehow, until that moment, I hadn't realized what difficulties the immediate future held for Vicki. She had a long road to recovery ahead of her, months and months. And how did a person manage with two broken legs? By wheelchair, of course. And she'd need someone to assist her with daily routines until she could walk again. I could help temporarily, but then I'd be returning to the States.

So much for my commitment to avoid caregiving in the future. But Vicki's situation was completely different than the nursemaid role I'd played in the past. My friend would recover.

"Does the hospital provide in-home care as well?" I asked, suddenly concerned that Vicki wouldn't be able to return to the farm for quite a while. What would that do to the claim she had staked at the farm? Would the other Mac-Brides manage to strip away all her rights to her inheritance, with Paul Turner firmly on their side? Or at the very least, would they manage to take away her control? They certainly were making a bold play for more power.

Charlotte sipped her tea before replying. "I assume the hospital will provide her with whatever she needs. Maybe they'll want tae keep her in the in-patient rehab program as long as possible."

A moment of silence stretched across the table before I asked, "Are you going to shear the sheep on this farm soon?" Although the sheep on the hills surrounding the farmhouse weren't at all shaggy, like some I'd seen coming and going from Glenkillen.

"No, they've had their haircuts," she said. "But I've got a few other farms in the area tae finish up."

"What do you do when you're not shearing sheep?"

"I've finished up my last year o' veterinary medicine studies in Glasgow," she told me. "And decided tae leave the care o' household pets fer others and go intae treating large domestic animals—sheep, cattle, horses. Working with Gavin has helped pay my expenses, as well as keeping me active in the countryside, where I practice with the local vet, who is thinking o' retiring soon. I never thought I'd take over fer Gavin, but fer now, until someone else can be found, I'll do it."

"Things will work out," I reassured her. "You have a sound plan in place." Then I turned the conversation to the conflicted family of MacBrides, hoping for some additional insight into the family. "You know the MacBrides well, then?"

"James and his son-in-law, John, mostly, since Gavin and me, we worked with the sheep, and those two liked tae stay involved, especially John."

"John does much better with animals than with people," I couldn't help pointing out.

"Some people are like that," Charlotte said. "You should meet some o' the more rural farmers. No social skills tae speak of at all."

"How about Kirstine?"

"I don't know her well. She's most interested in the shop—buying clothing and yarns and overseeing the wool products as well as keeping a presence on the shop's floor. So our paths don't usually cross."

I could have shared my own impressions of Kirstine Derry nee MacBride, but I restrained myself.

"What about Alec MacBride?" I asked next. "You said you ran into him in Inverness?"

Charlotte shrugged. "I only know him by sight. His mum lives in Inverness, and he was visiting her."

His mum? Oh right, that would be James MacBride's second wife. I hadn't given her a passing thought before now. She and James MacBride had divorced long ago. So, she was living close by in Inverness.

"I'm so sorry about Gavin," I told her. "I didn't have the pleasure of knowing him, but everyone says he was well loved throughout the countryside." Never mind that I had found the poor man dead in his cottage. I just wasn't up to telling that whole story. Let Charlotte find out from the locals.

"Gavin didn't have an enemy in the world that I knew o'," she said. "The night that James MacBride passed on, I went off looking for Gavin. I wasn't surprised tae find him at the pub, even as late as it was, drowning his sorrows. I tried tae convince him tae go home, but he hardly heard me. He was downing shots o' whisky, getting mighty drunk, and beside himself with grief over his good friend's death."

I almost said, "So you saw him right before he was killed," but caught myself in time. The pain in her eyes was intense enough as it was.

"Then I learned that Gavin was murdered sometime right after he left the pub. I should have stayed with him, but it was after midnight and I was exhausted."

"You can't blame yourself for what happened. You did everything you could."

"I remember thinking, 'Well, at least he isn't driving.' I made sure. All he had tae do was walk home. He couldn't get intae any trouble on that count. I remember thinking just that. And all along, someone must have been lying in wait.

"Three days it took tae finally find him!"

This was where I should probably have admitted that I had been there when he was found, but I just couldn't. Instead, I said, "I'm surprised no one missed him before then."

"His job took him out of Glenkillen fer days on end, and he dinnae bother tae tell a soul, always sayin' it was his business and nobody else's."

I couldn't think of a thing more to say to comfort her, so we sat a few minutes in awkward silence before she rose, and said, "Thank ye for the tea. I'll come by again once

Vicki MacBride is out o' hospital. I'm working close to Glenkillen fer a few weeks, and I'll hear when it happens from the town folks, along with every detail I missed till now, ye can count on that."

I walked outside with her, watching her drive off in her Jeep, thinking about our conversation.

Gavin had been in the pub the same night he'd met with Vicki. After they'd compared notes under a surveillance camera.

And sometime in the early hours of Tuesday morning, Gavin had been stabbed to death.

CHAPTER 38

The MacBride farm was a popular destination Thursday morning in more ways than one.

Aside from the normal activity of tour buses and shoppers arriving at Sheepish Expressions, the kettle on the stove hadn't even completely cooled from Charlotte Penn's visit before Inspector Jamieson presented himself at the door.

At my invitation, he sat down at the table while I prepared more tea, something I was becoming quite accomplished at. Practice, it turns out, really does make perfect.

He watched me fuss over the tea, placing the settings on the table, pouring, and finally sitting down across from him. "We Scots take our tea making extremely seriously," the inspector said when I'd placed it before him. "Best served in a small cup with a saucer, as ye've done."

"Forgetting the saucer is considered a serious breach of etiquette," I recited as I presented him with an assortment of extras. "Milk, never cream. White sugar. And here are a few more of Vicki's almond biscuits."

The inspector rewarded me with a smile. "Well done," he said.

He took a sip of tea from his cup and replaced it on the saucer with proper precision. "I've been banned from our patient's hospital room," he said. "Not that it came as much o' a surprise. And Sean was asked tae depart the premises as well. I'm not sure which is worse—being unable tae question the patient or having that bungler on the loose."

I smiled inwardly. The inspector would have to find other wild-goose chases for his volunteer assistant. "Why were you banished?" I asked.

"In the best interest o' the patient. Apparently, I make her nervous."

"She's more alert, then?"

"Alert enough for a wee bit o' questioning, I'm convinced."

I gave him a hard look, and said, "I tend to agree with the hospital's stance. You'll have plenty of time to interrogate her once she's released."

"Ye sound just like that snotty nurse. Yer tea, by the way, is getting better."

Implying it hadn't started out that way? "Thank you," I said, graciously. "To what do I owe this particular visit? Not that I'm complaining. I enjoy your company, but I'm also aware that you are in the middle of a murder investigation and this could hardly be a social visit."

"I know better than tae try tae fool ye, since yer always ontae me. So then I'd best not pretend it's strictly fer yer tea." He paused. "I'm fully aware that Vicki MacBride has been through a traumatic experience. But I need tae get tae the bottom o' this as quickly as possible. She hasnae even been allowed tae talk tae me about the accident. How it happened, why it happened, where she was going—not a single word."

The inspector was agitated. He was certainly not used to being told what he could and could not do.

"She wasn't lucid until now, anyway," I said, then remembered I shouldn't know anything about her current medical condition, so I quickly went on. "I don't see how I can be of any help."

"Ah, but you can," he answered. Was that smugness? As though I'd walked right into the lion's den? "Sean says yer a pro at slipping intae places where ye don't belong."

Wait just one minute. Sean! The snitch must have been more alert than I'd realized when I'd gone up to Vicki's room. "I can't imagine what he meant by that," I stammered.

The inspector went on as though I hadn't just denied it. "I was thinkin' we should put that talent tae good use," he suggested. "Ye could slip right up tae her room and give her some friendly comfort."

Oh, sure, like he cared about that. "You expect *me* to be the one to grill her?" Did he actually want me to spy on my own friend? What kind of person did he think I was?

"No need tae go off yer head," he said quickly, sensing that I wasn't happy with him. Or maybe it was the dagger eyes I threw at him. "I don't mean tae make ye angry."

"What makes you think I'm angry?"

"'Cuz yer head is steaming more than the kettle on the stovetop."

"I don't spy on my friends," I told him, making myself clear.

"And I'm not asking ye tae."

"Then what *are* you asking of me?"

"Simply that ye offer her yer support and counseling. Ask how the accident happened. That's harmless enough, isn't it? Besides, I'm guessing ye want tae find that out as much as I do."

"That's all you want from her? An accounting of the accident?" I regarded him through suspicious eyes. Was it possible that he was considering options other than just assuming she'd been running away? Could I even hope?

"I'm willing tae keep an open mind. Do ye still think Vicki MacBride was forced over the edge o' the road?"

I did an internal hop and skip, but on the exterior I stayed cool. "Is that what you think happened, too? You found evidence?"

He sighed. "Have ye noticed that ye answer every single one o' my questions with a question o' your own? We're never going tae get a thing accomplished at this rate."

I pressed my lips together and waited for him to reply to my question, ignoring the fact that he was absolutely right about my question-for-a-question responses. Although I hadn't realized it until he'd pointed it out.

"We don't have any proof that our patient was helped over the edge with a nudge or two," he admitted. "Her car was crumpled like an accordion, with enough dents tae qualify it fer the top o' the scrap heap and not a speck o' other colored paint tae prove anything. Nor any sign of tampering with the brakes. But, in spite o' all that, I have doubts."

"What made you change your mind?" I wanted to know.

"I haven't done anything o' the sort. But I have my concerns."

"And they are?"

"It wasn't dark, she hadn't been drinking, she knew these roads from her days in the Highlands, and I agree with ye that she wouldn't have left her dogs at the farm unless she intended tae return. Finally, all the tires on the vehicle were operational. We can't look tae a blowout fer the answer."

The inspector was a unique blend of keen external

observation and quiet introspection. And many of us trust our instincts. I know I do.

"Intuition has saved me plenty," he replied to my questioning look, "and at the moment, I'd like tae hear what Vicki MacBride has tae say."

So did I. More than anything. And a good part of me was really thrilled that the police inspector was asking for my assistance in his investigation, even if he was only using me to get in through a back door to which he had been denied the access code. Jamieson wasn't all-powerful at the moment, now, was he? Rather helpless, I'd have even ventured to say.

"The only way I'll cooperate," I told him, feeling the power, "is if Vicki knows up front that any information she offers will go directly to you. I won't play double spy."

"Aye," the inspector said.

I didn't mention that he also wouldn't hear any part of her story that I felt would incriminate her more than she already was.

"And there's one more line of questioning I'd like you tae—" the inspector started to say, but I cut him off.

"The accident is all for now. Her health is my main concern, and I'm not risking a setback by upsetting her. If I see that happening, I'm backing off."

"How did ye know what I was aboot to ask o' ye?"

"I have your number, Inspector."

And I did.

He also wanted me to find out about Vicki's clandestine meeting with Gavin. Why she'd lied. What they had discussed. He wanted it all.

So did I.

CHAPTER 39

My attempt to circumvent the hospital floor guards didn't go as well as the first time. I stepped off the elevator hiding behind a basket of lavender Peruvian lilies and pink mini carnations I'd purchased in the hospital's gift shop.

I heard a deep questioning male voice and was pretty sure it was addressing me, since I'd been alone on the ride up in the elevator. I peeked over the top of the basket.

"Are ye lost?" a sturdy, no-nonsense man asked again from his position at the desk. He had muscles the size of watermelons and a serious expression on his face, like a guard dog's: alert and ready.

Did I look lost?

This is exactly what happens when I fail to appear confident and directed while infiltrating a closed hospital ward. Confusion and nervousness had snuck in and sunk me. Or maybe it was the basket of flowers that had sent up red flags. It had been the very last one in the gift shop. Unfortunately, it contained an *It's a Girl!* balloon, which I hadn't been able to remove without ruining the entire bouquet. "Is this maternity?" I squeaked.

"One floor down," he said.

I whipped around to the elevator and punched the down button, glancing back at him from the corner of my eye. He stayed where he was at the front desk, guarding the hall passage, watching me to make sure I followed through.

Now what?

The truth and nothing but the truth was all I had left to try, so I spun back around and marched over to the desk. "Actually, I'm here to visit with Vicki MacBride."

"I thought as much. Ye were trying to sneak in. Ye had that air about ye. Did that inspector bloke send ye? Or that volunteer cop? He's been a real nuisance."

Astute on his part, but I wasn't admitting to anything. "Vicki doesn't have any family," I said instead, "and I'm her best friend—her only friend—in Glenkillen." There, that had the ring of truth to it, because it *was* true.

"Vicki MacBride has plenty o' family hereaboot." Now he had his bulgy arms crossed.

"I meant, any family that would visit. No one from the family has been up, have they?"

Mr. Nurse Ratched consulted a file, keeping one shrewd eye on me. "Not yet," he admitted. "Just that pesky cop and his superior, hovering like vultures."

I wasn't about to give up easily. Not for Inspector Jamieson's sake but for Vicki's. She really did need me. "You sent the police away, which was a wise decision," I said, surprised by the amount of passion in my voice. "But none of the other MacBrides have visited, nor will they. If you're from this village, then you've heard the gossip about the family feud. Right now, I'm all she has."

Had a flash of compassion flickered in his eyes?

I wrapped it up with: "You seem like a kind and caring man, someone concerned about your patient's best interest, someone who isn't hung up on visitation rules without taking circumstances into account."

I met his gaze and held it. "I only want to look in on her, cheer her up a bit. What harm would that do?"

He looked away first, glanced at the flowers, then back at me. I made a sad, pleading face.

"Five minutes," he warned. "And they begin right now."

I was already heading down the hallway.

"She's heavily medicated, so don't be surprised if she's a bit loopy." Then: "Don't ye need her room number?"

I waved my free hand before turning into Vicki's room.

Vicki was alert and looked slightly better than she had the last time I'd visited, though she was still connected to a tangle of wires and monitors that beeped and whose displays waved along.

I placed the flower basket on her nightstand where she could see them and bent down to give her cheek a kiss, hunting for a spot that wasn't banged up and bruised, and found a tiny one. Then I rose and said, "You look much better."

"Liar!" Vicki retorted, but she smiled with glazed eyes.

"How are you doing?"

"Great, now that you're here. How are my babies?"

"Spoiled."

"And Jasper?"

"Still ruling the roost."

"I'm moving to a regular room later today."

"That's great news!" And it was. Though the eternally optimistic side of me had wanted to hear that she was going home today. Tomorrow was the court hearing. In spite of my promise to Paul Turner to relate details of the hearing to Vicki, telling her right now would only upset her, and that was the last thing I wanted to do. Besides, she wasn't in a position to do anything about it.

"I wish you'd've brought Pepper and Coco for a visit."

"I had enough trouble getting in myself."

"Sit," Vicki said, patting a spot next to her on the bed.

I sat, and after relating a few Westie stories and assuring her that they were being well looked after, I ventured into the recent past. But first I told her outright, "Inspector Jamieson is anxious to question you, but he's been ordered to stay away from you for the time being."

Vicki smiled. "Then I'll stay here in this ward indefinitely."

I was having a hard time getting to the part where I admitted to her that the inspector had asked me to gather information. I just couldn't. Vicki would think I was visiting for that sole reason, and might feel I was misusing our friendship. So I decided I'd ask questions, get answers, and *then* suggest passing that information on to the proper authorities.

"Do you remember anything about the accident?" I asked.

Vicki dashed my hopes and dreams of a magical answer to all her problems by shaking her head. "Not a thing. It's like the slate has been wiped clean. I keep trying, but the doc says the moments leading up to the accident may never come back to me."

What a disappointment. But had I really expected it to be that easy? That Vicki would say that not only had she been forced off the road but she was also able to identify her attacker?

"Do you remember where you were going?" I tried next.

Vicki frowned in concentration. "I've been dreaming a lot since I've been here. So I'm having some trouble keeping everything straight. Let's see . . . I might have been on the way to Paul Turner's office," she said slowly, concentrating. "Yes, that's it. His secretary called to remind me of an appointment I was supposed to be at right then. I hadn't remembered making one, but she said he still had time if I hurried and that it was important."

That seemed odd. Paul Turner hadn't mentioned a missed meeting when we spoke. Although the man was far from friendly or forthcoming with me.

"Was this a female secretary?" I asked, remembering back to the meeting with the solicitor. Not only did he not have a secretary that day, there hadn't even been a workstation for one.

"Probably," Vicki answered.

"You couldn't tell?" Why was my heart pounding and my blood racing? Why was I so certain something was off-kilter? For all I knew, my friend was mistaking medically induced hallucinations for reality. Vicki said, "Okay, yes. A woman. Her voice was hoarse; she mentioned something about a sore throat."

"So it definitely was a she?"

Vicki shrugged, not caring. "Do you know what Turner wanted? What was so important that I missed?"

"Not a clue," I replied. If Paul Turner and Vicki had really had an appointment scheduled, I had no idea what it would have been about. It couldn't have been about the court hearing because Vicki hadn't been injured yet. The other Mac-Brides hadn't had a case at that time. Not yet anyway.

I'd been carefully watching my friend for any signs of tension or stress, but she remained calm.

I decided to ask. "Tell me about your meeting with Gavin Mitchell."

Vicki's outward calm vanished instantly and one of her monitors sped up. "I'm so sorry I lied."

"We can talk about that another time," I suggested. "It can wait."

"No, really. I wanted to tell you, but I was scared you wouldn't believe me and would start suspecting I'd had something to do with his death. And I knew for a fact the inspector would."

I could have responded that that might have been true, but covering it up had made it far worse. Instead, I said, "Tell me about it."

"Gavin phoned me the day my father died; that was true. He gave me the bad news that my father had just passed and urged me to come immediately. In fact, Gavin insisted that I hurry. So I caught the next flight from London, and checked into the Whistling Inn. I'd barely brought a thing with me except what I had on, a change of clothes, and a black dress."

"You hadn't expected to stay long," I said.

"Exactly. A note from Gavin was waiting for me along with keys to the farmhouse and a request to meet him first near the beach. I thought it odd that he suggested meeting that evening instead of waiting for morning, but I figured it must be really important."

"And what did he want?" I asked, when she paused.

"When we met up, he said he hadn't sent me any note! In fact, he said he'd received a note that was supposedly from me, requesting the same meeting—same time, same place. And he hadn't sent over the keys to the farmhouse either. We were both angry, thinking somebody was playing tricks. Who would do a thing like that? Except maybe

Kirstine, now that I see how resentful she is toward me. But
at the time, neither of us could take a guess."

"That explains why you both seemed angry," I muttered
out loud, remembering Sean's comment after watching the
video. "So when you and I found him murdered, you were
afraid."

"I couldn't have been more frightened. Here I'd been with
the poor man, maybe the last to see him alive, for all I
know."

"What did you do after meeting Gavin?"

"He told me to be at the solicitor's office first thing Tuesday morning, but he wouldn't say anything further. After
that, I hurried back to the inn. I was not about to go to the
farmhouse in the middle of the night if somebody was playing tricks. I wasn't even sure the key would work."

"Did he show you the note he said you wrote?"

"No, he hadn't brought it with him."

Vicki's account of the meeting with Gavin Mitchell was
solid. She hadn't displayed any confusion about the details,
and she'd answered each of my questions without hesitation.
"Do you still have the note that was supposedly from
Gavin?" I asked.

Vicki shook her head. "I gave it to Gavin. He said he'd
try to find out who'd do such a thing."

"And I'm guessing that neither of those notes has been
found. Otherwise, Inspector Jamieson would have been
around asking questions and demanding answers. And he'd
have learned that your handwriting didn't match the one on
the note to Gavin."

Didn't she realize that she'd been set up? Of course she
did, or she would have been honest about the meeting.

"So you went back to the inn."

"Yes, and Tuesday morning at the solicitor's, I found out

that I owned everything, that my da gave it all to me. I was stunned speechless, as you can imagine. Paul Turner told me he'd inform the rest of the family, which couldn't have gone well. Wednesday, Jeannie, bless her heart, gave me a ride to the farm. I took my father's car and drove it to the airport to go home to London to get my pets and pack for a longer stay."

"The next day we met on the plane on the way to your father's funeral." Everything made sense. The dots connected. Or so I thought. The inspector's opinion was a different matter.

"Do you mind if I share this information with the inspector?" I asked.

"Might as well. It can't hurt." Vicki peered at the basket on the nightstand, then her gaze rose to the balloon. "Why the baby balloon?"

"It's a rebirth for you. A new beginning," I joked.

One could only hope.

CHAPTER 40

Back at the farm, the Westies were again as excited to see me as if I'd been away for a month. I made a sandwich from slim pickings in the kitchen—a tin of tuna, a few wilted lettuce leaves, and two slices of bread. Then I called Paul Turner from the landline. A canned message informed me that the solicitor was unavailable and that I should leave a message. The recorded voice on the other end was definitely Turner's. If he had a personal secretary, one I hadn't met when Vicki and I visited his office, she didn't pick up, either. I left a brief message requesting that he call me back.

Next, I called Sean, and asked, "Were Vicki MacBride and Gavin Mitchell studying a piece of paper on that video?"

"The camera mighta been too grainy fer that. We identified them properly though, no question aboot identity."

"But you mentioned that they looked angry."

"Aye."

"Were they holding anything?"

"Didn't see anything like that."

"Can't you make the images clearer? You know, digitally?"

"This isn't one o' yer American movies, ye know. Jason Bourne might be able tae manage that, but the rest o' us have tae make do."

As soon as we disconnected, the phone rang. It was Paul Turner.

"You need a secretary," I suggested. "Someone to field calls for you and take proper messages."

"I can handle my own business," he said, with a dose of the condescension I'd learned to expect from him. "But thank you for the suggestion."

Aha! He didn't have a secretary. So who had really called Vicki about the fake meeting? "Did Vicki MacBride miss an appointment with you the day of her accident?"

"Are you suddenly her personal representative? Because the last time I checked, that role was mine."

"Please, just answer this one question. It's important. I won't ask any more after this."

"Very well. . . ." I heard papers rustling. "No," he said shortly after. "She did not have one, therefore she did not miss one."

I paused for a moment or two to give him time to ask me why I felt his answer was important. That would have been a perfectly normal response. But he didn't.

Instead, he said, "I'll call after court tomorrow. It's first thing in the morning."

An observer might think that gesture was very generous of him, a step in the right direction. But I knew it for what it really was. The man wanted to be the one to inform me of my eviction from the farmhouse.

I wished I could have seen the expression on his face

when I said, "That won't be necessary. I intend to be in court."

Silence. Then: "That's preposterous. You have no stake here. No business in the courtroom."

"Vicki's best interests are my stake in the outcome."

"Are you *suggesting* . . ."

I interrupted him. "No," I said, "I'm not suggesting anything. I'm convinced of it. You've already informed me that Kirstine and John have a solid argument for taking over management of the farm and are certain to win. You've either given up without even trying, or . . ." I let that hang as loosely as my temper. It felt good to let off a little bottled-up steam, and Turner was the perfect target. He, and Kirstine and John Derry.

After the solicitor hung up on me in a fit of pique, I stewed at the kitchen table over a cup of tea and the last of the almond biscuits.

It was looking more and more as if someone really had lured Vicki out onto the road—and then shoved her off it!

A call to the farmhouse from a fictitious secretary confirming a nonexistent appointment would have set Vicki on the collision course. And if the attack had gone as planned, the plot never would have been discovered. Because the only one who knew about the nonexistent appointment—other than the plotter—would have died in the crash. Except Vicki hadn't died.

But . . . if Turner was behind her accident, would he have volunteered information so freely now? Although it would be a simple matter to prove he didn't have office assistance, and a quick peek at his appointment calendar might show another client's name in that day's slot.

I marched down the lane to Sheepish Expressions for

another confrontation since I was on such a roll, only to discover that Kirstine wasn't at the shop.

"She's not expected today," said an unfamiliar woman behind the counter. "Can I say who called?"

"That won't be necessary."

I stood on the edge of the parking lot, hands on hips and breathing heavily, as though I'd just run a mile or two against a strong northern gale.

I wanted to strike out, to pulverize Paul Turner until the truth flew out of his mouth. Some days it's tough being a woman. Men settle their differences on equal terms.

Speaking of men . . .

Leith Cameron's white Land Rover pulled into the parking lot and stopped to the right of me. The passenger window slid down, and Kelly greeted me with a wagging tail and a glob of happy drool.

"You look like yer going tae kick something," Leith called out.

My anger zinged away into space at the sound of his voice.

"I'm going scouting fer a hot fishing spot on the River Spey," he continued. "Kelly's coming along fer a bit o' swimming. You should join us. I have plenty o' fishing gear."

The timing couldn't have been worse. I could trudge around with a major chip on my shoulder interviewing unpleasant locals. Or I could go fishing for the very first time in my life in a pristine outdoor setting with a great-looking and fun guy. Which to choose? "I'd love to, but right now I can't."

"And why is that?"

Where to even begin?

Because Vicki was in the hospital and couldn't defend herself.

Because I had to prepare for court tomorrow, when I would attempt to ride herd on a wily Paul Turner. Not to mention I might be out on the street with nowhere to go if our side lost.

Because I'd just found out someone might have lured Vicki onto the road so they could run her off a cliff and eliminate her permanently.

And because that somebody had to be Gavin Mitchell's murderer, and this was way more important than a fishing trip.

I had a whole lot of valid reasons.

Although . . . why couldn't I turn to Inspector Jamieson, dump the latest information in his lap, and be rid of it?

"I just changed my mind," I said to Leith. "Yes, I'd like to join you, very much. Just let me make a phone call first."

I called the inspector from the house while Leith and the border collie played fetch outside. Jamieson didn't answer, so I left a message explaining about the night Vicki met Gavin, about the fake notes that had brought them together, and the real reason she'd been on the road at the time of the accident—along with my conversation with the solicitor, which contradicted everything the pretend secretary had relayed.

I was aware, as I related our bedside conversation on the inspector's voice messaging, that the inspector was certain to doubt her claim. That was his job. He would require proof to back up her story. Without the notes, where the hand-writing wouldn't have matched Vicki's or the sheep shear-er's, the inspector wouldn't have proof that would allow him to ease off on Vicki as a suspect. Those notes also could explain why Gavin Mitchell's cottage had been searched and why Gavin's box of papers had been on the floor near the body. The killer had to find and destroy those incriminating notes. With a heavy heart, I had to acknowledge that he or she probably already had.

I wondered if Inspector Jamieson might be able to substantiate the origin of the phone call that had sent Vicki out onto the road right before her accident. What were the chances that a caller who wanted to remain anonymous had used an untraceable phone number? Probably pretty high; they were easy to get these days.

Which left it as Vicki's word against . . . well . . . against other proof that made her look guilty as sin.

I hung up and went off with a promise to myself to enjoy the rest of the day and leave the investigation to the police. And as for my writing, I justified that, too. Had I had one single carefree day since arriving in Scotland? No, I had not. I deserved one.

Little did I realize that Leith hadn't been talking about a lazy afternoon of casting from the shoreline. No watching bobbers gently tip with a warm summer breeze before disappearing beneath the surface, then pulling out tiny panfish on the end of the lines to be promptly released back into their habitats.

I'd fully expected Leith to do most of the work for me, the baiting and unhooking. Instead . . .

"You want me to wear this rubber suit?" I held the outfit, attached boots and all, up against my body.

"Unless ye want tae get wet as a trout."

"You mean I'm going *in* there?"

The river was something right out of *A River Runs Through It*. Bold, beautiful, unspoiled, and probably deep and dangerous.

"Can ye swim?" he asked.

"Yes, but why does that matter?" Was I going to end up trying to swim while wearing this? I'd sink for sure.

"Just checking. If ye cannae swim, I'd understand yer fear o' goin' in. But since ye can . . ."

"I'm not afraid," I said unconvincingly, watching the river bubble and boil along, clashing with boulders, flowing over and around them.

"The boots' soles have good grips," he assured me, while he wiggled into waders that matched the ones he'd handed to me. Kelly was already at the river's edge, lapping up the cool water. "Ye shouldn't have any trouble if ye stay close tae me. So put that thing on and let's see what's biting today."

I kicked off my shoes and wormed my way into the waders, adjusting the shoulder straps, then reluctantly following Leith into the rushing water. I had to brace myself with each step, feeling the force of the current, as powerful as the ocean's incoming tide. Or so I imagined.

I spent the rest of the afternoon learning to cast—fly-fishing, if you could call it that—catching and releasing a few trout while Kelly lounged on the riverbank.

As it turned out, I was more of a fisherwoman than a golfer. And not once did I think about murder and mayhem.

It was a wonderful afternoon, and it wasn't until much later, when I was back at the house preparing my defense for tomorrow's hearing, lying in bed with the windows and doors locked and Coco and Pepper cuddling at my feet, that I remembered an important detail about Leith Cameron.

He already had a girlfriend!

CHAPTER 41

The night passed without incident. No dogs barking in warning, no electrical outages or mysterious scratching at the windows. In the early morning, a light misty rain fell outside and the sky was gray. When I let Pepper and Coco out, a chill crept through the open door into the house. It was a day made specifically for wearing comfortable jeans, long sleeves, and a light rain jacket.

Instead, I slipped into a pair of black dress slacks and a somber top for this morning's courtroom appearance and the dramatic family dispute to be played out there.

What did the inside of a Scottish courtroom look like? Probably much like ours. I'd driven past Glenkillen's courthouse, a nondescript, weatherworn square building, where I understood civil disputes and minor lawbreaking offenses were heard. As I hurried to the car under my umbrella, preparing myself for the fight ahead, I pictured a bewigged magistrate with spectacles presiding from behind a towering bench.

The Peugeot started right up, but when I put it into first

gear and stepped on the gas, I heard and felt a *kerthunk* of some sort coming from the back end. On investigation, I found that the rear passenger tire was as flat as a two-pound coin.

Of all the times for something like this to happen!

I'd helped change a tire once, long ago. Okay, actually, I watched a tire get changed once. Big difference.

I didn't even know if this car had a spare or where it was located. Besides, court would be in session before I figured out how to change it. Better to find a ride.

To show the tire how ticked off I was, I gave it a kick reminiscent of the one I'd delivered to my late, unlamented rental car. Then I headed to the house to use the landline.

Which was dead.

And that caused me to upbraid myself for not following through on getting a mobile phone. Now I was totally stuck.

After a few moments of fuming and fussing and blaming myself, it struck me that perhaps this might not be an accident after all. No phone service. A flat tire. How convenient for someone.

Somebody wanted me stranded. Whether to keep me from attending the hearing or for a more sinister purpose, I didn't know. But I wasn't going to stick around to find out about that second option. Although, weren't all my murder suspects on their way to court? Kirstine and John Derry, and that pathetic excuse for an attorney. I was pretty sure Alec MacBride would be there as well. He might have a less rabid approach to the family concerns, but I expected he still might make an appearance to support his sister.

I calmed myself down. "Nobody is coming to get you," I said out loud, determined to find the spare tire and change it myself.

Only I couldn't find one anywhere.

Eventually I stopped to flip through the faded and torn owner's manual, where I managed to find the information I needed. Turned out that the emergency "tyre" wasn't in the "boot" as I'd expected, but rather *under* the vehicle, where it was suspended along with the jack. According to the manual, a bolt under the carpet inside the boot, when turned, would lower the spare to the ground for easy access.

Easy!

Ha!

By now I was more than a little damp.

The bolt was rusty and, when I peered under the car, there wasn't a spare to be found. There was an empty space where it had once been lodged—yes, that was right where it should have been—but a jack and tire, no. I pictured the courtroom filling up with MacBrides and solicitors. Any minute now, court would convene. A big part of me wanted to find a hefty piece of iron and pulverize the vehicle. Instead I ran inside the barn—flying right past Jasper, who jumped back in astonishment before slinking up the steps to the loft and disappearing—and to my surprise I actually found a tire iron beside a can of spray that said it was for fixing flats. I grabbed both and ran back to the car.

Why hadn't the can been in the car? It would have saved me critical time that had been spent searching and reading a stupid manual instead of heading for the Glenkillen courthouse.

The canned sealant worked like a charm. I was still tempted to give the car a whack with the tire iron, but instead I threw it into the passenger seat along with the empty can. Then I blew past Sheepish Expressions and headed for Glenkillen, windshield wipers flapping as it began to rain harder and harder.

The only one who cared about Vicki was me, and I was

covered in grime and soaking wet. Worse, I wasn't going to make it in time to put in an appeal. I'd even prepared a speech—a good one, I thought. If penning fiction didn't work out, I could always go into preparing closing arguments, if there was such a vocation.

Or was it the personal aspect of this case that had made me teary earlier, while reading over what I had written?

Regardless, it was all wasted now, my opportunity gone. There was no doubt who had won.

With a winter-chilled heart and not a spring of hope that I'd make it in time, I pressed on.

As I'd anticipated, both courtrooms were occupied by strangers. Not a MacBride to be found. That court session sure hadn't taken long. Feeling defeated, I stepped into the restroom and freshened up as best I could. The only bright spot was that I was wearing dark colors as opposed to lighter shades, which would have shown the full extent of the damage.

I considered the few options still left to me.

I could go back to the farm, pack my things, and prepare for the eviction. But they might be lying in wait for me like a pack of wolves about to slaughter this particular sheep.

I could visit Vicki in the hospital, but then I'd have to explain why I was down in the dumps, and I wasn't ready to face my friend knowing that I'd failed.

I could go to the pub, where I might possibly find the victorious conspirators celebrating their accomplishment and give them an opportunity to rub it in like salt in an open wound.

Of my options, the pub seemed the best. Before going inside, I checked out the cars parked on the street. None that I recognized. Not the inspector's or Sean's or any of the opposing sides'. So I felt safe slipping inside the Kilt &

Thistle, where Dale was in his routine spot behind the bar with a bar rag tossed over one shoulder.

"Eden Elliott, the Scottish lass with a knack fer the written word," he called out. "Looks like the weather got the best o' ye. What can I get fer ye? Something warm?"

Was it too early to start drinking? Could I hide in the deep warrens of the pub and nurse myself back to health with a dram or two or three of whisky? But that wouldn't solve my problems. And it certainly wouldn't improve my outlook. Perhaps temporarily, but in the long run I'd still have to deal with reality.

"Can you direct me to Inverness?" I heard myself asking.

A moment earlier, I hadn't had any idea which way to turn. Now I had found a direction, and even though I'd driven from Inverness that first day, I couldn't remember how to get back. "I . . . uh . . . need to buy a phone." *And look for a place to stay*, I thought, already missing the pub and Dale and all the other people I'd met in Glenkillen. Well, aside from those people I suspected of murder, of course. I wouldn't miss those people at all.

"It's not far," Dale said, spreading out a map. "We're here," he pointed, then went off explaining about a multitude of roundabouts and which wheel spoke to take on each, before eventually noticing my complete frustration.

"I have the answer," he told me. "Watch the till. I'll be right back."

And he walked out the front door. Watching the pub wasn't much of a job, since it was virtually empty. Except for, back in a dim corner, the figure of Bill Morris, who chose that moment to speak to me.

"While yer in Inverness, don't be attempting tae burn down the Hinterland B and B like ye almost did with my Whistling Inn."

I peered into the darkness. "First of all, I didn't have anything to do with the fire. And why would you think I was on my way to a B and B?"

"As if ye don't know. Moira MacBride, a proper and caring mum to Kirstine and Alec, owns the Hinterland, and ye been nosing around that family like a bloodhound on a trail. I'm warning ye away. She's a wonderful woman and doesn't deserve the likes of ye."

Thankfully, Dale came back with a GPS unit, which he programmed for me. "Ye can make the drive in about an hour's time. Just follow the voice tae the city center. You can't go wrong."

And with that overly optimistic reassurance, I cast a frown into Bill's corner and set off for Inverness.

CHAPTER 42

It's true that my driving had improved quite a bit since that first fateful day when I'd arrived on the outskirts of Glenkillen. Going to and from the farm and the village was now as close to routine as it could be, bearing in mind that left-side-of-the-road problem. I had figured out when to round and when to about. Driving to Inverness on what was basically unfamiliar terrain had me a little anxious. But I'd made it from Inverness to Glenkillen once. I could do it again.

I remembered too late the flat tire and the can of sealant I'd sprayed into it. I'd been so distraught when I realized I'd completely missed the court hearing that I had totally forgotten about the quick fix to the flat. Shouldn't I have it more thoroughly examined by a mechanic before taking off?

How long would the sealant hold?

Well, it was too late now, and I had more important driving issues to worry about.

Like cattle on the road, an occasional lamb, narrow byways, and undulating hills and valleys, all the while contending with the nonstop rain. Eventually I arrived at my destination, white-knuckled and with what I was sure was record high blood pressure.

Inverness is the capital of the Highlands, the most northern city, and it lies between great glens, the North Sea, and several lochs, including the infamous Loch Ness. It's a central location for booking tours. Many of the buses that arrived in Glenkillen and stopped off at Sheepish Expressions originated in Inverness.

The GPS had safely delivered me to the city center. Now I had to locate a store that carried mobile phones. How hard could that be?

The rain had stopped for the moment, but I tucked an umbrella into a tote for the next downpour. I abandoned the car and found the city center to be compact and easy to walk. I passed a rail station and beyond came to an area with street performers, and a little farther on discovered a covered market with all kinds of specialty shops.

I was standing in front of a kilt maker's shop admiring a window display filled with tartan patterns and wondering if I might find Elliott colors inside, when a man came out of the shop. It took me a moment to place him as the man who had attempted to speak with Alec MacBride at the private club after our golf game.

His name popped into my head from when Alec had brushed him off. "Warren!" I called out, and he turned and stared at me. I felt foolish. How would I explain our connection, since Alec had basically blown him off in a rude manner? But I needn't have worried.

"I know you," he said. "From the club. Doing a spot o' shopping, are ye?"

"Yes. What brings you to Inverness?"

"A business transaction." He frowned then, and said

grimly, "I should warn ye away from Alec MacBride. He's a bad egg."

"He's an acquaintance only, nothing more serious," I said, a little startled by his animosity. "But why do you feel the need to warn me?"

"He acts a high roller, but it's actually his mum foots his bills."

"I'm sure that isn't true," I said in Alec's defense. "He seems an independent man with his own career and resources."

Warren snorted. "He's good at deception. His dues are in arrears as well as his rent. I came to Inverness to pay a call on his mum, since her name is on the lease agreement. She refused to renew it, though. Not a bit happy about him and his ways."

I considered this new information. Alec and Kirstine's mother was James MacBride's second wife. Her children should have inherited at least two-thirds of their father's estate. Only they hadn't. What if she knew the reason why? It was worth exploring.

"Would you mind giving me her address?" I asked Warren.

"In the state she's in after my visit," he said, "she should be in a fine mood to set ye straight on the likes of her son. Coming into money, he says, as though I haven't heard *that* before."

He wrote out a name and address—Moira MacBride, Hinterland B and B, Hill Street—on one of his business cards, which identified Warren as the golf club manager.

"She owns and operates the bed-and-breakfast at that address," he said. "Do ye have navigation in yer auto?"

I nodded.

"Then plug in Hill Street. It's a short street, it is. Ye can't miss the B and B once ye get to Hill."

After thanking him, I hurried back to my car, fumbled through setting the address, waited for the self-assured voice to begin navigating, and started out following directions. Soon I turned onto Hill Street and slowly crept along until I found a small sign for Hinterland Bed-and-Breakfast. I pulled over and did a little planning.

I'd learned from the club manager that Alec MacBride was pretending to live the good life, but that it was all appearances—the clothes, the society, the expensive car— and that his mother had been footing his bills. His nonchalant attitude toward whether or not he inherited the family money must have been a ruse.

But so what? Alec wasn't the first person to pretend he was something other than what and who he really was. The world was filled with pretenders. And a fair share of them were probably just like Alec—eligible bachelors who were casting about for some promising catches.

The real issue was: How could I possibly broach such personal family questions to his mother? And more important, get honest answers? I was still pondering the issue as I went up the flower-edged walkway and rang the bell.

The attractive middle-aged woman who answered the door had the same pale Scottish complexion as her daughter Kirstine.

"Moira MacBride?"

"Aye."

"May I come in?"

"I'm full up for the evening," she told me.

Another area of concern cropped up. I probably needed a better introduction than "I'm a friend of your family's enemy. You remember her from her summers at the farm, the offspring of the first Mrs. MacBride? The one who inherited over your own children?"

That would send me packing for sure.

I'd also considered representing myself as part of the team investigating the murder of local sheep shearer Gavin Mitchell, but that might create a hostile environment, one not conducive to discussing family matters. Not to mention it might be illegal to impersonate a police officer, although I technically *was* assisting, wasn't I? The entire situation was complicated.

Amazingly, my mouth opened and the right words spilled out on their own. "I'm Eden Elliott," I told her. "I'm gathering information as assistant to the family solicitor." True— sort of—if you overlooked which particular side of the family I represented. I felt bad about that, but only briefly.

The door swung open, and I was invited inside, where I couldn't possibly refuse a nice cup of tea. That would be impolite. At one of several of the kitchen's broad, cheerful tables, we began.

"This seems rather late in the process," she said. "After all, isn't the hearing later this afternoon?"

I almost spit a mouthful of tea across the table before regaining my composure. Later this afternoon? Exactly who had told me it was scheduled for first thing in the morning? Paul Turner, that was who. That snake of a solicitor had tricked me. No wonder there hadn't been a MacBride to be found in the courthouse or surroundings. They hadn't been there yet.

"Assistants in a case like this work right up to the last minute," I sputtered, watching a black cat with silky long fur strut regally past us to a water bowl in the corner of the room. "Beautiful cat," I said.

"I hope I can keep her," Moira said wistfully, and in the

next few minutes I learned her life story in a nutshell. She and her son had that much in common. I learned she couldn't possibly survive without a feline companion, that she loved to read but only mysteries, and that she'd owned the B and B since her divorce from James MacBride. "And my little kitty is another reason why the children have to contest their father's will and win."

"You'll lose your cat if they don't?" How in the world did that make any difference?

Her face clouded over, and she said, "I refuse to give Alec any more money, not another pence. And his lease is up next month. If he moves here again, kitty will have to go."

"He's allergic?"

"I wish it were that simple. He hates cats. Thankfully James rescued Jasper, but at this time in my life, I couldn't bear to lose another precious pet."

Alec had been the source of Jasper's wariness, of his dislike of men? Charlotte Penn had spoken of abuse, but she hadn't identified the abuser. Perhaps she hadn't known. Something else about my conversation with the young sheep shearer tugged at my mind, but I couldn't place it.

Moira sipped her tea before saying, "Alec had scratches on his arm last time he came here, courtesy of Jasper. The man is my son, and I love him dearly, but he never seems to learn control."

What had she said? If only this conversation were rewindable. Or pausable, to give me more time to think. Hadn't Alec blamed his wounds under the bandages on thorny gorse that he'd encountered while searching for Vicki? Had he been out to the farm since, when I wasn't there, and had a run-in with Jasper?

Possibly, but still . . . what would he have been doing in the barn?

My heart began pounding around in my chest.

Moira continued. "But you didn't travel to Inverness from Glenkillen to listen to a mother bemoan the life choices of her son."

Oh, yes, I did, I wanted to say. *Tell me more.* Instead, I had to play the part. "Vicki remains hospitalized, and there is little doubt that Kirstine and Alec will walk out with a victory," I told her, watching her lips curve in satisfaction. "But we need to eliminate even that small amount of doubt. One of the questions we feel we should be prepared to address is: Why hasn't Alec taken a more active part in the family business?"

Moira sighed the way only a mother can. "Yes, the other side could use that against him. But why didn't you ask Alec that question?"

"He claims his income is substantial enough that he never needed or wanted to be part of the farm business."

She gave me a weak smile. "That sounds just like him."

"If the other side finds out the truth . . ." I took a moment to pat myself on the back for my quick responses, and waited for her next one. It came just as quickly.

"The truth is that Alec and James never got along. James wouldn't allow him to join the business. James is the reason my son has so many emotional issues, why I've tended to pamper the boy. I see my mistake more clearly now. If only James had made an effort to accept him. And to forgive me." She paused there, as though she'd said too much. Flustered, she jumped up and made excuses for ending our tea.

But she'd already given away more than she realized.

CHAPTER 43

I had to get back to Glenkillen in time for the court hearing!

What a huge relief to find out I hadn't missed it. "Later this afternoon," Moira MacBride had said, and I couldn't have just come out and asked her what time without creating suspicion. As one of the members of the MacBride team, I ought to have known that.

If nothing unforeseen happened, I would be back by two o'clock and could go right there. And wait as long as necessary.

Without warning, that little piece of my conversation with Charlotte Penn popped into my head.

Tuesday afternoon?

I hadn't caught the implication at the time, when Charlotte Penn said she'd run into Alec in Inverness on Tuesday afternoon. But wasn't that when the rest of us had been out searching for Vicki? He had told me he'd been out hunting for Vicki, too. Why had he lied? Why pretend to be helping when he hadn't been? Unless he'd been hunting for her in a much different way than the rest of us.

A man living beyond his means, with cat scratches and an abusive streak, didn't gain me much momentum in Vicki's appeal. None of that mattered as far as a judge was concerned. Neither did knowing that Alec MacBride had lied about searching for Vicki. Those new details didn't help one bit in the family's persistent efforts to destroy Vicki.

But maybe I was the one hunting this time. And for bigger game.

Alec had shown up at the farmhouse while I was doctoring my own gorse scratches, and right away he'd claimed that he'd had the exact same encounter with the prickly brush. But the ripped skin under his bandages had really been caused by the MacBride barn cat. Alec must have decided right on the spot that claiming an encounter with gorse was a perfect way to disguise them. It was a small inconsistency in the scheme of things, a small variation. What *was* Alec's dark secret? Had his encounter with Jasper occurred while tampering with the loft stairs to instigate a serious fall that might have permanently disabled or killed Vicki—or me?

Alec, with his short, stocky stature and his olive skin, looked so different than his sister. Right after his mother's closing remarks about a father who couldn't accept a son or forgive her, I'd begun to suspect the reason for divorce number two. I couldn't bring myself to ask Moira straight out, but I had a hunch that James MacBride wasn't Alec's real father. If Moira had had an affair that culminated in the birth of a child, had James disowned the child and divorced the mother?

I'd heard from several sources that James MacBride had been a very private man. He wouldn't have wanted the entire town to know those details. And his ex-wife wouldn't have spoken publicly of her indiscretion. Perhaps the bed-and-breakfast had been a gift in exchange for her silence. So who knew about this other than James, Moira, and, presumably, Alec? Had Gavin known?

First things first. I'd concentrate on this afternoon's court appearance. Focusing on the road was my top priority right this minute. I couldn't afford to have an accident. And of course, rain was falling again to make visibility difficult, so I had to flick on the wipers.

I'd completely forgotten about having the tire checked, but I didn't have time to have it looked at. Besides, it seemed to be holding up well enough.

If I'd been paying attention to the here and now, I wouldn't have been taken by surprise when I glanced in my rearview mirror and found another car right on my tail. Literally. It was shockingly close behind me, a car with tinted windows that obscured my view of the overly aggressive driver behind the wheel.

Crazy Scottish drivers!

Where did the tailgater expect me to pull over? There wasn't any place on this stretch. I began to watch for a place to turn off and tried not to look behind me again. *Eyes on the road ahead*. But I couldn't help noticing that the car hadn't backed off and loomed large in my mirror. How nerve-racking. I showered the driver with a few swear words that I reserve for a select few, all the while looking for a turnoff to get out of the maniac's way.

Instead, the scenery instantly changed—as it tends to do in the Highlands—and the full extent of the height of this road was apparent after a hasty side glance over the guardrail. A valley stretched out to the left of my lane, far below. A panic attack threatened to overcome me. I recognized the signs—rapid heartbeat, spinning sensation, difficulty breathing. I talked myself down from the emotional cliff by looking away quickly.

And that's when I felt the impact from the car behind me banging into my back bumper, but not with enough force to cause me to swerve. My first thought was rather smug. *That will teach the #@*#$ to tailgate!* My old Peugeot could take a heap of bashings and wouldn't be the worse for wear. It had already seen its fair share of vehicular combat. But the shiny black car appeared to be a much newer model.

I slowed down, still searching for a spot to pull off safely.

Crazy Driver and I would have to figure out the damage and exchange contact information. But what if this guy was as dangerous as his driving? If there was any chance our confrontation could accelerate into a show of road rage, stopping wouldn't be a smart move on my part. Even if he cooperated, I was in a hurry to get back to Glenkillen. How long would this take? Besides, the falling rain had become torrential. Which one of us would have to stand out in the rain while we traded information?

From the moment the other car had come up on my tail, I'd been fighting against a growing suspicion, one that was becoming full-blown. I didn't have proof yet, but I was almost positive that the other driver was Alec MacBride.

The other car slammed into my bumper again. This time I almost lost control of my car. It swerved into the oncoming lane, which luckily was empty of traffic, then it veered toward the other side of the road, where low-lying hills expanded in the distance.

The car righted itself and I was back in control, speeding up as though I could outrun him, because at this point I had to assume it was Alec and this was a full-fledged attempt on my life. Exactly as Vicki's had been, I was entirely certain now. There was no question about it. I heard the back tire blow before I felt it, the temporary patch picking a fine time to fail. I kept my foot on the accelerator anyway, until the car slowed in spite of my best efforts. Rather than risk the steep ledge to my left and being in a helpless position where my car could be easily pushed over the edge, I yanked the steering wheel to the other side, and shot across both lanes, bouncing down into a gully.

The car came to rest.

I stayed inside and hurriedly locked all the doors, keeping the motor running in case of a miracle.

I craned to see what was happening behind me. That's when I realized that I couldn't see the road, which meant my car couldn't be seen from the road, either. Not good. Awful news, really. The black vehicle came to rest beside me.

From the driver's seat, Alec MacBride gave me a wide grin. I probably gave him wild eyes back. *Stay calm,* I told my banging heart.

He must have followed me to Inverness, watched me meet up with the club manager, then continue on to his talkative mother's house.

Alec got out of the car with a golf club clutched in his right hand and came to stand in front of my car. I could see him clearly even through the sheets of rain. I jabbed my foot on the accelerator, hoping to run him down, but the car barely moved, the back tire and rim battered and mangled beyond all hope.

"We had an appointment at the farmhouse this morning," he said loudly, so I wouldn't miss a word. "Instead you managed to get the car moving and you passed me going the other way. Here's for being such a bad girl."

He swung and the golf iron connected with the

windshield. Spiderweb cracks rippled from one end of the glass to the other.

"And this is for not taking any of the warnings I sent your way. The fire, you dense woman; the fall. What's wrong with you stupid Americans? You were supposed to go back where you came from."

So he'd started the fire to get me out of town. Only Vicki had stepped in and offered me a place to stay. And the fall *had* been intended for me. That one had almost worked. I'd considered going back to Chicago after the hospital stay.

Alec paused to grin at me again, cocky and confident. And again raised the club.

The next blow sent shards of glass raining down on me where I'd scrunched behind the wheel. My only choice now was to make a run for the road. The tire iron was in the passenger seat, where I'd thrown it earlier. To think that I could out-bash Alec with a tire iron against his longer club was beyond foolish. But leaving it behind would be even more insane.

I didn't hang around for strike number three, instead grabbing the tire iron, leaping from the car, and making for the road. But Alec had anticipated my next move and circled around to the back of the car to block my way.

I brandished the tire iron.

He laughed.

I had no choice but to turn and run toward the hills.

He might have had more upper body strength, but I planned to outrun him. I pumped my arms, the weight of the tire iron a distinct disadvantage, but I didn't care. I was afraid to look back over my shoulder.

Ahead, slightly to my right, lay a field of waist-high gorse. I almost veered away from it, but then suddenly realized that Alec was dressed in shorts, while I had on long trousers. A small advantage, but I'd take it.

I stole a glance back. He was right behind me, in better shape than I'd expected. I ran directly for those branched thorns, flinching as I entered the thicket, not caring that the gorse's claws were pulling at my clothing, some of the longer thorns piercing my skin right through the fabric. I kept going. The mass of thorns began to slow me down, but I didn't stop pushing forward, ignoring the stabs.

Suddenly I was grabbed from behind. I whirled around to fight off Alec. Only he wasn't what was holding me back. I'd been completely entrapped around my waist in the dense thicket of gorse. Like an insect in the gooey grasp of a Venus flytrap. Like an ant on the slippery slope of a pitcher plant.

But so had he.

Alec had braved the gorse to chase me, but he hadn't gotten far, at least not far enough to reach me. He swung his club in frustration. I leaned away. It missed me by several feet. We both were working the thorns, hoping to break free, slowly moving forward inch by inch.

"Where's your little weapon?" he asked, referring to the tire iron I had lowered and hidden inside the gorse's yellow blooms.

"Accidentally dropped." I panted, trying to catch my breath. "Why did you kill the sheep shearer?"

"You know why." His lower legs were entombed in wickedly long thorns. He was bloody.

"How are you going to explain those?" I said, indicating his open wounds. "Or my smashed car window?"

"Everyone will just assume you were assaulted by some derelict passing on the road, a robbery-turned-murder."

I forced myself to slow my breathing. "James MacBride had a new will, didn't he?" I punted, about to put words in his mother's mouth that she hadn't actually spoken. "One you were specifically excluded from. Because you weren't his son. Your mother had an affair during her marriage to your father, and you were the product of that."

"She actually told you?" His face contorted with rage while he worked to bend away the thorns in his path. "How dare she! The woman was sworn to secrecy. Nobody was supposed to ever know that."

"Who else *did* know? Gavin Mitchell?" I kept going fast. "The old will had been filed with the solicitor before you and Kirstine were even a twinkle in anybody's eye. Not much you could do about the existence of that one. But Gavin Mitchell had witnessed the new one, at your father's deathbed, hadn't he?"

"I should have inherited half of the estate along with Kirstine. Instead, I found a copy of a new will on the old man's bed stand after he died. He made a big mistake in leaving all his earthly belongings to Kirstine and Vicki. He forced my hand."

"So you killed the only living witness to the new will. It would be much easier to murder your half sister later and let a court find in favor of you and your sister than to kill both of the women over the new one. That would have made you the obvious suspect."

"I hadn't planned to kill Vicki. Without your constant interference, she might have just been charged with murder, spent her life in prison, and Kirstine and I would have gotten what was owed us. That might still happen."

I nodded as though I agreed. "So you picked up Gavin when he left the pub and drove him to the MacBride barn, where you stabbed him to death before he had a chance to deliver the will to the solicitor. Then you moved his body and left clues for the inspector that ultimately led back to Vicki

MacBride. The pretend meeting you orchestrated between the two under surveillance cameras was a nice touch. And Vicki practically gave you that win when she lied."

"But you had to show up at the very beginning and insert yourself into the equation by cozying up to the authorities. I saw how you were trying to get in good with the inspector."

We'd both been inching along. Each time I'd manage to get free of a few thorns, others reached out and grabbed me.

"So you ran Vicki off the road," I continued, "before continuing on to Inverness to beg your mother for more money, a loan until the inheritance came through. She was smart to say no to you. Finally."

"The inspector would have had her under arrest by then if it weren't for you. I had to do something to hurry the process."

"Yes, you needed money to continue your lifestyle. So the plan changed. You'd eliminate the problem another way."

"There's more than one way to skin a cat," he said, reminding me of poor Jasper's brutal past, making me hate Alec even more. A feeling that increased when he continued. "Which reminds me. Jasper has used up eight of his lives. I'm going to take the last one after yours. I regret that we didn't get to know each other better first."

His smirk made me want to slap it off his face. I felt my blood boiling with a rage that only comes with the thought of animal abuse. I was afraid for myself, but I was beyond angry to hear about his plan for Jasper.

I managed to pry off some of the thorns embedded in the fabric of my trousers. He must have done the same, because at that moment he lunged toward me. He was closer now. The club began to rise, but became entangled in the gorse. Alec glanced at the club end and began to pull it out.

For one brief second I saw a narrow window of opportunity.

I raised the tire iron over my shoulder.

And let it fly with as much force as I could muster.

The iron connected with the side of Alec's face. His head jerked back as though I'd thrown a punch. He stopped struggling to free the golf club and looked at me with an expression of complete surprise. I stood motionless with renewed fear. Now I was weaponless, while he had two. I was out of ideas.

Then he grimaced before leaning forward and cupping his head in his hands.

This was my only chance.

I lurched toward him, reclaimed the tire iron, and hit him with every ounce of strength I could muster. He went down face-first in the gorse.

"That," I muttered under my ragged breath, "was for calling me a stupid American."

I considered hitting him again, but I didn't want to kill the man, so instead I struggled back the way we'd come, finding the path back easier, keeping an eye on my back in case he rose. I ran away as fast as I could.

I must have looked a sight to the occupants of the first car that happened along the road. Ripped clothing, scrapes and scratches, wielding a tire iron. No stranger in his right mind would have stopped for this madwoman.

Except the first vehicle that came along wasn't filled with strangers.

A familiar police vehicle screeched to a halt, and its emergency lights began flashing.

Inspector Jamieson, Sean Stevens, and Leith Cameron, followed by Kelly, poured out of the doors.

"Help!" I managed to stammer.

The three men surrounded me. The inspector relieved me of the weight of the tire iron. I'd never felt safer in my life as they dragged me from the middle of the road. Words wouldn't come; I was positively shocked into silence. With Leith holding my arm, I stumbled into the gully and past the two cars until Alec's prone body came into view. I would have crumpled to the ground if Leith hadn't had me firmly in his grip.

After that, Inspector Jamieson used his mobile phone to call for assistance, as we hurried down the slope and gathered near the gorse patch.

"Wha' did ye do tae the poor man's face?" Sean asked.

"Keep yerself quiet," the inspector told him. "Can't ye see there's been a struggle here?"

"How . . . did . . . you . . . find me?" I asked, still shaky.

The inspector answered. "I went tae the farm fer a wee visit and found ye gone. Sean, here, following along as usual, found the phone out o' order and traced the problem tae a cut line. Highly suspicious, that was. Then Leith here pulled up as we were heading out and insisted he join us in our search."

Sean was bursting to take over the story, and interrupted to say, "So next we went tae the pub and Dale told us ye went tae Inverness. We wouldn't o' thought anything o' it, except for the cut phone line at the farm."

"We decided tae come tae yer rescue," Leith said, staring at Alec, then glancing at the tire iron in the inspector's hand. "But apparently ye didn't need our help."

"Thank you for looking for me," I said, still shaky but with deep gratitude that they were there to support me at the end. "But ten minutes sooner would have been nice."

"Don't ye try tae get up," the inspector warned Alec when he began moving.

"He has a golf club," I told them. "And he isn't beyond using it."

The inspector addressed him again. "Ye just lie still. An ambulance is on the way."

Alec slumped and stayed on the ground, moaning.

When Sean went up to the road to wait for emergency backup to arrive, the inspector said in a low voice, "Constable Stevens has a sharp eye. I might have tae keep him after all."

With that welcome news, I felt strong enough to give them a brief overview of the day's events and how they had finally led me to suspect that Alec MacBride had murdered the sheep shearer. There would be plenty of time later to elaborate.

I ended with: "I should have realized earlier. In hindsight, there were signs."

"Ye know what they say aboot hindsight," the inspector said.

"Yes, that it's always twenty-twenty."

"That too, but also this: Hindsight is an exact science. It's always right."

Later, I thought about those small signs I'd overlooked. Like when I'd mentioned pig's blood to Alec. That particular detail hadn't become public knowledge yet. Alec couldn't have known. Unless he'd planted it there. But he hadn't been surprised, hadn't questioned me further. Anyone else, other than the killer, would have had a question or two. Vicki and I certainly had discussed it. Missing that clue could have been a fatal slipup on my part. It almost had been.

"You need to make another phone call for me," I told the inspector. "We need to stop a court proceeding."

So Inspector Jamieson, with new information to share with Kirstine and John Derry, managed to convince them to postpone the hearing until he could assess Alec's role in the death of their father.

Leith, with his arm still around mine, keeping me steady on my feet, said, "Ye turned out tae be a real thorn in this bloke's side."

The inspector, overhearing, laughed at the pun. "I couldn't have stated it better," he said.

CHAPTER 44

It was a fine morning two days later when Constable Sean Stevens drove up to the farmhouse, unloaded a wheelchair from the boot, and helped Vicki MacBride from the car to the chair. Our welcoming committee consisted of an unlikely trio: Inspector Jamieson, Kirstine MacBride, Jeannie Morris from the Whistling Inn, and myself.

And a menagerie of critters—Jasper from a guarded position inside the shadow of the barn door; Coco and Pepper, who were making slight progress in making friends with the shy cat; and Kelly, whose gaze strayed constantly to the sheep grazing in the pastures beyond and the towering figure of John Derry working amongst them.

"I want to apologize for my husband's bad behavior," Kirstine said to me. "He knew you were listening to our conversation that day, having seen you enter the shop. I had no idea you were there until later. John must have put quite the scare into you with his threatening words."

"I didn't take it too seriously," I said. Not the truth, of

course. He'd scared the wits nearly out of me. But we needed to move on.

"That volunteer officer o' mine," the inspector said next, "is acting the goat as usual."

That sounded bad for Sean. But the inspector had a warm smile on his face and seemed much more relaxed than he had while working the case.

"Acting the goat?" I asked.

"Goofing around again. It's a wee bit o' a joke. He's doing a good deed, and I think he likes his charge, don't ye?"

Ah, of course. Sean *did* look pleased to be wheeling Vicki around. "You'll keep him on then?"

"Knowing ye and yer ability tae win an argument, I don't have much o' a choice." His eyes twinkled.

Jeannie had arrived at the farmhouse a little earlier to refund my unused room charges, and she offered me a complimentary seven-day stay at the inn anytime in the future.

"Fer all the trouble I gave ye," she said. "And all along it was Alec MacBride who almost burned down the place."

I asked for a rain check. For the immediate future I would be here at the farmhouse, available to help Vicki recover, spending the rest of my time burrowed deep into the shadows of the Kilt & Thistle with my laptop and a story to write. One that had been seriously neglected until recently. The electricity between Gillian Fraser and Jack Ross was palpable, according to Ami's assessment after reading my most recent work on *Falling For You*.

But she wasn't nearly as happy about my procrastination over their sex scenes. "Something in your personal life is interfering," she wrote in her last e-mail. "A 'jolly good' romp in the hay might be required. I highly recommend it."

Leave it to Ami to come up with that solution.

She'd also wondered if I had firmed up my plans. Was I staying the six months my travel visa allowed?

I didn't have an answer for her. All I knew for sure was that I wasn't ready to go back yet. I couldn't face my mother's empty apartment, and I had already decided not to renew the lease. Ami would put me up temporarily once I returned to Chicago.

While Vicki arranged herself comfortably in the wheelchair, Kirstine approached her. Sean idled at the back of the wheelchair as the two women sized each other up.

"We got off to a bad start," Kirstine said, speaking first. "I thought the worst of you, and look how wrong I was. If you still want to add some of your handiwork to the shop, you're more than welcome to do that. We're partners now."

Kirstine extended her hand. Vicki stared at Kirstine, then took the offered hand in both of hers. She beamed. "Partners. I like the sound of that."

Vicki and Kirstine had a long way to go, but they were off to a great start.

While preparing charges against Alec MacBride for the murder of Gavin Mitchell, the inspector had sent a search team to Alec's apartment, where they had found evidence in the clubhouse trash—torn remnants of the notes between Gavin and Vicki that he had falsified. With that discovery, along with my incriminating statement, Alec had confessed to destroying the new will and to the murder.

So the two women would soon be in a court of law regarding the will again, but this time, they'd be on the same side.

"What about your husband?" Vicki asked Kirstine. "Won't he mind?"

Kirstine glanced out into the pasture. "He'll come around," she answered.

"What I'd really like to do is organize knitting classes," Vicki told her rather meekly, as though she expected a negative response. I caught a whiff of her signature perfume. Rose and jasmine assailed my senses and I realized how much I had missed that smell. "And I can spin, too. Maybe a class or two there as well."

"Would you believe I can't do either?" Kirstine said. "So, yes, that would be lovely. It would bring a whole new dimension to the shop."

Soon, the rest of the party moved indoors. Except me. I remained outside where I was, breathing in the wonderful aroma of fresh air and green earth. Leith had warned me that he would be late arriving to the celebration when he'd dropped off Kelly earlier. Something to do with wanting to bring his girl around.

To be frank, if I never met her, I'd be perfectly fine with it. But I couldn't say that.

Soon, the white Land Rover came into sight, traveling up the lane from the main road as if in slow motion. Part of me wanted to make a run for it and join Jasper in the barn's loft.

But I held my ground.

The Land Rover came to a stop and the driver's door swung open. Leith leapt out, wearing a kilt again, and ran around the front of the car to open the passenger door. He was so excited.

I plastered a welcoming smile on my lips.

She slid out, and Leith put his strong, protective arm around her. She was everything I'd imagined she would be—fair-skinned, perfect complexion, long blonde hair with a hint of natural reddish highlights, slim and trim, absolutely gorgeous.

And she stood about three and a half feet tall and was missing her two front teeth.

I couldn't help breaking out in a wide grin.

"I'd like ye tae meet Fia," Leith said when they stopped before me. I gazed down into her sky-blue eyes. "Her mum and I aren't together anymore, but we put aside our differences when it comes tae our daughter. Isn't that right, Fia?" He mussed her hair. She made a face at him.

"It's a pleasure, Fia," I said. "How old are you?"

"Six," she told me.

Six. About the same age I'd been when my father had abandoned me and my mother. Fia was luckier than I'd been. "And do you like parties?"

She nodded.

"Oh good, then you're in luck," I told her, "because I know where one is going on right this minute."

Tomorrow, I decided, I'd write that love scene I'd been avoiding.

Intuition told me the words would come this time.

And with that, we walked inside together to join the party.

ABOUT THE AUTHOR

Hannah Reed is the national bestselling author of the Queen Bee Mysteries, as well as the Scottish Highlands Mysteries. Her own Scottish ancestors were seventeenth-century rabble-rousers, who were eventually shipped to the New World, where they settled in the Michigan Upper Peninsula. Hannah has happily traveled back to her homeland several times, and in keeping with family tradition, enjoyed causing mayhem in the Highlands. Visit her website at hannahreedbooks.com.